FAMILY ALBUM

PENELOPE LIVELY

ISIS
LARGE PRINT
Oxford

First published in Great Britain 2009
by
Penguin Books Ltd.

Published in Large Print 2010 by ISIS Publishing Ltd.,
7 Centremead, Osney Mead, Oxford OX2 0ES
by arrangement with
Penguin Books Ltd.
a member of the Penguin Group

British Library Cataloguing in Publication Data
Lively, Penelope, 1933–
    Family album.
    1. Family secrets - - Fiction.
    2. Domestic fiction.
    3. Large type books.
    I. Title
    823.9'14–dc22

ISBN 978–0–7531–8588–9 (hb)
ISBN 978–0–7531–8589–6 (pb)

Printed and bound in Great Britain by
T. J. International Ltd., Padstow, Cornwall

FAMILY ALBUM

FAK

To Kay and Stephen

Contents

Allersmead

Gina turned the car off the road and into the driveway of Allersmead. At this point she seemed to see her entire life flash by. As the drowning are said to do. She thought of this, and that the genuinely drowning can never have been recorded on the matter.

Philip, in the passenger seat, saw a substantial Edwardian house, a wide flight of steps up to a front door with stained-glass panels, a weedy sweep of gravel in front. Emphatic trees all around. Sprawling shrubs. Stone urns that spilled lanky geraniums at the bottom of the steps. He had known Gina for six months and had been her lover for five of these.

Gina saw Alison standing on the top step, arms raised in rather theatrical greeting. She saw Charles emerge from the hall, staring down at them in what seemed mild surprise.

Philip saw a plump, smiling elderly woman with hair tumbling untidily from a bun, who was joined by a tall, stooped man wearing the kind of tweed jacket that you had thought was laid to rest by the 1970s. A large dog shambled at his heels, and slumped down on the top step.

Gina saw various spectres and dismissed them. Many people spoke, saying things they had been saying for years, and were also wiped. She brought the car to a stop, and got out, as did Philip. She said, "Hi, there. This is Philip."

Alison came down the steps, embraced Gina and beamed upon Philip. "I'm Alison. Lovely to meet you."

Charles simply stood. The dog thumped its tail.

Philip took the cases from the boot. He and Gina climbed the steps. Gina said, "Philip, this is Charles — my father."

Charles seemed to consider Philip, as though wondering if he might have seen him before. "And Ingrid," Gina continued.

Philip now saw another woman waiting in the large hall (black and white tiled floor, grandfather clock, umbrella stand, row of pegs loaded with raincoats, oak table strewn with junk mail), a statuesque and somewhat younger woman with straight fair hair and pink face, holding a garden trug full of greenery.

"Ingrid has such a splendid vegetable crop this year," said Alison. "We have broad beans coming out of our ears."

The house smelled of cooking. You could unravel the constituent ingredients: garlic, herbs, wine — some earthy casserole, a coq au vin perhaps, or a boeuf en daube.

Philip observed the staircase with oak banisters, the landing halfway up with window seat and further stained-glass window, the door open into a room apparently filled with books. A big house. A house from

2

the days when people — a kind of person — assumed a big house.

Gina experienced nostalgia, exasperation and a passionate need to be in their flat in Camden, with Philip opening a bottle of something after work.

Someone came galloping down the stairs, and halted at the bend, eyes on Gina. "Christ!" he said. "Not you again!"

"Sod off," said Gina amiably.

Philip saw grubby jeans, a frayed sweater and some eerie affinity with Gina.

"Honestly, Paul!" cried Alison. "Gina hasn't *been* here for over a year."

"It's called irony," said Gina. "Not that he'd know that. So how are things, you?"

Paul came down the stairs. "Why are you that brown colour?"

"Africa."

"We saw you on the news," said Ingrid. "Talking to those people fighting somewhere. Terrible."

"Indeed. Paul — this is Philip."

"Hi, Philip. Do you do Africa and stuff too?"

"I'm in editorial. I stay behind a desk mostly."

"Very wise." Charles was moving towards the book-filled room but now halted. "*The Times*, isn't it?"

"No," said Gina. "You haven't met Philip before. Not *The Times*."

"Forgive me." A kindly smile. "Not that I read it any longer. Once, it was the thinking man's paper. Now, one shops around, and is generally dissatisfied. What do you read?"

3

"The *Independent*," said Philip, after a moment. "By and large." He felt at a disadvantage, for reasons he could not identify.

"For the compost heap those small papers are better," said Ingrid. "The ones with big headlines — what do you call them?"

"Tabloids." Gina picked up her case. "Which room, Mum?"

"I do not know why," Ingrid went on. "It is perhaps to do with the ink. I am putting on the kettle now." She walked away through a door in the back of the hall.

"The big spare room, dear. And then come down and have tea. My orange and lemon cake. It used to be your favourite."

Gina and Philip climbed the stairs. Gina led the way into a bedroom. Philip glanced around and sensed a room that had remained the way it was for some time: functional rather than aspiring — an Indian-print bedspread, the walls in need of a lick of paint. He went to the window and saw a great sweep of garden: a terrace, and then a huge lawn skirted by trees, dropping away to other areas, furtive and invisible.

"Plenty of space."

"Just as well. There were six of us."

"Did David work on *The Times*?"

"At one point."

They were still at the stage when they skirted each other's impedimenta. Philip's ex-wife lurked in the wings. A former boyfriend of Gina's sometimes surfaced in this way, causing slight difficulty. And there was Allersmead, which Gina had decided had best be

4

confronted head-on. Philip's parents were in undemanding retirement in Cornwall, and had already been dealt with, over a weekend.

"So what's the difference?" Philip had said. "With your lot? Why is it apparently a bigger deal?"

"You'll see," she had replied.

Philip walked around the room. He picked up a photo on the mantelpiece. "Six. Only five here."

"Presumably someone wasn't yet born."

"Paul is . . .?"

"That one. He came before me. Eldest."

"And you had a brace on your teeth. Your fans would be aghast."

"Shut up." She was emptying her bag onto the bed. T-shirt, toilet things, not much else. She always travelled light. In the wardrobe at the flat, there was the other bag, permanently packed with basic clothes, passport, cash — in case she had to go somewhere at a moment's notice.

"Brace and all, you were a fetching little girl."

"No one thought so at the time. Sandra was the pretty one."

He moved back to the window. "Halcyon summer days. Hide and Seek. Picnics on the grass. It's the stuff of dreams."

"Huh! By the way, the bathroom's on the other side of the landing. The door sticks. You just push hard."

"Who does the cooking? Something smells amazing."

"My mother mostly, sometimes Ingrid." She had opened his case, and was taking out his things. "Which side of the bed do you want?"

"Left. I like that window. Who is Ingrid?"

"The au pair girl."

"But . . ."

"But she is no girl? Indeed. Ingrid has been the au pair girl for many years."

Philip appeared to consider this. "And she is . . . not exactly English?"

"Swedish or Danish or something. Once."

"No longer?"

"Well, look at her. She's Allersmead now, isn't she?"

Gina continued to hear voices; her life was still flashing at her. It seemed odd that Philip could be impervious to this, that a person with whom one had become so absolutely intimate could be so perversely ignorant. Not *know*. Not see and hear. One is sealed off, she thought. So is he. So's everyone. No wonder there's mayhem.

"We should go down."

"Of course. The orange and lemon cake." He had flung himself on the bed, arms behind his head. "How extraordinary — that you spring from here, and I know nothing about it."

"Rather what I was thinking. But I sprang some time ago, remember."

"Even so . . . I have to say, I don't see much physical resemblance. A hint of your father's nose, perhaps. Remind me again what exactly is his field."

"Field? Charles writes — wrote — books. Polymath — he'd probably buy that description. History, philosophy, sociology — a bit of everything."

"The name did ring a bell. When I met you."

"He'd be gratified."

"Wide readership?" enquired Philip, after a moment.

"Actually, yes. Accessible. More so than the academics, I suppose. Listen, we must go down."

He held out his arms. "Come here."

"Not now. Later."

The kitchen was the heartland of Allersmead. Of course. That is so in any well-adjusted family home, and Allersmead was a shrine to family. The kitchen was huge; once, some Edwardian cook would have presided here, serving up Sunday roasts to some prosperous Edwardian group. Now, there was — no, not an Aga but a big battered old gas cooker, a dresser cluttered with plates, cups, mugs, a scrubbed table that would seat a dozen. There were children's drawings still tucked behind the crockery on the dresser, a painted papier mâché tiger on a shelf alongside a row of indeterminate clay animals that someone made earlier. There were named mugs slung from hooks: Paul, Gina, Sandra, Katie, Roger, Clare.

Philip ate two slices of orange and lemon cake, with evident enthusiasm.

Gina eyed the papier mâché tiger. Katie made that. So where's my fish? We made them at school, and gave them to her for Christmas. The fish has not stayed the course, it would seem.

Tea was had. People came and went from the kitchen. Charles came, stood smiling benignly around, a cup in his hand, departed. Paul came, wolfed down cake and chocolate brownies, offered to service Gina's car — "For a consideration, mind." After he had gone, an engine revved outside. Gina looked alarmed.

"It's all right," said Alison. "That's his. He's got an old Golf, since he started with the job. And he's teaching himself about engines — so clever."

Ingrid sat at the end of the table, shelling broad beans. She and Alison had a discussion about pommes dauphinois or just mashed. A big round old station clock on the wall ticked, perhaps a touch too loudly.

"Show Philip the garden," said Alison. "Admire Ingrid's vegetables. She has some dahlias too. Of course, this has never been exactly a display garden." She beamed at Philip. "We grew children, not flowers."

Gina pushed her chair back noisily, stood, nodded at Philip. "Come on, then."

They went down the steps from the terrace. It was August. The wide, sloping lawn was shaggy, but also yellowing here and there. A couple of hydrangeas glowed, but the general effect was one of unconstrained greenery — rampant shrubs, the presiding trees. A fat branch that reached out over the grass supported a homely swing — a piece of plank slung from two ropes. As they walked down to the hidden areas beyond the lawn, Philip saw a rope ladder hung from another tree, a further swing, a sandpit with a crust of dead leaves.

"A sort of empty stage," he said. "Rather touching. No grandchildren yet?"

"No one has got around to it."

This area of the garden was more unkempt still, except for a disciplined vegetable garden at the far end — a wigwam of runner beans, bushy rows of broad

8

beans, lines of carrots, lettuces, onions. A bank topped by trees marked the boundary; in front of this, there were sprawling bushes, patches of overgrown grass, an ancient rubbish heap of branches and rotting vegetation, a flat place in the centre, just below the lawn, where a rectangle of fading grass seemed to have archaeological significance.

Philip eyed this. "What happened here?"

"Pond," said Gina. She walked over to the vegetables. "I am admiring you," she told them. "There. And the dahlias."

Philip joined her. "Have you really not been here for over a year?"

"Quite possibly. I do," she said, "lead quite a busy life. You may have noticed."

"This garden must have been paradise for kids."

"Paradise?" She laughed, for some reason. She was still looking at the vegetables. None of this stuff back then, she thought. Ingrid has found a new talent, a new use.

"There was one family of five at my school," said Philip. "I used to envy them — a sort of home-grown gang. I felt exposed by comparison, with just one mingy sister. Were you a gang?"

"Mafia activities were confined to the home. We ignored each other at school."

"And where *is* everyone? You don't make much reference, you know. Paul, once or twice, that's all."

"Dispersed." Gina crushed a sprig of marjoram, sniffed. "Wow — she's into herbs as well."

"Dispersed where? Remind me."

9

"Oh." She waved a hand, vaguely. "Roger's in Canada. Katie married an American. Clare — I'm not sure, right now. Sandra was last heard of in Italy, I believe. D'you fancy a walk around the neighbourhood? There's quite a nice park."

"Is Paul always in residence?"

"Paul comes and goes," she said. "The park — and the church is worth a glance — Victorian Gothic, likely to be defrocked at any moment, congregation of a dozen. Let's go." She walked away.

They lay in bed. The house creaked around them, as though subsiding. Boards groaned. A cupboard let out a small pistol shot. Gina remembered the place stuffed with ghosts, when she was eight. You crept to the bathroom at your peril.

"I have overeaten," said Philip. "Excellent food. Is it always like this?"

"My mother likes to cook."

After a moment Philip said. "He is quite a talker, when he decides to."

"Decides is the right word."

"One gets a bit left behind at points. I am not strong on German philosophers."

"He probably wouldn't like it if you were."

A pause. "How does Alison manage? And — um — Ingrid?"

"They are not required to."

"But he hasn't been an academic as such? No job in a university?"

"Regular employment would not have suited him, I guess."

"Did I overdo things a bit on Iraq? It was the one point when I felt relatively well informed. You can't now insist that Blair must have had information about WMD, when patently he didn't."

"My father can," said Gina.

"Do you," enquired Philip ". . . did you . . . tangle occasionally?"

She laughed. "I like 'tangle'. So delicate. Yes, I tangled. Head-on resistance, more like."

"All the same — stimulating for the young mind. My parents were short on opinions."

"I won't hear a word said against your parents."

He rolled onto his side, reached out. "Come here."

"I should warn you — this bed is noisy."

He squinted at her. "I thought this was the spare room. Oh — David . . ."

She sighed.

"Never mind — come here all the same."

The family tumbles through the house — happy, smiling faces preserved on mantelpieces and windowsills, on the piano, framed on walls. The swaddled chrysalis in Alison's arms becomes a sweet toddler with a mop of curls; another chrysalis arrives. The toddlers grow legs, wave from the branches of trees, turn cartwheels on the lawn. They are lined up in height order, each with an arm outstretched to another's shoulder, grinning. The big ones carry the little ones piggy-back. Their faces are dappled with the sunshine of summers past. Once, they have built a snowman, with Charles's pipe stuck in his mouth. They are preserved in an eternal childhood — ecstatic, absorbed, untroubled.

Philip studies this cavalcade, pausing on the staircase. "This is you? On the trampoline. With Paul?"

"Yes and yes."

"Do you remember that?"

"Remember?" said Gina. "I'm never sure if you remember or are told. The photo tells me Paul and I trampolined that day. So we must have done."

Philip eyed her. "What else are you told?"

Gina laughed. "Family history, of course. Everyone has one. We had selected extracts of yours at Fowey last month. Most edifying. That time you cut off your sister's ponytail."

"A calumny," said Philip. "She asked me to."

"Not in your mother's version. But there you go. Famously unreliable."

Philip abandoned the trampoline photograph and continued down the stairs. Gina was becoming attuned to indications of his state of mind — that uncanny achievement of coupledom; she sensed that he was alert and interested, but also ill at ease. The set of his shoulders indicated this, the way his fingers drummed on the banisters. He headed for the kitchen, without looking at her. There was the smell and sound of breakfast: toast, the chink of cup set down on saucer.

She had a headache. Her seven-year-old self beamed at her from the wall, lacking front teeth. She wondered if Philip was wanting to escape. I told you, she said to

12

his back. Bigger deal. I told you. His parents had been unexceptional to the point of anonymity. She had found them delightful.

Charles was seated in a big carver chair at the head of the table, wearing a plaid dressing gown and reading a book. He glanced up, raised a hand in some kind of greeting and continued to read.

Alison was at the cooker. "Tea or coffee? I'm doing bacon and fried egg for anyone who'd like."

Philip said that he would like.

Charles said, without looking up from his book, "This chap has the cold war all wrong. Would you subscribe to the theory that mutually assured destruction was the deciding factor, David?"

Alison turned, shot a rueful little smile at Gina and Philip. "Fried bread as well, Philip?"

Charles was not waiting for Philip's view on the cold war. "Apart from anything else, the man has the Soviet mind-set all wrong . . ."

"Are you reviewing the book?" enquired Gina.

Charles ignored this. He picked up his cup, drank and waved the empty cup in Ingrid's direction. She reached for the coffee pot and refilled it.

"Charles doesn't do much reviewing these days," said Alison. "It was always a bit of a chore."

From the hall, there came a rattle, and a thump. Evidently the newspaper had arrived. Charles had turned back to his book but now held out a hand, palm up. Alison left the room, returned with the paper and gave it to Charles.

"Time was," said Gina, "you were all over the *Sunday Times* and the *Observer* or whatever. I hadn't realized it was a chore."

Charles opened the newspaper, and became absorbed.

"One bacon and egg coming up," cried Alison gaily. "Yours, Philip."

Charles turned the pages of the paper with a lavish movement, sweeping a slice of toast to the floor. "Time was, Gina," he said, "you were interviewing town councillors on local radio. Now you're a television face. One moves on." He smiled; no reproof intended, it would seem.

Or off, thought Gina. You're not being asked any more, are you?

The dog had neatly secured the fallen toast and retreated under the table with it.

Ingrid spoke for the first time. "On television you do not notice the scar. Almost not at all."

"That's what make-up ladies are for," said Gina. "I'll pass on your commendation, Ingrid."

Philip was looking from her to Ingrid and back again. He seemed about to speak, and then to think better of it. He began to eat, vigorously.

Which scar story did I give him? Gina wondered. The accident-in-the-school-playground one or the fell-off-my-bike one? There was a repertoire, with which she had grown careless.

"You always look wonderful, dear," said Alison. "And you've always washed your hair, even when it's in a refugee camp or somewhere."

"And you do not make mistakes when you speak. Not even um and ah, very much." Ingrid was apparently warming to the theme.

Philip, in the middle of eating bacon and egg, set down his knife and fork, rather violently.

"I do my best," said Gina crisply. "I wonder if I could have some more coffee? And where is Paul?"

"In bed," said Charles, without looking up from the paper. "Where else? His natural habitat for many a year."

"He's finding the job quite demanding." There was the faintest note of reproach in Alison's voice. "He has to be there by eight thirty, so he rather needs his Sunday lie-in."

"Sometimes he can take from the garden centre things they do not want," said Ingrid. "Last week we had a camellia and some nice big pots."

"Damaged stock," explained Alison. "The pots were a bit chipped, and the camellia had been frosted."

"A career in horticulture is an unexpected departure. But of course there have been a number of new beginnings for Paul." It was hard to tell if Charles spoke sardonically or not. "None of them involving much by way of departure from here."

"What does he do at the garden centre?" asked Gina.

"He is on the till," said Ingrid. "And he moves plants about. I expect he has to go in this afternoon."

"And he labels new stock," added Alison. "And helps people find things. Poor dear, I dare say he *will* have to go in later — Sunday is their busy day. Now what do you two have in mind? We're having a roast for lunch,

15

of course, but we'll have it latish so you may just want to laze around till then."

"On your own, Philip," says Alison. "Where's Gina got to?"

"Gone to get a paper. She can't do Sunday without one."

"And Charles has taken ours off to his study, I suppose. I'll join you — lunch is looking after itself at the moment and the terrace is so lovely on a sunny morning." She plumps herself down. "Oops! I always forget this is the broken chair. Paul jumped on it once, years ago, naughty boy. And do you see all those chipped bits on the balustrades? That's where Katie and Roger used to bang their trikes into them, when they were small. This is a real *family* house and it's got all the scars. Such happy memories — everything reminds me of something. We planted that silver birch on Gina's first birthday — look at the size of it now. Were you in a large family, Philip? Ah . . . The thing is, I only ever wanted children, and what's wrong with that? say I." A gay laugh. "Such a wonderful base for them this was — a real old-fashioned family. The sight of them all trooping off to school; I can see them now. And I'd count them back in, later, and there'd be a proper tea waiting for them, and everyone had their special place at the table. I'm sure Gina's told you lots. It's the first ten years that count, isn't it? Ten, fifteen. That's what sets anyone up for life, isn't it? I had a blissful childhood myself, and I've always been thankful. It still feels like yesterday — theirs, I mean, not mine." More laughter. "I can never quite believe they've all grown up and . . . no, not *gone*, of course, not gone at all, just moved away a bit. Far as I'm concerned, they're all still here, like a lot of dear little ghosts." Alison sighs. "Such a happy time, Philip, you can't imagine. Of course, we've been so lucky. Nobody . . . well, just the occasional little upset, but that's normal, isn't it? Real old-fashioned family life — you can't beat it."

"I will make you coffee," says Ingrid. "And for Gina too? No, it is no bother, Please sit," she adds graciously.

Philip sits down at the kitchen table. Ingrid takes kettle to sink, with slow deliberation, reaches for coffee jar and mugs. "Here is for Gina her mug. That is nice. It is a pity she cannot come home more. It is a pity all of them cannot come home more. Now is rather empty in this house, but it is good Paul is still here. For Paul there has been going away and coming back. It is a pity there are no grandchildren but perhaps in the end. Alison would very much like children again. Charles I am not so sure but he has his work. I have been here now of course a long time but it is still funny in this house with no children. Do you have children, Philip? No. Well, perhaps one day. Six children was much work but we were two women always and that was good. This is a big house so plenty to do but plenty of room also — everyone has their space. Charles of course must have space, especially Charles. When there were children, some took more space than others, but that is how it is in a family, I think. Sometimes squabbling, sometimes some little bother. You remember the good times only. The bad times — well, the less that is said the better, isn't it? Do you like sugar, Philip? For Gina I think it is no sugar."

Philip meets Charles on the stairs.

Charles pauses. "Ah, David. Now, I put it to you — if Blair's briefings persuaded him of the existence of WMD, then he was morally bound to press for invasion. The man had no option."

Paul emerges from the bathroom, a towel round his waist. "Oh God — what's the time?"

"Half-past twelve," says Philip.

"Shit. I should have been at the garden centre an hour ago. Oh well — the car broke down again, I guess." He grins. "So what do you make of the ancestral nest? Home sweet home. Has Gina given you the conducted tour? The height-measurement wall? The dressing-up drawer? No? Shame on her. No sense of tradition. Has she told you about the cellar game and the scary cupboard? No? What's the matter with the girl? Oh — this house has seen a thing or two." Paul laughs, hitches the towel, moves off down the corridor.

Each room in the house is indeed branded. The tour that Gina has not proposed would perhaps start in the big drawing room. Here, there is the open fireplace up which, once, letters to Father Christmas were posted. Moving across the hall from the drawing room, we are in Charles's study, which is rather less imprinted with family life, and where a bolt on the inside of the door seems to suggest a certain fortress attitude. The kitchen is of course vibrant with references — the mugs, the handiwork — and if we climb the stairs we find the measurement wall at the far end of the landing. Here are six columns, with meticulous pencil marks alongside each — a column for each child, with a horizontal line marking the child's height at each birthday. Gina at six tops Paul at the same age, but Paul then rushes upwards, and outstrips everyone by sixteen, after which the record ceases. Katie seems always to have been the runt, while Clare's teenage growth spurt is remarkable. The deep bottom drawer of a huge tallboy close by contains the dressing-up clothes — a morass of cowboy outfits, witch's cloaks, tutus, masks, policeman's helmets, animal costumes and an assortment of adult discards by way of spangly dresses, shawls, junk jewellery and a battered top hat.

Each bedroom can be seen to be scarred, on close inspection. In one, someone has drawn a row of rudely naked figures under the windowsill, where you would only find them if you were looking hard. In another, there are ink blotches on the ceiling — an interesting achievement. It is clear that redecoration has never been a high priority at Allersmead. The master bedroom is shabby, with plum velvet curtains faded on the folds to beige, and a carpet with patches worn to the backing. There is a vast four-poster bed — the site, it must be supposed, of all that impressive procreation. And there is a cupboard in the wall, full of the parental clothes, a place of darkness and long shadowy shapes

— scary, indeed — into which once upon a time people pushed one another and shut the door upon the screams.

The cellar. At one side of the house there is a flight of steps leading down to a black door. The key is in the lock — an immense iron key. Turn it, open the door and you are in a dank, dark semi-subterranean space lit by a couple of murky windows, high up at ground level. The cellar has a damp brick floor and, against one wall, a huge wine rack in which presumably the Edwardian haute bourgeoisie once stored their tipple. Elsewhere there are wooden shelves crammed with detritus of one sort or another — mouldy cardboard boxes, rusty tools, an old mattress, cobwebbed milk bottles and jam jars, a bucket without a handle, a gas mask, a bird cage, some tin trays. In one corner stands a defunct lawnmower, apparently welded to the ground. Along one wall a packing case and a doorless cupboard have been turned into what seems like improvised housing, and above them there is a board with a wavering chalked scrawl. Headings — FORFITS and PENALTYS — and beneath them names and numbers: Paul 5, Gina 4, Sandra 5 . . . Paul 1, Gina 2 . . . Clare 16. Something went on here, once.

"What happens in the cellar?" enquires Philip, eyeing that door.

Gina shrugs. "Black beetles. Spiders. Cellar life."

They are wandering in the garden, after lunch — after too much lunch. Roast leg of lamb, mint sauce,

20

roast potatoes, broad beans — the works. Rhubarb crumble with cream. Cheese board for any survivors.

"Shall we think about going home soon?" says Gina.

Philip considers. "Of course, there is a sense in which you *are* at home."

"I am talking about the flat."

He puts his arm round her. "I know you are. Joke. Of a kind. All the same, say what you like, your mother is a crack cook. OK, let us get ourselves together. Do you want to take those newspapers back? Your father would no doubt use them."

Philip carried down their bags. Gina was in the hall with Alison and Ingrid. Alison was saying that it had been so good to meet Philip, and they must come again soon. Gina was saying yes, sure, of course, trouble is I never know when I'll have to be off somewhere. Ingrid had put beans, carrots, lettuce, herbs into a carrier bag: "The lettuce you must eat this evening, while it is fresh. The herbs put in water."

Alison called out. "Charles — they're going."

Charles emerged from his study. Gina took a step forward, kissed him. "We're off," she said. "Traffic — Sunday evening. Don't want to leave it too late."

Charles accepted the kiss, patted her arm. "Good to see you other than on a screen. Not that I look at much TV — I prefer to read the news — but we catch you occasionally." He held out his hand to Philip. "Nice to have met you . . . er. Hope I didn't go on too much last night." A quizzical glance. "Company can set me off."

Philip said that he had enjoyed their discussion.

21

Alison was waving a piece of paper at Gina. "Addresses, dear. Everyone's addresses — email and otherwise — since you're not sure if you've got them or not. Roger's moved to a new hospital in Toronto. And Katie's husband is being transferred to San Francisco — they're so pleased. Clare's touring at the moment with the dance company — in Japan — she sends such pretty postcards. So there's only her Paris address. Sandra of course has her flat in Rome."

"And we think there is perhaps an Italian man," said Ingrid.

"Do we?" said Charles. "I have not been told this. Are his intentions honourable?"

Alison laughed. "Really! Sandra is thirty-eight. I expect she can look after herself."

"No doubt. I was merely trying to be the responsible father. So there you are, Gina — that's the run-down on the family. Global displacement, you note."

"We have still Paul," said Ingrid.

"And are so thankful that we do." Alison embraced Gina, dabbed her face against Philip's. "I wish you could have seen more of him but of course the garden centre calls. Have a good journey. Come again soon."

Philip drove this time. As the car went through the gates, he saw the group on the steps reflected in the driving mirror — Alison and Ingrid waving, Charles simply standing, the dog at his feet, tongue lolling. He thought they looked firmly set in some other time — about 1975, maybe — and said so, intending no criticism.

22

"Seventy-seven, probably," said Gina. "The summer of my eighth birthday."

Except that they are not, she thought. She saw her young mother, her young father. She saw everybody in another incarnation — Paul, Sandra, Katie . . . all of them. Aunt Corinna — she was there then too. Not set fast — moved on and away. Except that it is all still there also, going on just as it did. That day. Other days.

Gina's Birthday Party

Corinna sits on the terrace, and looks down into the garden. She has arrived late; the party is in full swing. Black mark for that, no doubt — perhaps cancelling out the brownie points for being here. She is not Gina's godmother — this is an atheistic household — but her "patron", and patrons are required to attend birthdays. "Gina would be so hurt if you didn't come" — which means actually that Alison would be so hurt.

Children everywhere. The garden running with children. A display of Alison's fecundity. Not quite all are hers, of course — there are visitors, Gina's invitees. The family rule is that the birthday child alone is allowed guests, Corinna remembers, and a handful only, the family itself being so numerous. So Gina has the decreed smattering of friends.

Alison is joyous, Corinna sees. The earth mother. Dressed by Laura Ashley, or perhaps robed would be a better word — an acreage of sprigged cotton, top to toe, nicely concealing the lack of figure. Could she be . . .? Oh no, perish the thought. And the earth mother has provided — the kitchen table is testimony to her labours. Plate upon plate of tricksy little sandwiches, with identifying flags, bridge rolls, sausage rolls, tiny iced cakes in frilly cups, brandy snaps, chocolate biscuits and jugs of apple juice and lemonade. And, in the middle, the Cake — eighteen inches in diameter at least, home-made down to the last piped rosette and the neat calligraphy: Happy Birthday, Gina. Though the eight candles I imagine come from Woolworths, thinks Corinna. Oh, the earth mother has done her stuff.

Why does Alison so exasperate me? Is it because she has six children, and I have none? But this is 1977, and a woman's achievement is not measured by the output of her womb. In my circles, where people have heard of feminism, Alison is a throwback: she is entirely dependent on her husband, her skills and talents are limited to nappy-changing and birthday cakes, whereas I am a well-regarded scholar and teacher. I know more about Christina Rossetti than anyone except a tiresome man at Yale who will be trumped when my book comes out. In the modern world, it is I who am the achiever, not Alison.

All right, maybe the children come into it. Somehow. But it's more elemental than that. It's to do with that inexhaustible smile, and the way she pats your arm, and her general shapelessness and the fact that she's barely read a book in her life, and that slight stammer, and her majestic complacency.

Why ever did my brother pick her? Suddenly she was there, and he'd married her, and no sooner married than babies poured forth. What's in it for Charles? Amazing sex? Surely not. Three meals a day and room service when required, yes. Charles has never been asked to lift a domestic finger. Genetic prowess? Well, maybe. Who knows what dark unspoken urges he has. I'd be the last to say I know my brother.

Corinna has a cup of tea in her hand, supplied by Alison: "You must be parched after that drive, and we're not going to have the birthday tea till after they've finished the treasure hunt." Corinna drinks her tea and watches children eddy in and out of the bushes. Alison is in their midst, clapping her hands and exhorting them onwards. Ingrid wanders up from the pond garden, a baby on her hip. Her role today seems to be to keep the baby out of harm's way. When did this one arrive? One was barely aware that there had been another.

And now Charles has appeared, also coming from the pond garden. He joins Alison, who is consoling someone who has not yet found any treasure, and he stands beside her, looking somehow entirely detached, as though none of this were anything much to do with him, as though he had merely strayed upon the scene. But, paradoxically, he manages also to seem some kind of pivot; he commands attention, this tall man in jeans and a green checked shirt, slightly stooped, as though he condescended to the shorter folk about him, at whom he vaguely gazes through heavy-rimmed glasses. There they stand, Alison and Charles, in the middle of their suburban acreage, their progeny whooping around them.

Alison is skimming and floating. She skims about the garden, with the children; her skirts float around her; she is on a tide of pleasure. Her thoughts too skim and float: lovely day . . . sun . . . children . . . Sandra, don't push Katie, there's plenty of treasure for everyone . . . summer birthdays always best, poor Paul with January, one should have thought ahead . . . Paul's a bit forlorn, so many girls, with Gina's friends . . . will there be enough lemonade? . . . will they eat the paste sandwiches? Too savoury perhaps . . . Gina, do make sure the little ones find some treasure; I don't think Roger has *any* . . . sun . . . children . . . ah, here is Charles.

She skims to a stop, with Charles now beside her. "They're having *such* a lovely time," she tells him. But Charles is not here, she can see, he is concerned with matters of the mind, the things that go on in his head that she could not possibly follow. She puts her arm through his, smiling. Smiling and smiling.

"Who are all these children?" he says. "The ones that aren't ours?"

"They're Gina's friends from school," she tells him. "Just six of them, for her birthday. Rowena and Sally and Rosie and, um . . . Corinna is here. Having tea on the terrace. Why don't you join her?"

And here now is Ingrid, wandering over the grass, her hair glinting in the sun, the baby on her hip. Charles goes. Alison smiles at Ingrid. "Is Clare tired?" she says. "You could try putting her in her cot for a bit."

"She is fine," says Ingrid. "Shall I soon take the ice cream from the freezer?"

"Soon," says Alison. "They've nearly found all the treasure now."

★ ★ ★

27

She sits at the top of the grassy slope down to the pond garden, waiting. The treasure is hidden all over the garden — gold and silver chocolate coins. The little ones think the fairies hid it, but Gina knows better: she saw Alison, earlier, bustling in and out of the bushes, reaching up onto tree branches, pausing at the swing, the long bench, the steps up to the terrace. The treasure hunt is not to start till Alison shouts one, two, three — go! so they are all poised, dotted about the garden. She can see the bright flicker of their clothes, hither and thither, each pitched where they think they have a private hunting ground. There is Paul, over by the rhododendrons. Paul is not much enjoying himself, Gina knows; it is not his birthday, he has no friends here. She is sorry about that, because she is in bliss herself, but it is after all her turn. You wait a whole year for this, and he had his, as did all of them.

Bliss. She can't quite believe it — this is the day, her birthday, the day you wait for, that will never come. Better even than Christmas, because it is yours alone. The presents, the cards, the fact that you are eight, not seven. Eight, eight — she rolls the word around in her mouth. I am eight.

There is Dad, standing beside the pond with Ingrid. Usually when it is someone's birthday Dad stays in his study with the door shut, so Gina is pleased to see him. Ingrid is carrying Clare, and she now detaches Clare from her hip and appears to offer her to Dad, but Dad does not take her. Of course not — Ingrid should know by now that Dad does not carry babies.

Eight. Eight, eight, eight. And her big present, from Mum and Dad, is a new bike — green, with a bell and a saddle bag. Birthday. It is my birthday. And there is still the birthday tea to come, and this treasure hunt. But Mum has said she must not be greedy and find too many coins; she must help the younger ones to find some, and leave some for the visitors. Gina knows all the hiding places, because there have been treasure hunts before.

She waits, watching Alison, who is in the middle of the lawn. Beyond her, Gina can see Corinna — Aunt Corinna, except that they don't say Aunt, just Corinna — who has come out onto the terrace and is also watching — watching Alison, watching the whole garden. And now Alison is calling out one, two, three . . . and immediately Gina spots the gleam of a coin, there on that big stone.

She has five coins. Five treasures. But she must have eight — eight for her birthday. It doesn't matter if she is not the one with the most, but she must have eight. Where to look next? Not the big shrubbery — Rowena and Sally are in there, they will have found everything. She has already done the long grass around the swing, and the flower bed below the terrace wall. She runs down the lawn towards the pond garden; Ingrid is sitting on the grassy slope above, playing with Clare, and beyond her Gina can see Sandra busy among the bulrushes beside the big square stone pond. What is Sandra finding?

"Go away," says Sandra. "I'm looking here."

"I can look too," says Gina. "It's *my* birthday."

They scrabble in the rushes, a yard or so apart. Gina reaches out to search a thick clump and both at once see treasure. They are at the very edge of the pond; both fling themselves at the loot. They collide, Sandra is crying "I saw it first — it's mine", Gina has her hand out to grab . . . and that is all she remembers.

Not quite all. There is this dreamy subsequent footage of being carried on a flat bed thing by men in uniforms, of Alison's anxious face staring down at her, of Alison's mouth opening and shutting but Gina has no idea what she is saying, of being in another bed somewhere else, and her head is hurting and hurting and someone says, "It's all right, dear, you're going to go to sleep for a bit now."

"Ambulance," says Corinna crisply into the phone. "A child has a head injury. Allersmead — number 14 Temperley Avenue, driveway with white gateposts, on the right as you go east."

She returns to the terrace. Alison and Charles are beside the pond. Alison is kneeling. Charles is bending down. Ingrid is rounding up the other children. "Come, come," she calls gaily. "We go inside now — the treasure hunt is finished." But the children are uncompliant. Roger is saying that he wants Alison. The visitors are shocked and interested; queasily, they stare down towards the pond. Katie is asking if they can have tea now. Sandra seems not to be around. Ingrid has Roger by the hand, and is trying to herd the others onto the terrace. The baby is crying.

"What exactly happened?" asks Corinna.

Ingrid pauses. Her flat fair face, always rather impassive, has become even more so. "I think I did not really see," she says.

"Why the hell did you hide stuff right beside the pond?" says Charles.

Alison weeps. This is not happening. Things like this do not happen. Not in this family, not to her. It is all some sort of ghastly hallucination. In a moment she will come to, and the children will be rushing around again, and it will be time to call them in for tea.

Thus, the birthday, of which everyone will remember something different.

Gina will remember coming home, her head all bandaged. And it is not her birthday any more; her birthday has gone down the drain — written off, wiped out. There was never any birthday tea. Later, another day, they had the cake and she blew out the candles, but it did not count.

In due course, there is the scar, across one side of her forehead, where, it seems, she hit the stone wall of the pond. And the hospital visits.

"A wretched accident," says Alison. "A wretched silly accident. She slipped."

Katie says, "You can have my treasure. All of it. I've kept it for you."

Ingrid says nothing. Not then.

31

Paul will remember hating Gina's friends — those girls ganging up, whispering. He will remember the ambulancemen, advancing down the garden like alien invaders. He will remember watching out of the bedroom window, while the others swirl around in the hall and Ingrid cries, "Now we play a game — come in here and we play Pass the Parcel." He will remember that people sneaked into the kitchen and helped themselves to the birthday tea.

Alison will remember the ambulance ride, the siren, Gina's face, the voices of strangers, the doctors, the nurses, the hospital smell, the trolley taking Gina somewhere, the waiting, the waiting.

Corinna will remember telephoning someone's parent: "I'm afraid that the birthday party has had to be curtailed — Gina has had an accident. I wonder if you could come and fetch — um — Sally." She will remember Katie saying can we have tea now? Why aren't we having tea? She will remember thinking, Now I know, definitely. I am not having children, never. She will remember the arrival of concerned parents, the departure of their over-stimulated offspring, Ingrid saying "Oh — they did not have the party bags for going home", the baby wailing, the dog discovered wolfing down bridge rolls in the kitchen, the eventual return of Alison (fraught) and Charles (irritated). It will be some while before she again visits Allersmead.

Sandra will remember feeling sick.

Charles will remember saying to Alison, "Get that bloody pond filled in."

Katie, Roger and Clare will remember nothing.

Scissors

When the day begins, when the light swells and within the house some people turn over in bed, blink, burrow down for some more sleep (Sandra, Katie, Roger, Clare) and others yawn, stare at the window or the clock, return to yesterday's preoccupation (Charles, Paul, Ingrid) or simply pick up the thread of existence once more (Alison, Gina), when this spring morning gets up momentum there are nine at Allersmead, none of them more than a yard or two from someone else, but all poles apart within their heads, their hearts. The adults are incapable of recovering what it is that goes on inside the mind of a person of six and a half, or ten, or 15. The children have on the whole not the faintest idea of what it is that drives and motivates their elders, or of the landscape of their thoughts. The children have various instinctive understandings of why their siblings behave as they do; the adults retain the intimacy of daily association but have lost sight of one another in other ways — like most people, they know one another inside out, and not at all.

Thus, the beginning of the day, one day among so many, for each and all, though admittedly some have more under the belt than others — just over 15 thousand for Charles, a humble two thousand plus a few for

33

Clare. A day is a day is a day, but some pack more punch than others, and at eight in the morning there is no knowing. This one appears to be set fine — a blue early April sky with some thin veils of cirrus, the sun glinting on the chestnut buds, the radio by the matrimonial bed suggesting outbreaks of rain in northern Scotland but turning quickly to the more pressing matter of the task force steaming towards those southern Atlantic islands, and the war that is about to begin. There will be a lot of people down there for whom this day is not especially propitious.

At Allersmead, it is simply another day. It is nobody's birthday, there are no special arrangements for it. Some people have plans. Charles intends to work — he is at a crucial phase of his book, and wants to get on with this new chapter. Sandra must, simply must, get to a hairdresser and a jeans shop and to French Connection. Alison wakes thinking about a recipe for baked lemon chicken. Paul has a plan, about which he is apprehensive. Ingrid is not so much thinking as brooding; within her head there is a grey fog of discontent.

Clare sees, out of the bedroom window, the shining chestnut buds, the splendour in the grass, and is, for an instant, transfixed.

Gina also hears the news bulletin, on her own personal radio, the radio she had for Christmas, and forms an opinion.

The house itself has experienced around 43,000 days since first it rose from the mud of a late Victorian building site. It has known over a century of breakfasts, it has sat out decade upon decade of springs, of people saying, oh look, the trees are coming into bud, of the sun poking its way into the rooms, of the moths creeping into frock coats and plus-fours and twinsets and, today, into Alison's good tweed jacket that she keeps for best. It has weathered four-course meals served by parlourmaids, the arrival of the wind-up gramophone and the wireless, the departure of the parlourmaids, the onslaught of the Hoover; it has seen birth and death and a great deal of sex. Most of this it does not record; it keeps its counsel, it does not bear witness to the *Sturm und Drang*, to the raised voices and the tears, nor to the laughter, the exuberance, the expectations. It is merely the shell, the framework, the abiding presence that remains when all that evanescent human stuff has passed through and away. It is a triumph of impervious red brick, black and white tiles, oak woodwork, stained-glass lilies and acanthus. It neither knows nor cares. Its current market value would astonish its builders, but then so would much else about its leafy neighbourhood, this provincial suburb — the cars, the trousered women, the cars, the hatless men, the cars, the curious metal arms skewered to every roof or chimney. But they might also be astonished by — or complacent about — the stolid survival of the house, very much unchanged. It has seen off fashion, or, rather, it has risen above fashion. It is nailed firmly to a time, but has also floated free of its time, has accommodated itself to new habits and practices, has digested central heating and washing machines and agnosticism and voting women and children who are very much heard as well as seen. Created as a shrine to family life, it has remained as such, even if family life itself is a rather different construct.

The family, this morning, gets up according to personal taste. Sandra takes a bath, using Bliss Bubble Bath, and keeping others out of the bathroom for too long. Paul wipes his face with a flannel and leaves it at that. Alison showers while wondering how many of them will eat ratatouille if she plays down the garlic. Charles cuts himself shaving, and comes down to breakfast with a flake of Kleenex on his chin, which makes Clare giggle.

Ingrid does her hair in a complicated braid, which means that she is down rather later than usual. Katie, who precedes her, finds that the dog has made a mess in the cloakroom, and cleans up so that it will not get into trouble.

Roger does handstands in his bedroom until chivvied by Alison. Gina continues to listen to the radio while she dresses in jeans and the red jersey, and decides to write a letter of protest to Mrs Thatcher.

Charles is only partially in the here and now, which accounts for the shaving cut (Alison has advocated an electric shaver for years but Charles has his preference). He is on chapter twelve of his book, which deals with adolescent rites of passage in primal societies. The book itself is a general study of the cult of youth, in time and space. He is pleased with it. He has only a few more months of work to do, then the polishing and refining and checking, then the footnotes, then off to the publisher, and he can start thinking about the next, which so far is just a gleam in his eye but which will be a discussion of the concept of nostalgia. Charles prides himself on his eclecticism; he never writes the same book twice; he is known and regarded for his range, his ability to turn his mind to fresh fields. Not for him the carapace of a discipline; not for him some dusty academic label. Thank goodness. He tried a stint in academia once, and got out quick. Thanks to a godfather who made a fortune out of household cleaning products in the early part of the twentieth century, Charles has the cushion of a modest private income — not a princely one, but enough to keep them all if they are careful, when bolstered by what the books earn. Thank goodness for Vim and Dettol and Brasso.

So this morning he is thinking about male initiation ceremonies in sub-Saharan Africa, and about puberty in Samoa and New Guinea, and how to slot in the discrediting of Margaret Mead, and that he is minus a rather crucial reference, which means that he must go to the library this morning, instead of battening down in his study right away, Never mind — he can get back to the chapter in the afternoon. And then there is this drip of blood from his chin, which he barely notices, intent upon the day and what he will do with it.

On Saturdays, Charles eats breakfast with his children. Weekdays, the kitchen is a maelstrom of departure for school — of mislaid sports kits, of forgotten homework, of haste and crisis; he tends to snatch toast and coffee and seek the shelter of his study. At the weekend, he remains at the head of the big table, reading the paper, and from time to time paying benign attention to the conversation, to opinions, reports, demands, exchanges.

Gina announces that she thinks this war is crazy. The Falklands War. What is the point of people killing each other over some islands stuck out in the Atlantic where no one in their right mind would want to live anyway? Charles remarks that this can indeed be seen as a point of view, a not unreasonable one, but that there is an issue of international law, of sovereignty.

Roger is doing a school project on the ancient Greeks. Does Charles have a book with a picture of the Parthenon that he could copy? Charles ponders, and says that he does not think that he has. All those books you've got, and nothing with the Parthenon, says Roger, disgusted.

Clare tells the table that she has a loose tooth.

Katie tells Roger her year did that project too, and you don't *have* to have the Parthenon — any old temple will do.

Sandra needs to go shopping. She needs a blue tank top. She needs a haircut. Will Alison drive her into town?

Paul is rather silent. When, once, he asks for the bread, Charles is startled by his hoarse voice, as so often nowadays. His eldest son is mutating, becoming someone else. Charles finds this vaguely surprising, but he is not dismayed like Alison, who would like to tamp him down, to arrest development. She does not like this growing-up business. She was aghast when last she put Paul against the measurement wall.

Gradually, everyone seeps from the breakfast table. Except for Alison and Ingrid, who are clearing up. Except for Paul, who sits eyeing his father. Charles is immersed in this distant forthcoming war, in this new language of Exocets and exclusion zones. Eventually he becomes aware that Paul has spoken.

"Well, can I?"

"Can you what?" says Charles.

"Can I go to Amsterdam for a weekend with Nick and some other people from school?"

"Why?"

"Just to hang out there. See things and stuff."

"How much?"

"Thirty quid? Less, probably."

"No," says Charles, returning to the Exocets.

Alison, at the sink, is silent but evidently attentive. She seems about to speak, but does not. Ingrid removes Charles's empty cup, sweeps a damp cloth across the table.

"Nick's parents are letting him," says Paul. Sullen. Resentful. His voice now a growl.

Charles folds the paper, glances at Paul and then at his watch. "Do you have a particular interest in Van Gogh?"

"Who?"

"Quite," says Charles. He gets up, turns to Alison: "I'm going to the library, but I'll be back for lunch."

Paul is glaring at his father. "So it's absolute no?"

"'Fraid so," says Charles, quite kindly, "I can see no sensible reason for yes." He leaves the room.

Paul takes a great swipe at the table leg with his foot. "Shit!" The table rocks. Ingrid makes a tutting sound.

"I do understand, dear," says Alison. "But you *are* only just fourteen, and I'm not sure that Amsterdam is entirely . . . I mean, possibly a little trip to the coast sometime with your friends, Brighton perhaps . . . I'm surprised actually that Nick's parents . . . You're quite sure about that?"

"They said maybe," snarls Paul. "Maybe if I'm allowed to." He adds, conversationally now, "I hate Dad." He stalks out.

Ingrid says, "The milk is all finished. I shall go to the shop. Or will you go to Sainsbury later?"

Alone in the kitchen, the sunlit spring kitchen, Alison thinks food. At one level, she thinks fish fingers and beefburgers and chips, macaroni cheese, toad-in-the-hole, bubble and squeak; at another she rather wistfully conjures up coq au vin and cassoulet and the ratatouille that she proposes to infiltrate into this weekend's menu. There is family food, and there is grown-up food, which is what Alison would like to focus upon if that were feasible, but it is not because there would be trouble in the ranks. The ratatouille may just about pass unqueried, and she feels pretty sure she can get away with the lemon chicken, which is borderline between child-acceptable and properly grown-up. So she sits at the table, jotting down items, and realizes that she is short of this and that, which will necessitate a supermarket trip — tiresome on a Saturday.

Alison is a homemaker, a housewife, that now outmoded figure, but her management skills are not highly developed. She does not plan ahead enough, she runs out of things, she forgets to get the boiler serviced or the windows cleaned, children berate her because they have grown out of their school uniforms or she did not give them the money for the charity raffle. Ingrid is frequently reminding her ("What *would* I do without you?"); Charles merely looks resigned, and detached.

She is aware of these deficiencies but not particularly concerned. After all, everyone is fed, everyone is housed and cherished and listened to and helped and supplied with pocket money and birthday parties and love and attention and a real four-star family life, which is what matters, isn't it? Never mind if there is the occasional blip; never mind if this is not one of those homes that are run like a machine, what matters is being part of a family, isn't it? One lovely big family. For Alison, Allersmead is a kind of glowing archetypal hearth, and she is its guardian. This is all she ever wanted: children, and a house in which to stow them — a capacious, expansive house. And a husband, of course. And a dear old dog. And Denby ovenware and a Moulinex and a fish-kettle and a set of Sabatier knives. She has all of these things, and knows that she is lucky. Oh, so lucky.

Alison is not long alone in the kitchen. People come and go. Gina wants to know what Mrs Thatcher's address is. Alison supposes 10 Downing Street, and is shown the draft of Gina's letter, which is brief and to the point. Gina thinks this task force is a stupid idea and this war is a waste of money and people. She warns

Mrs Thatcher that she will not be voting for her when she is 18. Clare has lost her scissors, her cutting-out scissors, and wants to use the kitchen ones, which Alison forbids because they are real scissors, sharp, and Clare is not yet allowed to use real scissors. Clare gets petulant, and is diverted by Ingrid, who arrives at that moment: "Look, we will make pastry men." Clare becomes happy with flour and water and a rolling pin, and is only distracted by Roger and Katie, who drift in, dump themselves at the table and start to play that game with open hands, closed fists and snapping fingers — Paper, Stone, Scissors. Clare wants to play too. Katie explains, patiently: "Scissors cut paper, paper wraps stone, stone blunts scissors." Clare chooses scissors every time.

Sandra requires money for the bus. She is grumpy because Alison has refused a lift to the shops: Alison is going to the out-of-town supermarket later, which is in the opposite direction, and that is all the driving she proposes to do today.

Paul is not seen, but is heard slamming out of the front door, presumably in search of one of his local chums.

Charles does not have a good morning at the library. In fact, he is frustrated. The reference section is inadequate and fails to meet his needs. He does not much use the local library — he goes up to town to the British Library — but for some basic fact checking you would think a decent public library should serve the purpose. He pads around crossly for a couple of hours, harasses a librarian and comes away dissatisfied. He should have gone up to town. Too late now — he will have to do so on Monday, and fill in some crucial points later. He is twitching to get back to that chapter; he is in a writing frame of mind, the thing is flowing, he must seize the day. This particular day.

So he goes home, in time for lunch, which he smells as he opens the front door — an oveny, lemony smell. The dog (a sort of Labrador, from Battersea Dogs Home — Alison will only have rescue dogs) greets him, subservient and respectful in a way that his children never are. He turns left into his study to dump his briefcase, and finds Gina there, opening a drawer of his desk.

Gina is out of order. Right out of order. No child is allowed in the study. They are forbidden to disturb him when he is in there ("What if the house was on fire? What if Mum had dropped dead?") and under no circumstances do they go in if he is not. But here is Gina in front of an open drawer.

"What are you doing?" demands Charles.

Gina replies that she is looking for paper and an envelope. She has drafted a letter to Mrs Thatcher and she needs to copy it out in best handwriting onto that paper he has with the address at the top.

"You should have waited, and asked," says Charles. "You know you don't come in here. And it's not in that drawer anyway."

Gina shuts the drawer, rather roughly, and in so doing manages to sweep the top sheets off the pile of typescript beside the typewriter. Charles exclaims angrily and leaps forward to gather up the paper. "Gina, I really don't want you in here. Look, here's some paper and here's an envelope."

"Don't you want to read my letter?" says Gina, in a chilly voice.

Charles takes the draft from her, skims through it and hands it back. "Fine."

"Does she get a lot of letters?"

"Undoubtedly," says Charles. His attention is all on the typescript, the pages of which have got out of order.

Gina is silent for a moment. Then, "Is that the book you're writing?"

"Mmn."

"What's it about?"

"It's . . . it's about how people have behaved towards children and young people, in the past and in different parts of the world."

"What's that bit about?"

Charles hesitates. He decides not to elaborate on circumcision rituals in Namibia and elsewhere. "Oh — it's about what it's like to grow up in societies unlike our own."

"Actually," says Gina, "I read some of it. I thought it was disgusting." She stares at her father with cold disapproval. Charles, momentarily wrong-footed, feels personally responsible for these distressing practices. Then he recovers himself, moves back onto the moral high ground and says, "Gina, you have no business poking around on my desk. You're not to do that again."

There is a movement at the door. Both become aware that Clare is there, watching with interest. "It's lunchtime," she announces.

"Right," says Charles briskly. "Gina, take your paper and envelope. OK, Clare — tell Mum I'm just coming."

The lemon chicken does not go unchallenged.

"What's *this*?" demands Roger. "I don't like it."

"I don't like it too," says Clare.

Ingrid declares that the chicken is very nice. Others eat without comment. Paul has two helpings; Alison beams upon him. He makes a point of ignoring his father.

Charles does not notice that he is being ignored by Paul; he has developed a certain immunity to the reactions of his children over the years. It would otherwise be difficult to operate with independence. This does not mean that he is unaware, or uncaring, simply that these particular family circumstances require a certain spirit of self-preservation. In any case, Alison is more adept than he is at riding the emotional rollercoaster; motherhood is her *métier*. It is what she always intended. Occasionally he feels that he is incidental to her grand design. Sometimes he feels this quite strongly.

Right now, he is thinking of societies of which he has read in which the care and supervision of children is a more or less collective affair. The kibbutz has always seemed to him an eminently sensible arrangement, which reminds him that he needs to do more research on kibbutzim and their views. And then there are those

African tribal groups in which all women keep an eye on all children, and the men get on with whatever it is that they do, which again looks like a healthy system. Whereas the centuries-old western practice whereby children are hived off into individual family units looks both impractical — you have to have the workhouse or the orphanage as a safety net — and potentially lethal. The child cursed with inadequate or cruel parents is in a trap. Charles's book is not intended to be a vehicle for his personal views — it is to be a detached discussion of practices and attitudes — but, as he sits there thinking, at the head of the table, unimpeded (more or less) by the background clamour of his offspring, he decides that a careful selection of individual family experiences would nicely illustrate this point. The Tolstoys, for a start. All happy families . . . Yes, that would be the way to introduce local colour, and a colour in appropriate contrast to the set-up in Samoa or the forests of the Congo. How many Tolstoys were there? Did old Leo rise to six?

Charles looks along the table at his own brood. He is thinking now about heredity, about gene pools, about kinship. Very important, kinship, in primal societies. Your kinship network could determine whether you sank or swam. Whereas in twentieth-century Britain kinship obligations have been superseded by the welfare state, which props everyone up from the cradle to the grave. No need to go cap in hand to your mother's brother, by and large. Genes count for rather less, here and now. Charles eyes the storm of genes around him today, the kinship group arranged at either side of him

— lanky Paul, dark intense Gina, pubescent Sandra, Roger and Katie, who share freckles and a stocky build, Clare with her straw-coloured hair. A fair assortment, he thinks, no dominant feature, a bit of a job lot really. In aristocratic circles there would be the inherited nose, or the poached-egg eyes, as in Lely portraits. In Namibia there would be the fancy tribal marks.

"Why are you *staring*?" complains Sandra.

Charles's thoughts have been once again on ritual. "How old are you?"

Alison laughs. "Really, Charles! We had Sandra's birthday only two months ago. She's twelve."

"I apologize. I can't keep track. Now, if you had grown up in some parts of Africa," he tells Sandra, "you would have had some very pretty scars made on each cheek, at one time, and I would probably have been looking for a husband for you by now."

Paul snorts. Katie giggles. Sandra says, "Scars! Yuck!"

"All a question of taste." Charles considers his daughters. "You are offended by the idea of scars. Others would be appalled at jeans and trainers and" — a sharp glance at Sandra — "painted fingernails."

Alison says, "Sandra dear, you know I don't like that stuff."

"Specially green," says Roger.

"Shut up," says Sandra. To her mother, she explains, "Everyone's doing it, Mum. Everyone in my year."

Charles is back with ritual adornment. He sees the fingernails as a western version of all that tribal face-painting, tattooing and creative self-mutilation with which he has become familiar during recent research. In fact, he decides, Sandra is merely responding to an atavistic need to turn her body into a personal declaration — a statement about her affiliations and her aspirations. She is announcing that she is a late-twentieth-century western adolescent for whom appearance is of central significance. She is setting out her stall in a way that young people have done since prehistory; one can hardly take exception to this. One must accept the fingernails as the symbol that they are. Maybe he will share this perception with Alison, later.

The chicken is followed by jelly, which meets with approval from all except Charles, who declines it in favour of cheese and biscuits. The morning is now tipping into afternoon, the sun is high, the house is rich with occupation — the aroma of lemon chicken, the chatter of eight voices (only Charles is silent, pondering his various insights) — it is time for the next stage, when people will disperse. Sandra will catch the bus into town, Gina is going to copy out her letter to Mrs Thatcher and do some homework, Alison has her appointment with the supermarket, Ingrid is taking the three youngest to the local park, where there are swings and slides. Paul is frustrated because his best mate is off somewhere for the day; he will loaf around and see if he can find someone else.

Charles retires to his study. The front door bangs. Once: exit Sandra. Twice: exit Paul. A third time: exit Ingrid and the children. Gina thuds upstairs. The dog whines at the study door, wishing to join Charles, who ignores it, busy making a note of the points that occurred to him during lunch. Does he have a biography of Tolstoy? No. Add to the checklist for Monday's library session.

The front door again: Alison has gone.

The house seems now to subside a little, to settle itself to relative silence; the dog can be heard to slump down on its side in the hall, the grandfather clock ticks. Charles puts a sheet of paper into the typewriter and starts to type. Chapter eleven creeps ahead, line by line, paragraph by paragraph. Charles is immersed — in his train of thought, in the organization of words, of sentences. Time passes — but, for him, it seems to stand still. He looks out of the window occasionally, unseeing; thoughts tumble in his head. He is elsewhere, inside his mind, in pursuit of an argument, a sequence.

Alison returns. Charles barely registers the slam of the door.

Alison hauls the heavy bags through to the kitchen and unpacks the shopping. She is hot, tired and cross. The car kept stalling, she was stuck at a traffic light with everyone hooting at her, the car park was full and she had to circle for ten minutes, they were out of lamb so she couldn't get the shoulder she'd planned for tomorrow, there was no brown bread or olive oil. All right, one should avoid supermarkets on a Saturday afternoon, but she'd had no choice; somehow she hadn't been able to get there earlier in the week. This is turning out a bad day, a day when Alison feels submerged by the house, the family, instead of riding high, in her element, in control. There was that business with Paul, and Ingrid has been funny lately, and Gina is quite difficult, and there is something wrong with the top oven of the cooker, and the wretched car . . . Plus, she has her period.

She stands in the kitchen, out of sorts, surprisingly alone in this house in which one is never alone. She remembers that of course Charles is here, and there comes the urge — a fatal, irresistible urge — to involve Charles in her malaise. She knows that this is unwise, she knows better than to do this, but something drives her to abandon the last of the shopping on the kitchen table, to walk out of the room, to cross the hall, to open the door of the study.

Alison does not often go into Charles's study. When she does, she feels that in some eerie way she has stepped outside the house — her house, their house — and into some alien space. She is not at home here. The room is unfamiliar — the enormous desk covered with books and papers, the bookshelves that line the walls that she has never inspected, the fireplace with the tiled surround (De Morgan, Charles says, and Alison always repeats this to visitors because evidently De Morgan is something desirable), the oriental rug that came from Charles's family home, the old leather armchair — she knows its landscape but at the same time she feels a trespasser, a foreigner, a person who has left her own consoling habitat.

"I'm back, dear," she says.

"Mmn . . ." says Charles, typing.

Alison continues, in a rush. "The car's playing up, it keeps stopping, I had an awful time. I'll have to take it

50

to the garage but of course Sunday there won't be anyone there, it's a nuisance, I need it on Monday for Paul's dentist appointment. And, Charles, I wanted a word about Paul, that business this morning, I mean, I'm sure you're right, Amsterdam isn't a good idea, but I wondered if something a bit less, well, *foreign*, maybe Brighton . . ."

Charles ceases to type. The words cease to tumble in his head, the sentences to form. Alison's voice breaks in, reaching him as an incoherent sequence, something about a car, a dentist, Paul.

"What about Paul?" He scowls at the typewriter, rereading his last paragraph.

Alison repeats what she has just said, with extra points. Paul does need to do things with other boys; his friend Nick is really quite sensible; she wonders if they are giving Paul enough pocket money; boys that age are so hard to understand, of course one hasn't *had* a boy of fourteen before.

Charles hears most of this. He says tartly that he himself has been a boy of fourteen, and remembers the condition well. Paul will get over it, one trusts, most people do. In the meantime, it is just a question of stoicism all round. His hands return to the keys of the typewriter.

Alison judders with irritation — an unfamiliar reaction for her; you cannot be a good wife and mother and a prey to irritation.

"Well, yes, dear," she says. "Of course. I know that. But I do feel we should sometimes *discuss* things when there is a problem with the children, especially when it's you who had the, well, the little bother with Paul this morning . . ."

Charles cuts in. "Alison, I am working."

"Yes, I know that too," says Alison recklessly.

Charles takes a deep breath. He stares ahead for a moment, then turns to look at her. "Then why are you in my study?"

Alison stares back. "Because I live here."

There is tension now. Something dark has stalked into the room.

Charles lays a hand on the pile of typescript on the desk. "This book," he says, "is —"

"I know," says Alison, cutting him off. "This book, and all the other books."

"I was about to say — this book, which I dare say you will not read — happens to be nearly finished. I am on the final, crucial, stretch."

"What's it about?" says Alison.

Second time today, that question. "It is about . . . concepts of youth, of the young."

Alison laughs.

"An amusing subject?"

"Oh, no," says Alison. "Just that it seems rather suitable."

They eye one another.

"I have children," says Alison. "And you have books. Except that of course you have children too."

"Of course."

That dark presence hovers.

"Fortunately," says Alison, "I love children. *Any* child." Her gaze is now intent.

Charles looks away. "Indeed you do."

When Alison came into the room she was panting slightly — bothered, disordered. Now, she has cooled. She is stiff, contained; she is not her usual self at all. No wonder that Charles seems uneasy.

"Alison," he says, "I realize you're having a difficult day. These things will sort themselves out, I'm sure."

Alison smiles now — a small, unedifying smile. "Oh, yes. Things do, don't they? Even the most tiresome things. I'll leave you to your book."

Alison goes. Charles blinks, frowns. He stares out of the window, and then at the sheet of paper in the typewriter. Minutes pass. He begins again to type, haltingly at first, then more fluently. With an effort, he recovers his train of thought, and once again becomes impervious to the world. Half an hour goes by. He is unaware of Alison going up the stairs, and stopping for a moment to talk to Gina. He is unaware that Ingrid and the children have returned, loudly welcomed by the dog.

In fact, Charles is deaf. He has to be. He has trained himself in deafness. Within his study, he switches over to deaf mode, and the house obediently recedes. He does not hear cries; shouts; the thud, thud of the stairs; the phone; the dog.

Accordingly he does not, after a while, hear Ingrid's knock. Nor does he hear when, eventually, she comes into the room. Just, he hears what she says: "Shall I bring you tea?"

He does not look up. "Mmn? Oh — yes. Yes, do."

Presently, a mug arrives beside him. He types, halts for a moment, reaches for the mug, drinks, types on.

Ingrid stands there. After a moment, she says, "I am a servant."

Charles does not at once hear that. Then an echo reaches him. In the echo, it is not quite clear if Ingrid has put a question or made a statement. Charles's attention is caught by this ambiguity as much as by the content; he is something of a pedant. His hands leave the keyboard. "Don't be silly."

"It is true," says Ingrid.

Charles sighs. "Oh, come on, Ingrid. Don't be like that. Have the children been playing up?"

"The children are like always."

Ingrid continues to stand, slightly behind Charles's chair. He is obliged to swivel in order to look at her. Her face is, as usual, short on expression, but there is something in her eyes that has him seeking cover. He turns away.

"Look," he says. "You know we . . . You know I . . ."

"I do not know anything," says Ingrid.

Charles frowns. "Oh dear, I'm sorry you're feeling like this." His hands drift back to the typewriter. But something else has stalked into the room, alongside Ingrid. Discomfort looms. "Ingrid, I'm in the middle of something just now," he says. "Where's Alison?"

"I do not know. I think she is upstairs."

Silence. Ingrid does not go. Charles lifts a page from his piled typescript, puts it down again, waits, glances round and meets once more Ingrid's cool blue stare.

"Ingrid," he says. "Really — I don't know what I'm supposed to . . ." His voice trails away.

"I know you don't know," says Ingrid. "You do not know, and I do not know."

She leaves the room.

Alone, Charles glares at the sheet in the typewriter. He glares, scowls, types furiously for about 20 seconds and then stops. He is finding that he is no longer deaf; he can hear kitchen noises, a child yelling to another child, the slam of a door. The house seethes around him, the world is too much with him, what is a man to do?

It is now late afternoon. The light is softer, the shadows longer; everyone is home and the house is alive with activity. Paul has failed to locate any of his friends and thunders up the stairs to his room, where he flings himself upon the bed for a bout of morose self-pity. Gina takes her letter to the postbox on the corner. Katie and Roger are playing in the garden, with Clare trailing around after them. Sandra is back from the shops, in possession of some satisfactory loot, and a new hairstyle. Alison and Ingrid are in the kitchen, starting to prepare supper, both of them unusually quiet.

Charles struggles for an hour. He has dried up. He types, and then throws away the sheet, types some more, and wastes another sheet. He cannot recover that productive flow. At last he gives up. He shuffles together the completed pages, frustrated. He must get out, walk for a while. Perhaps that will clear his head, but he suspects that the rest of today will go down the drain. He had hoped to get far into this chapter.

He goes into the hall, and puts on his coat. The dog nudges the study door open, and climbs onto the leather armchair, a favourite refuge. Charles goes through the kitchen to fetch his keys from the dresser hook where all household keys hang. Both women glance at him but do not speak.

Charles says, "I am going out. I may be some time."

As he crosses the road, he hears his own voice again, and his words sound a touch inappropriate: he is not leaving a cabin in the Antarctic in pursuit of a heroic death, he is merely escaping briefly from his family. That said, there is no chance that either Alison or Ingrid will pick up on the reference.

Charles walks purposelessly around the neighbourhood, trying to focus upon the rest of this chapter, to marshal material and arguments, to work out the thread of the thing. Various neighbours notice him — that man who lives at Allersmead with all those kids — but he is not much aware of others. Some people know him as Alison's husband — Alison is more gregarious — and remember that they have really never exchanged more than two words with him. What is it that he does? Works at home in some way, it seems. This sets him apart from all those who have offices and working hours, and provokes mild contempt or suppressed envy, according to inclination. Whatever, he is perceived as somehow not a chap you'd have a pint with, or a chat about the local council's latest cock-up. One woman eyes him and thinks furtively that he is rather good-looking, a bit like that American writer who married Marilyn Monroe, but the wife at Allersmead is no Marilyn Monroe — oh, dear me, no.

In fact, Charles is not in this affluent English suburb on a spring evening in 1982, but amongst the Bushmen of the Kalahari, to which he has never been, and in an Israeli kibbutz, and scrutinizing the lifestyle of seventeenth-century French peasantry, and casting a speculative eye on the family of Queen Victoria — didn't some rather odd child management go on there? He is getting back into the chapter, this walk is doing him good, the malaise of the last hour or two has eased. He wonders what Alison has for supper. He thinks that he might be able to get back to his desk later — he often finds the evenings conducive to work.

Macaroni cheese. He recognizes supper as he comes in through the front door. A favourite with the children. He turns into his study, minded to make some quick notes.

At once, as he steps into the room, he knows that something is awry. There is a sense of invasion, of disorder. The dog flops off the armchair, tail wagging. But the dog is not an issue. Charles has seen, now — he has seen the floor, the desk.

Paper. But paper as paper should never be. What he sees is paper in ribbons, in shreds, in a blizzard of long white fragments — a spaghetti blizzard of paper, spread out on the carpet, sliding from the desk. A paper storm that has replaced the neat pile of typescript that he left.

He flings himself upon it. He finds some intact pages beneath. But much is blitzed, blasted, scissored into a porridge of white strips on which dance bits of words, letters, punctuation marks. There can be no recovery, no first aid; whoever did this was assiduous.

Charles grabs a handful of paper and bursts into the kitchen. The family is assembled, most already sitting at the table, Alison at the cooker in front of a steaming dish of crusty golden macaroni cheese. She turns: "*There* you are, dear . . ." Then she stares: "*Oh* . . ."

"*Who?*" roars Charles. "*Which* of you?" Strips of paper stream from his fist. Every face is now turned to him. All are apparently amazed, aghast.

"*Who?*" demands Charles — calmer now, intent, focused. "*Who* has been in my study and cut up my typescript?" His gaze sweeps across the eight faces, and there floats through his head the realization that today he has offended at least four of those present; four have looked at him with eyes that registered — at that particular moment — deep resentment.

Silence. Alison's hand is apparently frozen in mid-air, serving spoon in hand. Paul is looking out of the window. Gina stares at her father. Time is suspended.

Clare says, "Aren't we going to have supper now?"

The Silver Wedding

"Did you do it?" asks Philip.

"No."

They are in the flat, in bed. Gina stares at the ceiling.

"So who did?"

"Actually," she says, "I don't know. Perhaps Paul. Maybe not Paul."

"Haven't you ever asked him?"

"We don't discuss it," says Gina.

"Why ever not?"

Gina shrugs. "Who knows?"

There is a pause. Philip says, "It has its funny side. In retrospect. Not at the time, I imagine."

"No. Nobody laughed, I can tell you that. No way."

Philip considers. "Sandra? She comes across as a bit . . . devious."

"No. She wouldn't have been interested in something like that."

A further pause. Philip is evidently intrigued. "An adult? Surely not?"

"Ingrid or my mother?" Gina is impassive. "Not inconceivable."

"Whew! That would put an interesting spin on things. Actually I reckon it was the kids — Katie and Roger. For a laugh."

Gina shakes her head. "Katie and Roger were the good ones. And Clare was only five or six."

"Did he publish the book?"

"Oh, yes. It did rather well. He was much on Radio 4, talking about the cult of youth." Gina smiles.

"And meanwhile, back at the ranch . . . Tell me more. Sometimes I think you hold things back."

"Of course," says Gina.

He turns his head to look at her. "Aha. I thought so."

"And anyway, I don't know it all, do I? There were six of us. Eight, with them."

"And Ingrid. Nine. I take your point. But at least I can have one version."

Gina now looks at him. "Why are you so interested?"

He grins. "It's happy families, isn't it? Everyone's fascinated by someone else's family. And it's you, far as I'm concerned — it's where you've come from."

"Ah," says Gina. "I see. You're after insights. Why I'm how I am."

"Nothing so vulgar. I just want the fuller picture. What you've got in your head."

"Oh, that. Untransferable, fortunately."

"When did everybody go? I mean, by when?"

Gina reflects. "In dribs and drabs. Me first, in fact. But there was never a finite going. There were compulsory attendances. Christmas. Anniversaries. Their silver wedding. That. Oh yes, that."

"Some people I don't see very well — they're in the shadows. Katie, for instance."

"Katie was kind. Is, I suppose. I haven't seen her for a long time."

★ ★ ★

Her present to them is a silver bowl, bought in the Saturday antique market. She went there specially, searching, two Saturdays running, and it cost more than she can afford. She will have to cut back for a while, though there is not much back into which to cut. Her student grant is rapidly eaten up, and the bit extra that she has from her parents doesn't go far, and of course they can't do more, not with Roger and Clare still to come.

She has wrapped the bowl in blue tissue paper, with a little silver label that says, "For Mum and Dad with love from Katie." It is in her backpack, up in the rack, and from time to time she glances up to check — the train is crowded; someone might grab it.

She is having to miss her best friend's birthday party. Oh well. Can't be helped. All the same, she thinks about this, right now, and that Mike, whom she is beginning to rather like, would be there, and so will Sophie, who also rather likes Mike. She tries to shake off this thought, and stares at the window, beyond which twilight landscape rushes past, overlaid by her own face — a small, worried-looking face framed in untidy curly hair, looking both familiar and profoundly unfamiliar. Katie is sometimes astonished to be 20; part of her seems to be eight, or ten, or twelve, at Allersmead still, everything going on there as it always had. She can feel almost guilty, waking up in her room in the hall of residence — someone else.

And now it feels strange, going back. Of course, she hasn't really left — she goes back every vacation. But it is as though she were only there by courtesy. She is

61

poised now for flight. In a year or so she will be properly gone — to wherever she is going to go, a job somewhere, a bedsit, a flatshare. Is this scary? Or exciting? She does not know. Her face, flying along beside her, seems uneasy.

Everyone is coming, apparently. "Yeah," Roger had said, on the phone last night. After a fractional pause, to which Katie's ear was tuned. She knows Roger; she grew up with Roger. Oh, they all grew up together, but she and Roger were a unit. She knows his responses, his turn of thought.

"Everyone?"

"Yeah," he said again. "Fair amount of aggro."

He had lowered his voice. She knew exactly where he was: in the hall, where the phone had forever been sited. There would be others within earshot — Mum and Ingrid in the kitchen. Dad in his study, maybe Clare somewhere.

She sighed. "Paul?"

"Yup. Not returning phone calls. Couldn't be reached. Mum going spare. Then eventually a message saying he'll probably make it. Probably. Mum very spare still."

"Sandra?"

"A fuss about some do she'd miss. But she's coming."

"Gina?"

"Gina's coming."

So they will all be there. Probably. Oh, and Corinna and Martin, apparently. That's a turn-up for the books. They do not come to Allersmead often. Katie is

nervous of Corinna; she's so clever, and she looks at
you as though you are being assessed. Martin's not
much better. He knows everything there is to know
about Shakespeare — he's written all these books —
what are you to talk to him about? Katie has always
slunk into the background when Corinna and Martin
show up. Gina copes with them better, and Sandra,
who doesn't give a hang about anyone assessing her.

There is to be a family supper this evening, for which
she will be in reasonable time, and then tomorrow a
buffet lunch for some friends and neighbours. A couple
of people who were at school with Mum, and her
kitchen class — the group who come to Allersmead
once a week to learn higher cooking, Mum's first ever
earning endeavour, and why not? And a few other
people Mum knows and . . . well, Dad doesn't really
have any friends, when you think about it.

25 years. That is a seriously long time. A seriously
long marriage. Sitting there in the train, Katie inspects
this expanse of time, reeling back like a length of track,
as long as her life, and then more. At the far end of it
stand her young parents, but these are people she
cannot imagine. A young Dad? Goodness, no. A
thinner, fresher Mum? A *childless* Mum? No, no. Her
parents are unchanging figures, unchangeable, set fast
at some point long ago, much as they are now, much as
they were — are — for the Katies who are still playing
in the Allersmead garden, digging with Roger in the
sandpit, being pushed into the scary cupboard, getting
the fairy costume out of the dressing-up drawer,
trooping down into the cellar.

Actually, I never liked the cellar game, she thinks, But you had to play, if everyone else was. And she didn't like it when Gina and Sandra fought, and when Paul got told off by Dad, and when . . . When what? When there was something stalking around, something uncomfortable, like shadows outside the window on a dark night, but not that, something inside the house. What do I mean? thinks Katie. I don't know now, and I didn't know then.

The train pulls into the station. She reaches for her backpack, gets off, goes outside to where the buses are, and oh good — there is a home bus waiting.

She gets off the bus at the end of the road and walks the last stretch to Allersmead. How many times has she done that? Every school day. Twelve school years. So multiply by . . . Oh, thousands, anyway. She has walked along here aged five, and then up and up and up until 18, and it's after A levels and she has an A and two Bs and Manchester will have her. That wall where there used to be a ginger cat sitting, and that lamppost to which she used to race Roger, and the drain into which they used to drop sweetie papers. She and Roger always waited for each other, and walked together. When Clare started school, they waited for her too. The others went separately, for the most part, as though they had nothing to do with one another. Paul, Gina, Sandra — solitary figures trailing a few yards apart. Sometimes Paul and Gina would join up, sometimes Gina and Sandra — generally, they straggled. She can see them still, in different incarnations — smaller, larger. Gina and Sandra in those maroon school tunics, but Sandra manages to make hers look elegant, something about the way she ties the belt, the way she walks.

If I have children, thinks Katie — maybe not so many. But such thoughts immediately evaporate — she cannot see beyond finals, sometimes not even as far as that. She lives still from week to week, month to month. Her head is full of her friends, the kaleidoscope of her relationships, of Chaucer and Donne and *Middlemarch*, and if she gets a vac job might she be able to save enough to go to France with people in the summer? She is tethered still to Allersmead, but it is a light tether which soon will break. She will be out there on her own, and will make the best of it; she knows she'll do that — she's not bad at managing. But right now she doesn't much think about all that; there's too much going on anyway.

She can see the white gateposts now — Allersmead. Almost, she can already smell it — comforting cooking smells, the hall smell of raincoat, a whiff of dog and something unidentifiable that is just the Allersmead aroma — lifting somehow from woodwork and stone tiles and stained glass and people.

She climbs the steps and pushes open the front door. The dog heaves itself up and acknowledges her, tail swishing.

Ingrid comes down the stairs.

"Hi!" says Katie. "Are the others here yet?"

"You are the first," says Ingrid. "Except of course Roger and Clare already here. It is good that you have come. Charles has gone out; I do not know where. Alison is in the kitchen. Crying, I think."

★ ★ ★

Clare hears the front door slam. Someone. One of them. But she's busy right now; she can't go down. She lifts her right leg and places the toes delicately against the mantelpiece. Then the left. Again. And again. She bends over backwards, slowly, floating her hands down to rest on the floor and stays there, thus arched, to a count of ten. She does the splits. Again. And again. And more.

The routine completed, she looks at herself in the mirror. Sideways on. She is thin, but not nearly thin enough. There is a suggestion of bum, the slightest curve of stomach. What to do? She has tried living on lettuce leaves and not much else, until Roger pointed out that dancers need muscle, and you don't build up muscle on a starvation diet. So now she eats, sparingly, and eyes her body with distaste.

She knows what she wants. She has a goal, an ideal. She saw the Frankfurt Ballet on the telly, and from that moment her life changed. Those lithe androgynous figures, like pieces of string, apparently boneless; those dances that were unlike anything she had ever seen — startling, capricious, furiously inventive. She hadn't known dancing could be like this. It is a world away from *Nutcracker* on the South Bank at Christmas, and the Saturday dance class at the leisure centre. Where do you learn to dance like a piece of string? How do you melt your bones?

There is an ongoing argument. May she leave school at the end of the year and go to dance school? Dad just rolls his eyes and sighs. Mum sees her in a tutu, flittering around in *Swan Lake*, and says, well, ballet is lovely, of course, but don't they sort of peter out at 30? Ingrid says to dance is nice, but there are also A levels and college.

Roger is not at Allersmead. He is in the Casualty Department of the local hospital. He has had the most tremendous piece of luck. His friend Luke got his hand stamped on during the afternoon rugby match against a rival school — emphatically stamped on, broken in all probability — so Roger was able to step forward and offer to go with him to the hospital, which meant an enthralling couple of hours observing what goes on in Casualty. He has had a road accident (man with a head injury, woman with cuts), a couple of burns, an electric hedge-clipper misfortune and various people just looking ill about whom he would have liked to know more. His interest is forensic, though he is also sympathetic. He longs to get behind the curtains with the medics and really learn something, watch an examination, have a go himself at an assessment, a diagnosis. His only chance comes when it is Luke's turn for a cubicle and a brisk young houseman, whom Roger is able to chat up and thus gets to have a good look at Luke's X-ray, over which he pores. There is no fracture, which would have made it more interesting yet, but massive bruising and swelling. Luke is by now thoroughly pissed off, and takes a dim view of Roger's evident appreciation of the afternoon. When his mother arrives and is effusive in her thanks to Roger for his solicitous attendance, Luke sits scowling, aware only that this means he will miss next week's match.

It is half-past six. Roger remembers with a jolt that this is the evening of the family gathering, and he had better leg it back to Allersmead pronto, or he will be in serious trouble. He gives Luke a kindly cuff on the shoulder, says goodbye to his mother and gallops off.

He has known that he wanted to be a doctor since he was about ten. He loved visits to the surgery, watched (and suffered) with interest as one or other of the family had chicken pox, flu, insect bites, gashed knees, scalds and sties. One minute people are running around, just fine, he noted, and the next they are felled by this or that, and the effects are impressive, but something can be done. He was going to be a part of this process. Oh, wanting to help people came into it, to make them better, but just as impelling was the fascinating business of cause and effect, of seeing what happens to someone when ill or injured, and then being the person who works out how to frustrate misfortune. Biology became his favourite subject; by the time he got to GCSEs he was already on course, sails set for medical school. With luck, and hard work, in a few years' time he will be the guy in the white coat, dispensing expertise in Casualty.

He belts up the steps and into the house. Smell of food, sound of voices from the kitchen — help! are they already eating? He opens the kitchen door a touch furtively, and sees that all is well. The table is not even set. Katie is there, and Ingrid, and Mum is stirring something on the cooker. She turns sharply as she hears him, and her face falls.

"Oh, it's you, dear," she says.

Sandra sees Roger hurtling up the steps as she arrives. She often forgets about Roger. Katie too. They were always on the fringes of her vision back then, of little interest unless you needed them to make up the numbers in some game. And now Roger is taller than she is, with a gruff male voice.

She takes her time, switching on the car's interior light to do her face. She is pleased with the car; it is second-hand — of course — but a lovely metallic blue, with sun roof, radio and cassette player. She can barely afford the payments, but what the hell. She's going to put in for a rise at the magazine. The editor likes her; she may even get to cover the Paris shows next spring.

Allersmead is fading for Sandra. From where she is now, Allersmead seems a long way away, an alternative universe where they do things differently, a place that has no conception of the fashion world, of the *vie et mouvement* of a vibrant office, of photo shoots and travel and being busy, busy, busy. Last Christmas, she'd brought a copy of the magazine. Her mother had eyed it with some alarm, turned over the page and said, "Goodness, those girls are so *thin*." Her father picked it up, stared at the cover, put it down again. Ingrid said, "These clothes are strange — I could not wear them but I suppose in London it is different." Clare said, "Wow!"

Gina had flipped through the pages. Was that a curled lip? "Not your scene," said Sandra. "I shouldn't bother. How's Radio Swindon?"

Sandra applies mascara. She glances at the house. Allersmead is alive with light. It may have faded in the mind, but within its context it is still very much in business. Someone walks past the sitting room window — she cannot see who. Are they all here? Is Gina here?

Gina and I, she thinks, are fish and fowl. Cat and dog. Sisters? Technically. Opposites. Rivals. Anything she liked I didn't. Anything I did she despised. Same still, really, except that it doesn't matter now. We don't have to live together.

She fixes her hair, steps from the car, takes her overnight bag from the back, and the flowers for Mum — the bouquet from Harrods — and runs up the steps, heels clicking on the stone. She pushes open the door, smells dinner — a thousand dinners — fends off the dog, which threatens her skirt with dirty paws, and Charles comes out of his study.

"Hi, Dad," says Sandra. "Happy anniversary."

Charles appears to consider this. "Ah. Yes. Much is being made of it."

"Of course. An event. Is everyone here yet?"

"The front door has been active. I have not counted."

"Dad," says Sandra, "you are out to lunch, as usual."

"I beg your pardon?"

Sandra shrugs. "An expression. You're not entirely . . . with it."

"I apologize," says Charles. "In fact, I was about to go up and put on a clean shirt in honour of the occasion."

"Good idea," says Sandra. She is thinking that a *new* shirt would be appropriate. That blue thing with the frayed button-down collar dates from when she was about ten. Does he even *own* a suit?

Charles is in no hurry. He eyes her. "How much are you paid?"

Sandra is affronted. "No way am I telling you."

"My interest is purely academic. I am writing about economic expectations. What people feel themselves to be worth. What are you worth then?"

"About thirty K," says Sandra crisply. This is significantly more than her present pay packet.

Charles raises an eyebrow. "Impressive. You can buy a university lecturer for that, I believe. Remind me how old you are?"

"Oh, *Dad* . . . " cries Sandra.

The kitchen door opens and here is Alison.

"Oh . . . Sandra dear. I thought it might be Paul. We're a bit worried that he . . ."

The front door, now. It swings open, and frames Gina.

"Gina dear . . ." says Alison. Her voice falls away.

Mum is in a tizz. Dad is not. Sandra has blonde highlights and a pricey-looking car.

Gina closes the door behind her and is digested into Allersmead. Clare shimmies down the stairs. Katie's voice sounds from the kitchen, and Roger, interrupted by Ingrid, who is saying something about laying the table now. Gina holds out her bunch of lilies to Alison, and at the same moment spots Sandra's bouquet on the hall table. Upstaged. Wouldn't you know?

"Oh, goodness," says Alison vaguely. "And you too, Sandra! How lovely. I must put them in water right away. You're both in your own rooms, of course, but remember you're sharing the bathroom with Corinna and Martin. I hope they won't be late — the pheasants have to come out of the oven by eight thirty. And Paul . . . At the worst I suppose we'll have to start without him. He didn't seem able to say definitely about coming and he hasn't rung again. I think I'll just pop up and change before Corinna gets here. Ingrid has been having a struggle with the sitting room fire — would you have a look at it, one of you?"

Alison goes upstairs, followed by Charles. Sandra and Gina contemplate one another.

"I'm not much good at fires," says Sandra with a silky smile. She too heads upstairs, bag in hand.

Gina goes into the sitting room where the fireplace sullenly smoulders. Once, she sent a letter to Father Christmas asking him to bring her a real typewriter. He did not comply, any more than God attended to her request that Sandra be transferred to another family; these failures induced a permanent scepticism about the powers of vaunted agencies. The United Nations can also fail to deliver, one has observed.

She adds some kindling to the sulky flames, applies the bellows and coaxes forth a gush of flame. She sits back on her heels, watching.

72

Katie comes into the room. "Can you remember where flower vases are? Mum's told me to do them."

"Top shelf of the pantry cupboard."

Katie sits down on the fireside stool. "Mum was in tears when I arrived."

"Why?"

"Don't know. Dad didn't seem to be anywhere and there's a fuss about Paul."

Gina pokes a log. Sparks fly up. "Fingers crossed," she says.

"What?"

"Just — I wouldn't bet on Paul, one way and another."

"Oh, dear." Katie sighs. "Mum's rather set her heart on tonight."

"I know. Half a dozen pheasants have died for this." Gina hands Katie the bellows. "Here, you blow for a bit."

Katie squats by the fire. The logs flare up. "What do you *do* at the radio place?"

"I chase fire engines," says Gina. "Strictly local fire engines. I record outrage about the vandalism of park benches. I interview centenarians."

"Is it fun?"

"You can certainly find some fun."

"You were always going to do something like that," says Katie. "Remember the *Allersmead Weekly Herald*?"

Gina laughs. "Editor, lead writer and reporter. The rest of you were hopeless. Lost interest after issue number one."

"You're so lucky. I don't know what I want to do."

"Don't worry. Things have a way of simply happening."

"But suppose the wrong things happen."

"Evasive action," says Gina. "Spot the dead end. Mind, I can talk. Some would say local radio is just that. I'm giving it one year."

"There are these postgraduate scholarships to America. I've been wondering."

"So go for it."

Katie sighs again, gets up. "I'd better do the flowers."

The fire is developing a heart. Gina puts on another log. In this suburban home, she tells the mike — no, in this suburban mansion a family is gathered for a sacred ritual, the celebration of the passage of time. 25 years have been knocked on the head; 25 years are under the belt. Parents and children have come together to wonder at this amazing mastery of the calendar, to congratulate one another on having got older, on having refused to stay still. Animals have been sacrificed, there will be festive exchanges — not too much let's hope, there will be statements of individual beliefs and tastes — again, let's hope no one overdoes it, the old home will echo with merriment and no doubt, frankly, the occasional discordant aside. Let's talk to some of the key players . . .

Clare comes in. "Look," she says.

Clare leans over backwards, drops her hands to the ground, and rests thus, a poised arch.

"Fantastic," says Gina.

74

Clare straightens up. She lifts one leg up to the level of her shoulder, and holds her foot lightly in one hand.

"Impressive."

Clare sits cross-legged by the hearth. "Have you ever heard of the Frankfurt Ballet?"

"I'm afraid not." Gina purses her lips, tilts her head to one side. "You're a young student of dance, Clare," she says. "Tell me, do you see yourself as the Sugar Plum Fairy or a member of Hot Gospel?"

Clare giggles. "What's the funny voice for?"

"It's an interview voice. Clare, as a sixteen-year-old mover and shaker, how would you change the world?"

"I don't believe you really ask people things like that."

"Sadly, no. I ask them if they're in favour of a new bypass and how they feel about winning the dog show. With luck, you can slip in the occasional subversive item."

Clare gets up, does the splits, and rests thus on the hearthrug.

"Don't," says Gina. "It makes me sore just to look at you."

Clare swings to her feet, wanders over to the window. "Here's a car."

"Aha. Corinna and Martin."

"There's been huge commotion about tonight."

"So it seems."

"Massive. Mum and Ingrid. Dad not. There's a cake, silver things all over it. Mum was icing till midnight."

Gina pokes the fire, which is going nicely now. She stares through sparks into the shuddering red embers across which flit a procession of other cakes, other celebrations — the birthdays, the bonfire parties, the ceremonial cooking of two decades. The family that eats together stays together.

The front door opens. Voices.

"Come on," says Gina, getting up. "We'd better do hostess stuff if Mum's still upstairs."

"The fatted calf has been slain," says Corinna as she opens the front door. "I could smell it from outside."

Martin follows her, carrying the bags. "I forget," he says. "Have we brought an offering?"

"Of course. Silver candle snuffer. They'll wonder how they did without one for so long."

Gina and Clare appear from the sitting room. Greetings. Kisses. Martin deals awkwardly with the kissing. He and Corinna are childless, and never wished to be otherwise. The Allersmead environment is as alien as you can get, as far as he is concerned. Charles should be a fellow spirit — he is a scholar, after all, of a sort, he leads the life of the mind — but Martin has never achieved more than desultory exchanges. From his viewpoint, in the heart of academia, someone like Charles is a bit of a lightweight, a dilettante. Charles, on the other hand, has an aura of unjustifiable complacency and is clearly unimpressed by status. Neither he nor Alison wrote to congratulate Martin on his chair.

"They're upstairs changing," Gina explains. "Down in a minute."

76

"Oh, my goodness," says Corinna. "Is it black tie? Have we boobed?"

Gina ignores this quip which she considers facetious. She offers to show Corinna and Martin to their room. Corinna says that actually she is dying for a drink.

"It's champagne," Clare announces. "I've seen it in the fridge. There's a tray out with the glasses."

Alison now appears on the bend of the staircase, with cries of welcome. She is wearing something long and flowery that looks to Corinna like a converted curtain, and is followed by Charles, who is in brown cord trousers, shirt and a pullover that can be seen to be delicately laced with moth-holes, if you look closely. He is followed by Sandra. Roger, Katie and Ingrid now emerge from the kitchen and the Allersmead hall is suddenly full of people and talk. The dog barks hysterically. Alison sends Roger back to the kitchen for the champagne and starts to herd everyone into the sitting room.

"Still no Paul — oh, dear. Well, we'll just have to start anyway, tiresome boy. Clare, get the nibbles, would you — on the kitchen dresser. And Dad will need a cloth for the champagne; it always overflows, doesn't it? Oh, you did get the fire going — well done. Now that there are so few of us we hardly ever seem to *use* this room. We've got the telly in the old study now, where people did their homework; it's so much cosier. Corinna, we haven't seen you for *such* a long time; you're going to find everyone so different, so *grown-up*."

Grown-up? Corinna eyes the group. Indeed yes, though she glimpses too their younger selves. The small boy somewhere beyond Roger. Katie's expression, which is still that of a wide-eyed eight-year-old. Sandra is elegant, poised and out of kilter with the rest; that was perhaps heralded years ago. Gina — well, Gina always did have an air of shrewd appraisal and she has it now; Corinna feels judged and found wanting, something of an unusual experience for her. Clare is rapier thin and undeniably pretty. Ah — Clare.

Charles is opening champagne and making a hash of it. There is mopping up to be done. At last everyone is furnished with a glass.

Corinna raises hers. "Here's to marriage!" She and Martin are not married, so is there a hint of irony here?

Alison puts her arm through Charles's. "I really can't quite believe it. 25 years! It feels like much less — and then in other ways much more. I mean, the wedding seems like yesterday, I remember everything . . . that register office — of course they are a bit sort of official and a church wedding is lovely but out of the question for us, Charles felt you really have to be paid up C of E — and the lunch at that hotel, my mother's *hat*, she always overdid things, my father forgetting his speech . . ."

Corinna remembers Alison pink-faced with excitement, wearing a sort of smock, flowers in her hair.

". . . the icing on the cake so hard I couldn't get the knife in . . ."

78

"Did anything go right?" asks Gina.

Alison is merrily indignant. "Things aren't *meant* to go right at weddings — that's part of the fun. It was a lovely day, wasn't it?" She beams up at Charles, who is wearing what his offspring recognize as his expression of contained endurance. It is his Christmas expression; they know it well. He inclines his head in reply to Alison, which might mean anything.

Clare is circulating with the nibbles which, this being Allersmead, are not nuts or olives but exquisite little savoury confections made by Alison. Corinna takes several. At least you eat well here, which can somewhat mitigate whatever circumstance has arisen — the birthday, the calendar ritual. Alison now holds cookery classes, it seems. Next thing, she'll be on the telly. One can just see her, the earth mother radiating into every home, wooden spoon in hand. Except that Charles would never allow it. Sees the telly as beneath contempt, I seem to remember.

"So you've got a dedicated TV room now?" she remarks. "I thought you scorned the telly, Charles?"

"He got hooked on the Gulf War," says Roger. "Kate Adie in a flak jacket and missiles whizzing down ventilator shafts."

"Six o'clock news every evening," says Clare. "He was sitting waiting for it."

Alison chips in. "Now that's silly. Of course Dad wanted to know what was going on, like we all did. It's true that he doesn't normally watch television very much."

Charles smiles. "I will admit that there was a certain awful fascination. The language alone. Scuds and Exocets."

"Well, it is good that it is finished," says Ingrid. "All those poor men getting killed. Iraq men mostly."

Corinna stares for a moment at Ingrid. One has never really got to grips with Ingrid.

Alison now hurries from the room; the pheasants need attention. Corinna tells everyone that she and Martin are having a sabbatical in the States — a semester at Berkeley. She'll be able to get on with her book and Martin is giving a lecture series, a rather prestigious one, as it happens. This does not prompt much response; Clare asks what sabbatical means, and is told, at some length. Charles appears uninterested.

"So how's Leeds, Katie?" says Martin, in a hearty tone.

Katie, apologetic, says that actually it's Manchester, and it's fine. Martin refers to a colleague of his there and wonders if Katie has come across him. The colleague in question is the vice chancellor, and you do not come across the vice chancellor if you are a second-year student. Katie is once more apologetic. Martin loses impetus and turns to Charles. Katie slinks from the limelight and goes to join Roger on the window seat.

"Well done," says Roger.

"I've always been scared of him."

"I'm not good with Corinna. She used to make me feel as though I'd got dirty ears and breakfast between my teeth."

"You probably had," says Katie amiably. "Thing is, she couldn't do children."

"Perhaps she'll come round to us now we're maturing." Roger grins. "She's having a try with Sandra, anyway."

Corinna has never heard of the magazine, so Sandra tells her about it, a touch laconically. She is well aware that fashion mags are not on Corinna's radar, and she doesn't care, one way or the other. Corinna isn't really on her radar, for that matter, except in the way that everything back then — everything pertaining to family and Allersmead — glimmers away in the mind and there's nothing you can do about that. She describes a fashion shoot, amused by Corinna's expression of disdain.

"These girls are paid *how* much? It's outrageous!"

Martin has asked Charles what he is working on at the moment, thus inviting an extended account of some book on the eighteenth-century Enlightenment. Charles is a popularizer, in Martin's opinion — potboilers, Sunday newspaper fodder. Martin himself produces the sort of work that provokes intense discussion amongst about a dozen people and is bought only by academic libraries. For some reason, Charles's projects both intrigue and exasperate Martin and he is always driven to make enquiries, through clenched teeth. Some years ago, he discovered that Charles's book on cults of youth sold in tens of thousands; he has never got over this.

Gina attends to the fire, which threatens to sulk again. Corinna is talking to Sandra, Martin is engaged with Charles — Ingrid apparently listening. Katie and

Roger are in a huddle on the window seat, with Clare on the floor beside them. Gina wonders about going to the kitchen to see if Alison needs a hand, and then decides against it. Alison would probably decline help — she always has kitchen matters perfectly under control — and also she is in a fuss, which intrusion might make worse.

Gina sits down on the hearth stool, and considers the room. Hello and welcome to the family programme. Last week we looked at what it means to be an only child. Today, we're going to get inside a *large* family — a family of six, a throwback some might say to the Victorian age, but there is nothing Victorian about the Harpers, from fashionable Sandra to leggy schoolgirl Clare. Gina is number two, but when I asked her about the dynamics of such a family she was curiously reticent. I forget, she says. You forget. They forget, I suppose. That's the thing. There's a whole lot of oblivion, and then out of it occasionally something floats up, quite sharp and clear. Someone saying something, doing something. And, anyway, it's not so much dynamics, it's a climate. I asked about the importance of position in the family. Oh, eldest or youngest, says Gina, that's the place to be — in the middle is just rank and file. She is reluctant to be specific about the part that parents play. Let's just say they have leading roles, she comments.

Alison returns. "Dinner's ready!" she cries. "Come through, everyone. Gina, put the fireguard in front of the fire. Bring your glasses, please — and those plates, Roger dear."

82

They troop into the kitchen. Alison has a *placement*. "You there, Corinna, by Charles. Martin at the other end. I'm giving up on Paul, I suppose — oh, dear, what can have happened? Sit, everyone. Charles, do the wine, will you?"

The starter is a smoked-salmon pâté, one of Alison's specialities. At last she's able to say goodbye to fish fingers and beefburgers, thinks Gina. Poor Mum, she had to cook below her level for years and years.

They are ten round the table in the Allersmead kitchen. Alison has turned off the overhead light and lit candles. They are eating off the Limoges china, which belonged to Alison's mother and the appearance of which always signals some significant occasion. Alison explains its provenance to Corinna — how her parents bought the set in France on their honeymoon and miraculously she has been able to maintain it intact: "Not that it comes out *that* often, but even so . . . Twelve place-settings and the soup tureen, so pretty — the pink and gold. My mother was torn between this and a blue and green, apparently."

"We wash always by hand," says Ingrid. "Not in the dishwasher."

Martin is wearing a glazed expression. Katie and Roger are engaged in cosy banter across the table. Sandra is telling Clare that she should try wearing her hair up, she'll show her how tomorrow. Charles has just asked Gina how much she gets paid at the radio station.

Corinna has heard all about the Limoges china on previous occasions and considers it hideous. She tucks into the pâté, eyes Charles and decides that he looks distinctly middle-aged these days — and then remembers that if he does then so presumably does she. He is two years younger.

"Great pâté, Mum," says Roger. "Is there any more going?"

Beaming, Alison hands the bowl round for seconds.

"Very good," says Martin.

Alison beams further. "I'll give Corinna the recipe."

Corinna gulps.

Sandra says, "Oh, are you a crack cook too, like Mum?"

Corinna manages a wintry smile, and suppresses comment. It occurs to her that perhaps there is more to Sandra than meets the eye.

Clare is exercised about the matter of her hair. She twists a long blonde lock and holds it round her head. She addresses the table. "What do you think? Up?"

"Either way is nice," says Ingrid, "but up will fall down when you dance."

"You skewer it," says Sandra. "Trust me — I know about hair."

Corinna sighs. Martin is thinking of High Table dinner at his college.

Alison reckons up would be lovely. "So sweet and old-fashioned. Of course, mine has been up for ever." She waves a hand at her frazzled bun. "The trouble is you can't get proper hairpins these days, or kirby grips, just these peculiar clamp things, but I have got a little store, I'll let you have some, dear, to experiment with."

84

"*Mum . . .*" cries Clare, "I don't mean to be rude but no way is it going to be anything like yours."

Charles rises, reaching for the wine bottle.

"Yes, please," says Corinna, holding out her glass. "What is it, incidentally?" She is not in fact interested in the wine but is determined to put a stopper on this hair debate.

Charles peers at the label. "Sainsbury's."

"Boxes are cheaper," says Ingrid. "But for special occasions always a bottle."

Martin's expression is unfathomable. Roger tells everyone that actually cheap plonk is laced with anti-freeze, everybody knows that, Katie is saying that she and her friends drink beer anyway — plonk's too expensive, anti-freeze or not. Sandra says that now she knows why she steered clear of uni. Gina has begun to take away the dirty plates, and Alison is opening the door of the oven. There is a gust of roast pheasant.

Charles is required to carve. Ingrid and Alison dish up vegetables. There is bustle now, people getting up and down, Charles complaining about the anatomy of pheasants, Roger offering advice, Alison putting finishing touches to the gravy, Ingrid handing out the servings. "Sit *down*," orders Alison. "Everyone who's getting in the way."

At last all are provided with a plateful of pheasant, all are once more seated. The vegetables circulate. And from the hall the dog begins to bark. Alison freezes, gravy boat in hand.

The door opens. Paul. He stands there, eyeing the room.

85

"*There* you are!" cries Alison. "Better late than never. Whatever happened? Why didn't you *ring*? I tried and tried to reach you. Anyway — here you are. Pull up that chair — Sandra, you and Roger shunt up and make room between you. Charles, another helping, please."

Gina observes Paul. Oh, dear. Glazed look, slightly swaying motion. Pissed or stoned? Both, possibly.

"Sit *down*, dear," says Alison.

Paul continues to stand. He has everyone's attention, except for Charles, who is once more addressing himself to a pheasant carcass, with irritation.

Paul says, "I want to sit next to Gina."

"OK, OK," says Roger. "No prob. Shove up, Clare." He hauls the chair around the table, then steers his brother into it. "There." He fills a glass with water from the tap and sets it down in front of Paul.

"I want some wine," says Paul.

Martin has begun to talk with pointed loudness about the summer that he and Corinna have just spent in Italy: ". . . lent this villa by a colleague of mine. Perfect place in which to get down to some work . . ." Clare and Katie, having registered Paul, raise their eyebrows at one another, and are exchanging opinions about a film.

Gina fetches a glass and half fills it with wine. "That's the ration," she says to Paul quietly. "Right? Now eat, there's a good boy."

Paul appears to subside. He eats, in a desultory way. Alison is watching him with an anxious expression.

"You do look tired, dear. What *have* you been doing with yourself?"

Roger snorts. Clare rolls her eyes. "Mum," says Gina. "This pheasant is amazing. And how do you do potatoes this way? You must write it down for me. I'm really trying to get into cooking now I've got a flat. Could I have a Le Creuset thing for my birthday?"

". . . Piero della Francesca country, of course . . ." Martin is saying.

Paul puts down his knife and fork. He takes a swig of his wine, and gazes vaguely round the table. "Is it someone's birthday?" he enquires.

"*Honestly*, Paul . . . For goodness' sake! I've been writing you cards and leaving messages for weeks. It's our *anniversary*. Silver wedding. 25 years!" Alison is indignant, though indulgently so.

"Sorry, sorry . . ." Paul stares at his mother. "Congratulations. 25 years . . ." He appears to reflect on this. "So that makes me 24, right?"

"Well, of course," says Alison brightly.

"And I am 22," says Gina in a rush. "And so forth and so on right down to Clare who is all of . . . ten, is it, Clare?" And don't let us get into exactly when Paul's birthday is, just don't let's go there, time-honoured no-go area. "And here we all are gathered together to celebrate Mum and Dad and all of us and here's to the next 25 years." She raises her glass. So do others. So does Paul.

He says, "I want some more wine."

Gina says, *sotto voce*, "I want doesn't get. Just cool it, right?"

Corinna is wearing a speculative look. Martin is pursuing the Italian theme. He tells Charles that he and Corinna are looking for a permanent bolt-hole over there. Corinna interrupts to say well, maybe, but there's also the Dordogne, our French is better than our Italian. Charles stares at them as though wondering who they are. Alison says, "Of course there's a lot to be said for abroad but we always loved Cornwall when the children were young, we had such a nice house at Crackington Haven, several summers, it was there Paul climbed the cliff and got stuck, such a panic, we thought he'd fall, oh dear — do you remember, Charles?"

"All too vividly."

There is a brief hiatus, into which Paul speaks, looking at his mother. "Which of us was your favourite? Who did you love best?"

All know that they should not look at Alison, and most do so. Clare drops her fork. Sandra takes a deep and audible breath. Gina kicks Paul on the shin. Charles gazes down the table, impassive.

"Really, dear! What a silly question!" says Alison merrily. She gets up. "Now, who's for seconds? There's plenty of vegetables, and I think Charles can squeeze out a bit more pheasant. Martin? Corinna?"

Seconds are had, by those who wish. Paul declines, and stares moodily at the empty glass in front of him. He mutters to Gina. "You *kicked* me."

Gina murmurs back that indeed she did. "Could you, do you think, cool it? Just do me a favour and shut up until the booze or whatever has worn off.

Incidentally, where *are* you hanging out at the moment? Do you have such a thing as an address?"

Paul's reply is indistinct.

"And work?"

"Bit of a problem there," mutters Paul. "Got the sack from Starbucks."

"Ah. Cash-flow difficulty?"

Paul grunts.

"Here's a deal. Keep your head down for the rest of the evening and I'll give you a tenner as an advance Christmas present."

The pudding is one of Alison's signature confections, a raspberry-cream meringue. "Frozen raspberries, of course, but our own; we had a wonderful crop this summer. Ingrid's doing so much gardening these days — now we haven't got small people running us off our feet, she planted new canes a couple of years ago and they're doing wonderfully."

Clare declines the meringue with a sigh; cream is a no-no. Roger says in that case he'll have hers, please. Martin seems to have driven Italian retreats into the ground and is sitting silent. Corinna is recalling her parents' practice of games after a family meal: "Remember, Charles? Pencil and paper games and at Christmas always charades. Dressing up and acting. It seems weird now but of course very much what some people still did then — a Victorian/Edwardian survival, the last gasp of home entertainment. Charles, I distinctly remember you in a tablecloth, aged about ten, being a Roman emperor."

There are giggles around the table. "Can we have a repeat performance?" says Roger.

Charles smiles blandly, and addresses Corinna. "And I remember you as Titania, in a net curtain."

This image reduces Clare to suppressed hysteria. She has to bite on her napkin.

Paul speaks. "I think we should play a game after dinner. We should play the cellar game."

Silence.

"No way," says Clare.

"Wrap up, Paul, OK?" says Roger.

"The cellar game?" says Alison. She looks around, brightly. "What was the cellar game? You all used to troop off and I'd worry that you'd hurt yourselves on the junk there is down there."

"Since you're asking," says Paul, "the cellar game . . ."

Gina cuts him off. "Nobody wants to play anything after dinner. We're going to help clear up and then have coffee or whatever and those who wish will be allowed to slump in front of the telly. Is there any more of this yummy pud, Mum?"

Paul has been sidelined. The raspberry meringue is finished off and then there is much pushing back of chairs and gathering up of plates and glasses. Alison tells Charles, Corinna and Martin to go through to the sitting room: "Make yourselves comfortable — Charles dear, see to the fire, would you. Sandra, the glasses can go straight into the dishwasher. Someone pass me those plates." She waves at the pile of Limoges dessert plates on the table.

Paul picks up the plates. He lurches in Alison's direction. He stumbles. The plates slither from his hands and smash upon the floor.

At midnight, in the privacy of the matrimonial bathroom, Alison mops tears from her face, for the second time that day. The first occasion had been to do with frustration over Paul's failure to say whether he would turn up or not, with irritation because her favourite kitchen knife had gone missing and the accumulated stress of preparation. Now, she is mourning the Limoges china, she has just realized that Paul was drunk or something and a great suppressed stew of aggravation and discontent simmers within. She scrubs her face with the flannel and returns to the bedroom; her long-sleeved nightie with ruffled neck and the unpinned hair around her shoulders make her seem faintly girlish.

Charles, in maroon pyjamas, is sitting on the edge of the bed, hunting through the pile of books on the bedside table.

Alison goes to the dressing table and brushes her hair. "We could have done with an extra pheasant," she says. "But the pudding went down well and Corinna wants the recipe for the salmon pâté."

"Your usual gastronomic triumph," says Charles, selecting a book and getting into bed.

Alison turns round. "And Paul was drunk and most of the Limoges dessert plates are smashed and Corinna is so patronizing and we have been married for 25 years."

"Indeed yes," says Charles. "To all of that, I suppose."

"Why?"

He looks at her over his glasses, finger in the book. "Why what?"

"Why did we get married?"

A brief silence.

"I seem to recall you were pregnant."

"Oh, of course," says Alison. "I knew there was something."

She gets into bed, the tears rolling once more.

The Cellar Game

The house hears everything. The house knows. It knows all that has been said, all that has been done. Silent speech hangs in the air, and repeats the words that hang in people's heads: "I am a servant", "I seem to recall that you were pregnant", "Who did you love best?" The house stows away this inaccessible archive; people store also, because they cannot help it. They hear the same things said, time and again. They take this personal cargo away from Allersmead, to wherever they go next; they cannot relinquish it. Past and future become one — what has been said, what will be said, the silent witness of this place.

Gina sits in a television studio, waiting for her moment, and for no reason at all Paul speaks, his voice invades the present, comes swimming up from another day, another world: "Eat a spider," he orders.

The cellar is not a cellar at all. It is, variously, the Pacific Ocean, the Antarctic, the open prairie and much else. When they go down there, it undergoes a metamorphosis — the damp Edwardian brick walls dissolve, the cindery floor melts away. The packing cases, the broken ping-pong table, the doorless

93

cupboard all become habitations; the old lawnmower is a sledge, a horse, a ship. They are adrift on a raft, they sledge to the South Pole, they fight off the Indians from their covered wagon — for this is 1979, cowboys and Indians are still around. As are other things. The far end of the cellar, the dark end, the end which the light from the windows does not penetrate, that end is Dalek country; the Daleks are there, lurking invisible in the gloom. They may come out, if provoked. James Bond owns the stone stairway; from the top step he guns down the enemy, and then leaps to safety with one practised bound.

Paul is always James Bond. Until . . . Until the day Sandra says, "I'm going to be James Bond this time."

"You can't. You're a girl."

Sandra retorts, "If we can pretend someone's James Bond then we can pretend I'm a boy."

Paul is silenced, trying to ferret a way round the logic of this. At last he says, grudgingly, "All right. Just this time." He is struck by a dismaying thought. "But I'm not being James Bond's girl."

There can be arguments, there can be dissent, but at the moment they all pile down the steps to play the game there is united purpose. Somehow, a collective decision has been made: today it is the cowboys and Indians game, today it is the ship game.

And there is another game. This is a more low-key game, but it is an abiding game; they come back to it time and again. It does not have a name — it is simply an arrangement into which they slip, almost without discussion. The packing case becomes a house, the home. Paul is always the father. Gina, usually, is the mother but sometimes Sandra wants the role. More often, Sandra prefers to be a child — one of the children, and usually a subversive child, who answers back, who disobeys. It is Sandra, more often than not, who has to pay a forfeit. Clare is the baby; sometimes she has to submit to being wrapped up in a piece of damp sacking and placed in the orange-box cot. Actually, she does not too much mind; she lies there smiling peacefully, even sucking her thumb. Katie and Roger are simply children, they bulk out the family.

Family life is not particularly tranquil. Paul is a Victorian paterfamilias. He demands absolute obedience, absolute compliance. There is a draconian education system in force: people have to learn bits of a tattered telephone directory by heart, they have to add up columns of figures. But there is a certain tacit agreement here: protest is ritual: it is stylized. Children sigh and groan and roll their eyes. Only when things go too far — Sandra — is a price exacted.

Gina is a peculiar sort of mother. She does not cook; meals are conjured from the air, and eaten with relish — it is always bangers and mash with tomato ketchup. She is interested in story-telling; people have to sit in a circle and now the story will begin, and it will go on at some length, sometimes incorporating themselves — themselves in that other, above-ground, Allersmead life — so that things become interestingly confused; they do not know quite who or where they are.

It is Gina, on the whole, who devises the cellar games, whether it is home life in the packing case or a bout on the high seas. She directs the narrative, such as it is, and proposes who does what and when, though others have an input here. Paul requires plenty of action, while both Katie and Roger have been known to object if their roles are too insignificant or too challenging.

"I don't want to play," says Katie.

"You have to," says Paul kindly. "Everyone has to. You know that."

"I'm not going to be the one who gets eaten by the sharks."

Gina intervenes. "She can get rescued. We throw her a rope."

Paul frowns. This spoils things. He does not have an anticlimax in mind. "Clare, then."

Clare beams. She is not sure what a shark is.

Actually, Clare can be a problem. She is inclined to start doing her own thing, to introduce an element of four-year-old mayhem. She has only recently been included at all, and has not yet grasped the imperative requirement for team work. There is a form of democracy in operation — people can raise objections about what is demanded of them personally, they can make suggestions and proposals, but nobody may go off at a tangent, introducing their own sub-plot or, indeed, engaging in some completely different operation. They may not — Clare may not — start to play with the stack of jam jars on the shelf of the broken bookcase, or go off to jump on the mattress which is not a mattress but a boat or a covered wagon or a sledge. It is just as well that the cellar has its own hidden malevolence, and Clare is aware of this; she does not like spiders and woodlice, still less does she fancy the snakes that she has been told lurk in dark places, let alone the invisible Daleks. Clare has to hide behind the sofa during *Doctor Who*. So, on the whole, Clare stays close to everyone else and does what she is told, frequently bemused about what is going on.

Sometimes visiting children are obliged to play the cellar game. Usually, they do not enjoy it. There is the feeling that you are on the edge of things, you do not quite understand, you are inadequate, you are an outsider. And when it comes to forfeits they find that they would like to go home.

"Eat a spider!" orders Paul. There are gasps. This is new, and harsh. Everyone looks at Sandra. Will she decide to take a penalty? Evidently not: "OK," she says calmly. She goes over to the cobwebby place under the window. She searches.

Forfeits are not quite the whole point of the cellar game. On some occasions, no forfeits arise. Rather, they are a kind of embellishment, a peak of creativity and excitement which things attain from time to time. Someone will overstep the mark — deliberately as often as not, provocatively — and there will be no alternative. In the house game, one of the children will be subversive, disobedient, and must be brought to heel.

Or there will be mutiny on the ship, or someone fails a test of bravery. Some forfeits are mild enough: sit blindfold for ten minutes, squat for five minutes, walk right round the house in nothing but your knickers, sing "God Save the Queen". Others are more demanding: go into the back garden and dig up a worm and bring it back, steal one of Mum's hairpins, stay in the Dalek corner for five minutes. Forfeits are both challenge and entertainment. The challenged will win status by accepting and successfully carrying out the forfeit; the spectators will be diverted but also titillated by the thought that next time it might be them.

There is an escape route. Anyone can refuse to accept a forfeit, but in that case they must take a penalty. They lose face, and their penalty mark is chalked up on the board, to be there in perpetuity. Clare has never really understood about this, and her penalty marks are in double figures, despite the fact that her penalties are customized. "No," she says. "I don't want to do a somersault. Not now."

There is a continual search for new forfeits. Paul's various proposals involving matches and lighters have been vetoed; some primitive instinct about health and safety seems to operate.

"Show us!"

"It's in my hand," says Sandra. "If I show you, it'll get away."

"How big is it?" demands Roger.

Katie is worried. "I think this is cruel. It's really cruel to the spider."

98

Paul says, "I don't believe you've got one at all."

Sandra eyes him coolly. "Suit yourself," she says. She raises her hand to her mouth, opens it. She swallows, gags dramatically, stares at them in triumph.

Gina realizes that they will never know. Did she or didn't she?

The appeal of the cellar game is privacy and secrecy; it is never mentioned above ground, no grown-up knows what goes on. If it has been noticed that they have gone down there Paul, or Gina, or Sandra will say airily — oh, we go down there and read to the little ones. Reading always earns brownie points at Allersmead. Or — we're making a museum down there (creative, cultural, good). Or — we thought we'd tidy it up a bit (positively virtuous). Alison does not care for the cellar and virtually never visits it. Charles is perhaps barely aware that it exists.

The cellar is their territory. And the cellar game is an alternative universe into which, occasionally, they withdraw. It has nothing to do with real life; they are licensed to become other people, though their above-ground status and personalities continue to direct and inform the game. Paul is still the eldest, and thus entitled to pull rank. Gina supplies the most productive ideas, and devises storylines and props. Katie and Roger remain something of a unit, and like to have roles that reflect this. Sandra is wayward and independent; if she feels like rocking the boat, she will. And Clare is occasionally a liability, an uncontrollable element.

★ ★ ★

Today it is the family game. Gina is mother. Paul has shot a bison, so Gina has served bison bangers and mash, and now it is story-time. "Are you sitting comfortably?" she says.

Sandra groans, and gets a look to kill.

The story begins. It is a story about six children, who sound eerily familiar. There are smiles and nudges. There is an episode in which they swim the Channel; Clare is nearly drowned, Roger carries out a valiant rescue. And then the story veers in an unexpected direction. Everyone has grown up. Katie has eight children. Roger is a British Airways pilot. Clare is a pop star. Paul is prime minister (much hilarity at this point). Sandra . . . Sandra is a head teacher.

"I absolutely am not," says Sandra. "Absolutely no way."

Gina is firm. "In the story you are."

"Then I'm not in the story," says Sandra.

Paul says that she has to be. Paul is inflexible when it comes to rules.

Sandra shrugs. "You can have this head teacher if you want to, but she's not me. And, anyway, what are you?"

Gina says that she is a writer. She is telling the story.

"Then you can't be a very good one," says Sandra. "It's obvious I'm not the sort of person who is ever going to be a head teacher."

Gina is getting angry. "In the story that's what you are. And, anyway, you don't know what you're going to be like when you're grown-up."

"Actually," says Sandra easily, "you've only thought up this head-teacher stuff because you know it would annoy me."

Ah. A home truth, maybe. Something has happened. Reality has invaded the game. The game has lost its potency, its immunity; the real world has muscled in, asserting itself.

The cellar game is doomed, in fact — the Damoclean sword of time hangs over it. At twelve, Paul is still in there; at 13, he will not be. Sandra, a sophisticate, has perhaps already sprung clear. Quite soon, the cellar will become just that once more. The mattress, the packing case, the broken cupboard will sit out the decades — unconsidered, unrequired. The Daleks will sink into the murk of their corner. But the wooden board under the window will continue to record FORFITS and PENALTYS.

Crackington Haven

Katie does not have eight children. She has no children. Roger is not a British Airways pilot; he is a paediatrician in a hospital in Toronto. Katie has flown up from Boston to see him, because it is his birthday, and she is unhappy — she needs to get away for a couple of days; she needs a quick fix of family, this bit of family in particular. They are having a celebratory lunch in the restaurant at the top of the CN Tower, which is turning out to be a mistake because Katie is finding that she gets vertigo. She has to sit with her back to the stupendous view that is the whole point of the place.

"So adopt, then," says Roger.

"Oh, we've thought of that. Of course. I would, but Al's not so keen. He feels he might not . . . Oh, I don't know quite what he feels."

"You've done all the stuff?"

"All of it," says Katie grimly. "IVF — all that. Every possible test, tried everything. It seems to be me, by the way, not him. Which makes it worse, somehow."

Roger nods. "Yeah — I can see you'd feel that. Not that you should."

"You would think, wouldn't you, that I'd have inherited something of the family fertility?"

"Doesn't follow, I'm afraid. Actually, come to think of it, none of us has managed to reproduce so far."

"Gina wouldn't have time. Can't see Sandra with kids — they'd cramp her style. Nor Clare. Paul — well, better not, I should think. What about you?"

Roger spreads his hands. "I'm waiting for the love of my life. She doesn't seem to show up."

"Sorry to *whinge*," says Katie. "Enough of that, anyway. We'll get over it. *I'll* get over it. Al more or less has, I think."

"There's a sort of woman for whom having a child — children — is the only thing that matters. I know — I see them. I don't think you're like that."

"I know who was," says Katie, after a moment. "Mum."

Roger nods.

"Mum without kids is unthinkable. Whereas Dad . . ."

"We happened to Dad," says Roger.

"Oh, come on. It wasn't parthenogenesis."

"Short of celibacy, I assume he didn't have much say in the matter."

Katie looks slightly shocked. "You mean Mum just went ahead and *bred*, for personal satisfaction?"

Roger shrugs. "Maybe. Or just sheer inefficiency."

"Not that," says Katie. "It was the more the merrier."

"Indeed. To a fault."

They look at one another for a moment.

"Yup," says Katie. "So was Dad put upon in a big way, or did he — um — fight back?"

Roger is thoughtful. "There is the matter of Paul's birthday."

"She was pregnant, you mean?"

"Well, presumably."

"So?" says Katie. "Accidents happen."

"Or not."

"Oh!" she cries. "You shouldn't say that."

Roger inclines his head. "It's been known. An old ploy."

"But *Mum* . . ."

For both, their parents seem to hover — presences that are entirely known, familiar — and also unreachable, enigmatic.

"She had people do what she wanted, somehow," says Roger.

Katie disputes this. "That's not right. She wasn't as *organized* as that. And Dad never did anything he didn't want to do. He stood on one side."

"Or found it was the only place to be."

"That's not quite how I see it. He went into that study and pulled up the drawbridge. She did everything. She and Ingrid."

"The harem? Or monstrous regiment of women?"

"Roger, *honestly* . . ."

"Both? I wonder . . . We're not the ones who can know."

"We were *there*," says Katie.

"Six of us were there. Nine. Would we all tell the same story? Take that summer holiday in Cornwall. Crackington Haven."

They contemplate an August that is dead and gone, but not so at all, shimmering in their heads, and presumably in other heads, an assemblage of fragments, of sea and rock and sand and faces and voices, things said and done, things seen and thought.

"Oh, goodness," says Katie. "It was one commotion after another. Paul and the police. Sandra going off with that boy all the time. Ingrid's man turning up."

"On the contrary, it was an amazing summer. I had that kite. I got seriously into marine biology."

"Smelly dead things in buckets. That I do remember."

"Police?" says Roger. "Boy? Man? I do have a vague memory of small local disturbances, on the edge of one's vision. That's my point, you see. Your Cornwall evidently was not my Cornwall. Nor, I suppose, was anyone else's. Mum's. His."

Cornwall flickers — an old film rerun, degraded by time.

"So who's right?" says Roger. "Who sees all of it?"

The rented holiday house has five bedrooms. Paul and Roger must share, Katie and Clare, Gina and Sandra (under protest). Charles and Alison. Ingrid alone has a room to herself, but it is a sliver of a thing, next to the kitchen, perhaps once a pantry. The whole place is over-furnished: hefty armchairs rub shoulders in the large sitting room; you fight your way through a thicket of occasional tables, magazine racks and pouffes. The conservatory/dining room with view over the sea has stacked white plastic chairs and a deal table. The kitchen is under-equipped, but that is not a problem because Alison has brought her own *batterie de cuisine* — the most cherished pans and casseroles, the knives, the implements. The mattresses on the beds all have plastic covers; Alison finds these offensive and removes them. There is a forest of spider-plants on every surface in the sitting room; these she banishes to the cloakroom, which is cluttered with other people's abandoned pac-a-macs (torn), beach balls (punctured) and buckets (leaky). Further legacies from previous occupants of the house include a shelf of paperbacks (which Charles inspects with disdain), and detritus such as playing cards that have got underneath chairs and cupboards, forgotten shampoo in the shower, magazines, a postcard from Portugal to someone called Ella reporting that Joey can swim now and a pink cotton sunhat with daisy trim.

Gina considers the magazines, the postcard and the sunhat and tries to imagine their previous owners: what were last month's voices like, last month's faces?

Sandra examines the shampoo, and then bins it: an inferior brand.

Paul finds a bus timetable on the shelf under the telephone, and perks up.

Crackington Haven is a small resort: a scatter of houses and cottages, most of them summer rentals, a village shop, a couple of daily ice-cream vans, an itinerant burger bar. No cafés, pubs or shopping malls, which is why Alison has chosen it. A lovely, lovely family sort of place, quite unspoilt, off the beaten track, just heavenly sea and the dear little beach and gorgeous walks along the cliffs.

There are a few things she has not reckoned with: that bus timetable, the telephone, other holiday folk.

Roger's life is hitched to the tides. He needs low tide. He waits — daily, hourly — for low tide. He goes out first thing to assess the state of play. Waves rippling up the beach are bad news: high tide, that will take hours to recede, hours before the rock pools are revealed, hours before he can get out there and get stuck in, eyes down, net in hand, the buckets and the jars lined up on a convenient slab.

In the evening, he pores over the book, the guide to the seashore. He is getting good at identification. He has a notebook, and he lists what he has caught and identified. The daily catch heaves, crawls and wriggles in the containers that Alison insists must be left outside. In the morning, he returns the lot to their proper environment, but there are often a few casualties. He regrets these, but scientific enquiry necessarily involves a degree of detachment. He is immersed, absorbed, away in an intellectual frenzy. He thinks of nothing but sea anemones and sea urchins, limpets and whelks, shrimps and sea slugs. He has had a red cushion star and a spider crab, a sea lemon and a shore rockling. He is desperate for a butterfly blenny. The guide has put him on his mettle; its illustrations offer alluring creatures that he has not yet met. He must have a rock goby and a velvet swimming crab. Will he achieve these before the end of the holiday? He cannot afford to lose a single moment of low tide, even when it is windy and the kite also calls. The best days are when wind and high tide coincide and he can take to the cliff, with the kite dancing overhead and the sea waiting to be harvested in due course.

Horse mussel? Dog whelk? He squats outside the kitchen door, staring into the bucket, the book open alongside. He hears Alison's voice, a background noise to which he is impervious, as irrelevant as a bluebottle on a window pane. "Where is Paul?" she is crying. "Where on earth has he got to? Has anyone seen Paul?"

Sandra has spent the day stretched out on the sand in her pink bikini. When, at points, she becomes too unbearably cold, she sits up and huddles her towel around her, eyes trained on the far side of the beach where the boy's family is encamped, where he is idly kicking a ball around with a younger brother.

It is working. One has not suffered in vain. He glances towards her more and more frequently. The ball is kicked in her direction again and again. Once, it skims across her legs. "*Sorry!*" he calls. Sandra glimmers at him, sideways.

This is day three. Day one was a dead loss. The beach had nothing to offer but kids building sandcastles, lolloping dogs and parents erecting wind breaks and staking out territories. She sat morosely on a rock, in shorts and a sweater, glaring at the sea. Other families go to the Algarve, or Majorca, where there's proper sun and you can get a decent tan; *we* have to come to bloody Crackington Haven.

At the end of day two everything changes. She has spotted him. Eighteen, probably — even nineteen. *Very nice.* Suddenly Crackington Haven takes on a different complexion. The sun is not as feeble as one had thought; the beach and the cliffs are really very pretty. Now it is just a question of the pink bikini, and perseverance.

Katie knows where Paul is. Paul is either in Bude, or on his way there. She knows this because she saw him at the bus stop. "You haven't seen me, right?" he tells her, and now she is in a quandary, as Alison bounces around the house in escalating distress. Where should her loyalties lie?

Paul is grounded this summer because of the trouble at college. Paul did not make it to what Alison calls "one of the nice universities", and is doing an engineering course at a place that he says is utterly crap but actually he quite likes it because they leave you pretty well alone. Perhaps in consequence of this there has been trouble. The lower-grade trouble is that Paul has not applied himself, and has failed the end-of-year exams. The higher-grade trouble is referred to by Alison only in whispered asides to Charles, but Katie knows what it is, as does Sandra, as does Gina. Paul has been caught doing drugs. So Paul is grounded for the summer; he has to do remedial studies at evening classes run by the council, and he is to account for his movements. Bude is not accounted for.

Supper is ready and Alison is still keening. In fact, the way things are going, supper will be put on hold altogether and Alison will be on the phone to the coastguards. It is only three years since the episode of Paul and the cliff rescue. Katie realizes that common sense dictates a single course of action: she must shop Paul.

Clare too needs low tide. She needs that expanse of hard wet sand. Even so, she will have to compete for possession with the cricket-playing family and the volleyball lot.

She does handstands. She walks on her hands. She does cartwheels. She wheels over and over until Crackington Haven spins around her and, when eventually she stops, she staggers.

She has made a friend. Emma. Emma is hopeless at handstands and cartwheels but she is audience, and they are digging a trench, when Clare is through with cartwheels — for the moment.

"So he's gone to Bude . . ." says Gina. "So? It's not Las Vegas. He's *nineteen*, Mum."

"He should have said. He *knows* what the agreement is. What the rules are. He should have talked it over. We could have gone there all together, for a family outing. There's no need to go off like that on his own. Bude is horrid, by all accounts: crowds of people, and rubbishy shops and bars. You get those leather bikers there, apparently, and goodness knows what else. That's exactly why we come to Crackington Haven."

The conservatory/dining room reverberates with Alison's dismay. Supper is being eaten by those unaffected. "Is there any more?" enquires Roger. Sandra has just realized with disgust that she forgot to take her watch off while sun-bathing, and now she has a watchstrap mark.

Gina turns to Charles. "Where do you stand on this, Dad?"

A challenge. Get involved — one way or the other.

Charles appears to reflect. "I have never been to Bude."

"Oh, you *have*," cries Alison. "We went there once when the car had to have a new exhaust. But never mind that. It's the *principle*. He *knows*."

Gina sighs. We have been here before. Many times. Mum going berserk (and usually about Paul); Dad standing back.

Alison continues, at length. When she draws breath, Charles speaks. He says, "Paul will presumably return, in due course. At that point, there can be discussion." He puts his knife and fork together, rises and leaves the table.

Gina watches him. Does he have a point? What is the view from Dad? We hear a lot about the view from Mum, but what does he see? What is there to be seen?

Charles has brought with him on the holiday three boxes of books, his typewriter and a sheaf of paper. This baggage, along with everyone else's, Alison's cooking equipment, Paul's guitar and other essentials meant that the family car — a Volkswagen bus which can seat ten — was so crammed that all except Charles, Alison and Clare had to travel by train.

111

Charles plans to work, in so far as this is possible. He has always found the summer holiday particularly taxing. He has no dedicated study to which to retreat, he cannot escape from a degree of communal activity (sandcastle building, thank God, is done with), he must take part in outings to places of interest. In fact, he is not entirely averse to these last — a castle or stately home is fine — but the definition of a place of interest is a matter of impassioned argument within the family; he is equally likely to find himself at an ice rink or a funfair. He likes to walk, and does so, though usually alone since the concept of walking for pleasure has not caught on with his offspring, and Alison finds that she gets out of breath rather soon.

He is 47. Age has never been of great interest, but occasionally he finds himself looking at this figure: an awful lot of life seems to have leaked away. He is reasonably satisfied with his achievements, but has the feeling that his *magnum opus* is still to come. What will it be? He is known for his range. He is waiting — for a consuming new interest to sneak up on him. In the meantime, there is a thing on the Romantic poets; something of a potboiler, in fact. In the service of this, Charles walks on the cliffs above Crackington Haven, thinking about the Romantic Revival.

Or trying to. But today there are distractions. He is distracted by the view — the serenely sailing fleet of clouds, the soft rim of the horizon on which sits the grey shape of some ship, Tennyson's crawling sea down there below the cliff. He is distracted by last night's scene with Paul, which hangs in his head. And he is distracted by thoughts that have no bearing on the Romantic poets but stem from their very existence: the concurrence of things, the fact that the Romantics march on because he and a mass of others are interested in them, Tennyson too for that matter, the sea for ever hitched to his words, if you are that way inclined. Concurrence, juxtaposition, the absence of any sequence.

Could the *magnum opus* be lurking here? If so, it is an effective lurk; Charles cannot see beyond that single intriguing perception. And, oddly, it translates to a vision of his own children, whom he sees suddenly as multiple creatures, each of them still present in many incarnations — smaller, larger, babies, lumpen teenagers, any of them to be summoned up at will.

He contemplates this, picking his way along the cliff path, past clumps of thrift, little thickets of gorse, outcrops like rocky gardens, none of which he notices, locked into these thoughts. It occurs to him that a novelist would make more of this sequence problem, if that is what it is, rather than a serious analytical worker like himself.

Ingrid receives a phone call. She talks for some while in a low voice, in her own language.

Ingrid says, "My friend is in Cornwall and would like to come to stay for a few days. All right?"

"Of course," says Alison. "How nice. She won't mind going in with you, will she? There's that extra fold-up bed."

113

"He will not mind at all," says Ingrid.

People stare. Sandra claps her hand over her mouth; she is impressed — well! Who'd have thought it!

Alison blinks. "Oh. Yes — right, then."

Charles alone does not react. Perhaps he did not hear.

Alison is oppressed by age. Not her own. The children, who are no longer children, except for Clare, and perhaps Roger, who is on the cusp. The others are disappearing over the horizon, and she is aghast. This should not be happening. Not yet. Oh, of course they grow up but somehow one had always felt that that was way, way off. And now, suddenly, this summer, it no longer is. It is not just their size, their new concerns — it is the sense that they are moving into foreign territory, places of which she knows nothing. Once, they were infinitely familiar, predictable; now they are alarmingly volatile. One does not know what they are thinking, or, half the time, what they are doing.

Paul. He has been led astray, undoubtedly. He has fallen in with some bad types at that college place. He has been turned into someone else. This is not the old, known Paul — a bit naughty sometimes but nothing you couldn't cope with. Evil outsiders have fed him drugs and distracted him from his studies and turned him into a person who takes buses to Bude all the time instead of being part of the lovely family holiday.

Sandra and that boy on the beach.

Katie does not exactly give cause for alarm, but she is disconcerting all the same, in a different way. She is

114

as tall as Alison, she has breasts, she has her own quiet decisiveness. You feel that you can't any more tell her what she should do. She has probably already done it, or done something else.

And Gina. The way she *talks* now. Sometimes Alison feels that Gina is in fact much older than she is. Much cleverer. Knows much more. Gina takes Charles on — argues with him, has opinions of her own. It's not that she's rude or anything, just that she has become this *person*. This person who seems only tenuously connected to child Gina, and who makes Alison feel inadequate. One is somehow on the edge of things now, trying to get a word in, trying to be listened to. Time was, they *needed* you, even Gina. Now, they do not. They are not just self-sufficient, they have raced off to some other incarnation; there are moments when Alison hardly recognizes them.

Ingrid.

This man. It's not going to be like that time back then, is it?

Oh, this holiday is running off the rails. She has lost control of it; there are daily subversions, intrusions. After all the careful planning — the house booked way back in *January*, the lists of stuff to bring, the Volkswagen serviced, the rail tickets sorted, the excursions noted.

Alison stands at the kitchen table rolling pastry and watching the rain that snakes down the windowpane and reduces the hillside opposite to a quivering green blur. At least when it rains you know where everyone is. Paul is still in bed, the rest are scattered around that

115

uncompromising sitting room, walled off from one another by bulbous furniture. Gina has her feet up on a sofa, reading. Roger is on the floor with his nature book and his notebook and one of those buckets that are supposed to be left outside. Katie is writing a letter. Sandra is painting her toenails. Clare is in the only open space, jiggling about to the tinny racket that emanates from the Walkman she has borrowed from Sandra.

Charles is in their bedroom, which has to serve also as his study.

Ingrid is peeling potatoes at the sink and humming to herself. This is not a familiar sound. What has she got to hum about?

Alison cuts the pastry lid to size and fits it over the dish already filled with steak and kidney. She crimps the edge, arranges a pastry flower in the centre, slashes a couple of air vents. Then she washes and dries her hands, and takes off her apron.

She walks across into the sitting room, bright, brisk, in charge.

"What about a game of Scrabble?"

Alison and Ingrid are in the kitchen, assembling the next meal. Alison drops her knife; she is on edge, it seems.

She says, "Of course, Jan is charming, but what is it that he does in London?"

Ingrid replies that he is studying.

Alison expresses surprise. She had thought that, well, he'd have a job; he's over thirty, isn't he? But of course

116

some people do go on with studying for quite a while. What is it that he studies?

"He is studying linguistics," says Ingrid.

Alison supposes that Ingrid has, well, seen something of him when she goes up to London?

Ingrid has been going up to London quite a lot recently. It was understood that she had developed an interest in art, and was visiting galleries.

Ingrid says blandly that she has seen much of Jan. "We like to go to exhibitions."

Is linguistics something to do with art? Alison decides not to pursue this, and also to be cheerful, and neutral. "Well, that's nice," she says. "Now, have we done enough potatoes?"

Jan is large and silent. He has blonde stubble all over his face and a surprisingly weathered look for someone so devoted to his studies. He arrived riding an elderly motorcycle, on which he and Ingrid sputter off on expeditions, Ingrid clutching a little metal hoop in front of the pillion seat. Jan smiles a great deal but says little. Cornwall is very beautiful, he agrees. Yes, he likes the sea very much. After the initial astonishment at Ingrid's *coup* nobody except Alison is much interested in Jan. Most people have other fish to fry.

In a turfy hollow up on the cliff, well screened from the path by some bushes, Sandra loses her virginity. The event is a bit of a let-down: hurried, messy and faintly embarrassing. She hopes this does not mean that sex is just not what it is cracked up to be, but suspects that he is as inexperienced as she is, though he suggests otherwise. Probably they will get better at it.

Gina is reading, writing and waiting. She is waiting for the results of her A levels, on which depends her place at York, and in the meantime she is reading *War and Peace*, because this is the last chance — she'll be too busy from October onwards, possibly for the rest of her life — and she is writing a diary. The diary is not a confessional one but a record of her reactions to current events. She is thinking these days that she just might want to become a politician, in which case she needs to sort out where she stands on various contemporary issues. She is seriously deprived of news material down here; she has her radio but newspapers are hard to come by in Crackington Haven, and she needs print stories. The village shop does not stock the *Guardian*, the few copies of the *Telegraph* have all been snapped up by five past nine, and in any case Gina wouldn't be seen dead with the *Telegraph*. She asks Paul to bring her back a paper from his forays into Bude, but he usually forgets.

At night, before they put the light out, Gina is at the Battle of Borodino, while Sandra is immersed in *Cosmopolitan*, locked behind her Walkman. They get on best if they don't much bother to talk. Silence can be really quite amicable. And Sandra is in excellent humour. Gina knows why. She knows about Sandra's boy. You could hardly fail to — they are inseparable, snogging behind the rocks, or mooching around the cliff path. They have been to Bude together — he has his driving licence, and was allowed to borrow the family car. Bude is where the action is, says Sandra — in so far as you can call it action, in Cornwall.

It occurs to Gina that this is probably the last family holiday, or at least the last in which she will be involved. This time next year she will be a student, and when you are a student you spend the vacation backpacking on the continent, don't you? That's what Paul should be doing, by rights, if he wasn't grounded because of the fuss at his college place, no cash flow, no option but to stick to home. Gina is sorry for him, but also concerned. He has been on drugs, no question, and probably still is, given half a chance. There was a scheme to find him a summer job, and indeed he did a week shelf-stacking at the supermarket at home until he was cheeky to the manager and got fired.

"That was stupid," she told him. "You should have stuck it out."

He shrugged. "It was a crap job. What's the point?"

"Cash," said Gina. "Gainful employment. It's what we all have to come to."

Paul rolled his eyes. "Not just yet, for Christ's sake." He grinned at her. "How about you take me to the pub after supper? We can tell Mum we're going for a walk."

Gina reckons something will have to be done about Paul, sooner or later, but she is not her brother's keeper, and she has enough on at the moment anyway, what with the looming A-level results, and the prospect of York — fingers crossed — and this realization, both heady and sobering, that she is at a brink, that she is about to step into a new world, a new life, in which there will no longer be August in Cornwall, and the smothering embrace of Allersmead.

Katie is worried. She worries about these spots she gets, she worries about her maths — she's sure she's going to flunk maths at GCSE, she worries because Mum's so het up this summer, not that anyone else ever seems to notice. She worries also about this worrying; she does too much of it, she should be more laid back, like Gina and Sandra, or indeed Paul, who is practically horizontal and that's not particularly good either.

Mum is in a lather about Paul. He keeps schlepping off to Bude and she can't stop him. He's not supposed to have any money but somehow he has; he says he's going surfing, but Paul has never shown the faintest interest in surfing before. So Mum agitates each time until he gets back. Plus, she is for some reason fussed about Ingrid having this man turn up. She is lavishly nice to Jan, and to Ingrid too, but it's clear enough that she is not happy about things. Does she mind that they are, well, having a relationship obviously? Surely not. Ingrid is a grown-up person, after all, very grown-up you might say. Does Mum think that Ingrid is going to go off? Like that time (which Katie remembers only rather vaguely), and after all she came back, didn't she?

And Mum is fidgety too about Sandra and her boy. The amount of time they spend together, what they may be getting up to — and that's clear enough, frankly. They're doing it; Katie feels pretty sure about that. So of course Mum is in a stew in case Sandra gets pregnant. Katie is a bit anxious about this too. That would be a serious problem. Except that once there was a real-life baby Mum would simply take it over and digest it into the family, wouldn't she? But it won't happen, because Sandra will see that it doesn't, somehow. Girls like Sandra do not get pregnant.

Is Dad even *noticing* any of this? He seems to be aware of Jan, but only because he's someone different to talk to at meals, except that Jan doesn't talk back. Dad gives his views on whatever and Jan nods and says, "Ah, indeed, yes." Mum made sure that Dad got drawn into the first row with Paul about Bude, but one notes that it is not he who is always asking where Paul is — has anyone seen Paul? Sandra's boy is not even on his horizon.

Dad is not like other people's fathers; one has always known that. Fair enough — you wouldn't want an assembly-line father. He never did father things like playing football with the boys. Looking back, he is there but also not there; you somehow didn't take difficulties to Dad, though to be fair he would be quite onside when it came to questions about school things. Other people's fathers go out to work; Dad goes into his study. And out of his study, in due course, comes a book.

Katie has tried to read a couple of Dad's books. She finds that it is the kind of reading where you follow the words, punctiliously, line by line and page by page, and suddenly you realize that they haven't added up to anything of which you could give an account. Which is

121

your fault, of course: you are not bright enough, or old enough.

We are not a usual kind of family, thinks Katie. There are so many of us, and Mum does most of the parenting, but is that because she wants to and Dad is kind of an accessory, or is it that Dad opts out? And we have someone who is sort of the au pair girl but also isn't because she has always been there, which I suppose looks odd from outside.

But it's other families who are strange. Two children and synchronized parents. Where you are is what is normal.

Charles is suffering from proximity. The proximity of his family, which is so much more so here than in the relative spaciousness of Allersmead; the proximity of the sea, which should lend itself to the pursuit of Romanticism, but does not. It occurs to him, irritatingly, that most of the Romantics lived in extreme proximity with family, and seem to have managed. So does he have a problem?

Oh yes, he does. He knows that. He is a man to whom family has happened, unstoppably, or so it seemed and, yes, of course he is responsible; he has begotten this tribe, and in his way he loves them. If anything happened . . . That time Paul got stuck on the cliff he was berserk. But he is a man also who needs solitude, who needs silent communion with language, with ideas. Just now, silent communion is not on offer. Two days ago, he bought a half bottle of whisky from the hotel and took it for an evening walk.

He came back anaesthetized, and full of self-disgust. No, he must not succumb to that again. That way lies disaster, as he well knows.

Roger finds a butterfly blenny. O frabjous day! Callooh! Callay!

Sandra and her boy have another go; there is marked improvement.

Paul scores, on a street corner in Bude.

Clare perfects her back flip, discards Emma and takes up with Lucy.

The holiday is into its third week but where Charles is concerned it is a continuous present, without chronology. Since he seldom acquires a newspaper, he seldom knows what day it is. This does not particularly matter — though the absence of a paper does. What does matter is that he is not getting much work done. This is partly because he has no proper study, but seems to be also to do with an onset of mental inertia. He is bored with Romanticism. This present undertaking is one of a series of brief books on concepts, for the aspirational reader; probably he should never have agreed to do it, or have picked a different concept. Fascism would have had more bite.

As it is, he reads perfunctorily, rapidly mired by Coleridge, maddened by Wordsworth, only too willing to put the rest of them down after five minutes. What is the matter? He is not a man who reads perfunctorily; he is a man who reads with application, with perception, with absolute attention. This was a misguided project, no question, but he is stuck with it now. It is a short book, an inessential one, to be honest — the only thing is to get on and deal with it.

Which is what he seems unable to do. During the day, when it is fine and everyone else is out and about, the house is relatively peaceful, but he is still unable to apply himself. He goes for walks, to clear the head, or at least that is the intention, but instead the head becomes further muddied by idle observation of gulls, plants, the moody sea, which offers a different humour each day — wild and wave-whipped, calm and contemplative. Pathetic fallacy stuff — the sea is not moody, it simply is. This is what comes of immersion in the Romantics.

Charles is irritable; that is the state of his own humour just now. This is not unusual, and he is aware of this, and would challenge any man in similar family circumstances who claimed to be otherwise. But holiday conditions somehow exacerbate things; back at Allersmead, he can keep his irritation contained, indeed quite often he is not irritated at all. He is able largely to ignore the vicissitudes of family life, and to take a genial interest when that seems appropriate. But down here in this wind-rattled house with its monstrous furniture, where there is a fine grit of sand on every floor (why doesn't someone sweep it up?) and heaving marine life in buckets outside the back door (he has tripped over one of these), the annoyance level is racked up to new heights. Alison is over-concerned about Paul, and permanently distracted. Gina is determinedly argumentative, which is not in itself a fault and Charles is well disposed to discussion, but somehow she seems always to outmanoeuvre him. He has been conscious of losing face on occasion. This taciturn Scandinavian has appeared; there is no question of losing face where he is concerned, but there is not much point in offering one's views to someone whose only reply is a compliant smile. Ingrid is tiresomely smug.

All in all, Charles would like to go home. But one must sit it out. At points he wonders if he is having some sort of mid-life crisis (he has learned this term from casting his eye over the sort of article by women journalists that he does not usually read). He would like to think himself superior to that sort of weakness, but we are all human, and he is conscious that he suffered a brief lapse of sanity some years ago, which will never be forgotten.

So he tramps the cliff paths, exchanging polite greetings with other walkers; on one occasion he comes across a pair of teenagers canoodling behind a gorse bush, and passes quickly by. There is something vaguely emotive about the back of the girl's head, but he is lost in his own discontents.

Jan leaves. After he has gone, Katie says to Roger, "Ask Ingrid if she is going to marry Jan." "Ask her yourself," says Roger. "She won't tell me," says Katie. "She's more likely to tell you because she'll know you're not particularly interested." Roger shrugs: "OK, then." And in due course he throws this casual query at Ingrid when he comes across her alone, sunning herself on the beach. Ingrid laughs. "Jan is not a person you marry," she says. Roger does not pursue the matter, and is told off for this later by Katie.

Jan is not a person you marry because as it happens he is married to someone else. This suits Ingrid well enough, and presumably it suits Jan also. Neither wishes to change their present circumstances — just, it is nice for Ingrid to have a friend in London, and nice too for Jan to have some solace while he pursues his studies. There is no need for explanations, to anyone.

Sandra's boy is becoming a touch possessive. He wants to continue their arrangement after the holiday, and is full of plans for further meetings. Sandra is evasive. She has now got the measure of sex, which was the whole point. If her period arrives as it should at the end of the week she thinks she may well call a halt, very sweetly and kindly. It's all a bit risky, she doesn't want to have to go on watching the calendar indefinitely, she likes him but not enough to go for broke with him. She will have to tell him that this was a holiday romance and that is all, it's been fantastic, so no hard feelings, right?

It happens to be Roger who answers the phone when the call comes from Bude police station. Everyone else — bar Paul — is dumped in front of the television, it being a damp evening, including Charles, who has noticed a documentary he would quite like to watch

126

after the current programme, and intends to assert his rights. Roger is outside the back door, with his buckets, and so is the only one to hear the phone ring in the hall and pick it up. He is too intent upon his researches to register the significance of what comes down the line to him, and so simply puts his head round the sitting room door and announces: "It's the police in Bude, for Mum or Dad."

Alison gasps. An awful, yelping gasp. Charles gets up and goes out of the room to where the phone is. Someone switches off the television. They hear him say, "Yes . . . Yes . . . No . . . Yes." Then he comes back into the room, and looks at Alison. "We shall have to go to Bude," he says.

Alison is speechless. She has risen, and simply stands there, staring. At last she manages, "Is he *hurt*?"

"Paul is unhurt," says Charles crisply. "He is at the police station."

There is a hunt for car keys, for Alison's jacket. Charles is silent; Alison is incoherent. The others watch them get into the car, Charles at the wheel. They watch the Volkswagen make its way out of the drive and up the hill.

"Oh, dear," says Sandra.

Paul has been caught. Possession of drugs. This had to happen, thinks Gina. Maybe it'll sort him out. Alison weeps; Charles seems resigned rather than enraged. Paul himself is sullen, but not especially repentant. "I'm not going to *prison*," he says to Gina. "It's a *caution*, that's all. Could happen to anyone. Does happen to anyone."

Gina points out that he had better watch it, in future. Paul says cheerfully that he will, of course he will. Just, he had to do *something* down here, didn't he? He couldn't just sit about in this godforsaken place all day. He'd made quite a few mates in Bude, and one thing led to another.

Gina sighs. One thing has always led to another, with Paul. Progress is a dog-leg affair for him, rather than a smooth trajectory; he shoots off in one direction on impulse, then switches course once again. It depends who he comes across, what he hears, what grabs his attention. He is borne along on some incorruptible current of optimism: it will all work out in the end, something will turn up, no one's going to find out, are they?

Unfortunately they do, on occasion. The stolid spoilsport Cornish police, for instance. So now Paul is not so much grounded as under house arrest. For the rest of the holiday he will remain at Crackington Haven 24 hours a day. Surprisingly, he becomes quite docile about this. He flies Roger's kite with him, he admires Clare's cartwheels. He offers to help Alison in the kitchen, and spends a messy afternoon making drop scones for tea. Alison is tearful with gratitude and relief. She tells Gina that it is just so unfair, always someone turns up to lead Paul astray, left to himself he would just get on with things, there is no problem, it is other people who are his undoing.

★ ★ ★

128

So that was the summer at Crackington Haven. Katie and Roger, at the top of the CN Tower in Toronto, reflect upon it across the years. Each sees just their own facet, but in any case they are other people now — those distant early selves can be summoned up, it is just possible still to see what they saw, but they are also unreachable. Katie looks across the table at her brother and sees this *man*, who is somehow a product of that boy in shorts and a T-shirt, fishing in rock pools. She sees this man with open face, thatch of gingery hair, this really rather nice-looking fellow (why hasn't some girl snapped him up?), who deals daily with matters of life and death, a useful person, a necessary person. Roger sees a woman with a small, neat-featured appealing face (does that Al realize how fortunate he is?) and a faintly worried expression — but she always had that, he remembers.

"How's work?" he says.

"Oh, fine. I'm a commissioning editor now — a step up."

There is a silence.

"Do you know?" says Roger. "Even now, I get a thrill when I think of a butterfly blenny."

Katie smiles. "Those crawling buckets. I can see them now. And you. Blue shorts and sunburn."

"Careful. This is getting close to nostalgia."

"One of Dad's books is about that. I've read it. Tried to read it."

"Said to be a bad thing, nostalgia. I have immigrant patients who suffer from it — yearning for somewhere else."

"No way do I yearn for Crackington Haven," says Katie. "Fuss and bother and an uncomfortable house is what I remember. We went there more than once."

"Allersmead?"

"Allersmead what?"

"Nostalgia."

Katie considers. "No," she decides. "Not if nostalgia means what I think it does. Kind of glamorizing something. Allersmead just is. Was."

"Inescapable."

They smile, wryly.

"Coffee?" says Roger. "And then I have to get back to the nostalgic immigrants."

Ingrid

"Your mother rang," says Philip.

Gina is just back from turbulent events half the world away. She is jetlagged and displaced; a part of her is still scurrying, at work. Mother? What mother?

"She wanted to tell you that Roger is getting married, and wondered when we'll be coming down to Allersmead for a weekend."

Gina surfaces. "Ah. Who is Roger marrying?"

"A perfectly sweet Canadian girl."

"Of course. Good for him."

"So when?"

"When what?" says Gina, throwing dirty clothes into the washing machine. Philip has wandered after her, and offers a glass of wine.

"When are we going there? Just so I can clear my diary."

Gina sighs.

"You're prejudiced, that's the trouble," he says. "From my point of view the whole set-up has a certain fascination. And the food is amazing."

"This is my family," says Gina coldly, "not a set-up."

He puts his arm round her. "Sorry. Sorry. There was further news. Your father has had a beastly cold. The

131

dog dug up Ingrid's asparagus bed and Ingrid was much displeased."

Gina switches on the washing machine and picks up her glass. "Talking of nosh, we have none. Shall we go to the Turkish place?"

"You have to understand," says Philip, "that for those of us who grew up with the most bland of family circumstances, yours are exotic. Six of you. That house. Where I come from everyone had two point five children and lived in a semi. No one had heard of such a thing as an au pair girl, let alone one who stays forty years and grows asparagus. Forty years?"

"Thereabouts," says Gina.

"Were you fond of her?"

"Fond?" Gina gazes at him. "I've no idea. She was there, and that was that. Part of the landscape."

Indeed yes. So that when she wasn't there you noticed. That time.

"When's Ingrid coming back?" someone would say, once in a while. Postcards came, bright and shiny in blues and greens — sea and sky and Scandinavian forests — addressed to All at Allersmead, or to individuals: some rugged fishermen with creels for Paul, lasses in national costume for Katie, kittens in a basket for Clare. Gina was eleven, with concerns of her own, but she was aware that things were somehow awry. There was a gap, and Mum was all on edge.

"Soon," she would say. "In a week or two, I expect." And when one day Sandra said, "Actually, *is* Ingrid coming back?" she flew into a temper.

132

"Will you not go *on* about this. Of course Ingrid's coming back. She had to see to family business, that's all."

"Did you know?" asks Philip, later that evening, in the Turkish place.

"Not consciously. Not till later, when one put two and two together."

Alison remembers that time with absolute clarity. That is to say, she remembers seminal moments. She remembers being locked in dispute with Ingrid somewhere in the garden, where they cannot be overheard. Dispute? She is the supplicant. Ingrid is rock hard, immoveable. "I am not sure," she says. "If I come back. Perhaps."

"You *must* come back," cries Alison. "The children would be devastated, you know that, the little ones especially. Clare is so young still. They've never known Allersmead without you."

Ingrid shrugs. "Perhaps I take . . ."

"*No!*" says Alison violently.

They stare at one another.

"This is a *family*," wails Alison. "You know that."

"*Talk* to her," she says to Charles.

Charles looks out of the window. "She is a free agent, Alison."

"Just so it's clear to her how much *everyone* wants to be sure she's coming back."

Charles is silent. After a while he says, "I dare say things will work out somehow."

Alison makes a wild gesture. "That's what you said . . . then."

"And I suppose that is what has happened, if you look at it objectively, which is why we are having this conversation."

How long? Months, rather than weeks. One postcard says that Ingrid is having a holiday with some cousins on this pretty fjord, another that she is doing for a while some work in a restaurant, she has made chocolate brownies just like Alison's! These periodic reminders mean that no one is able to forget that Ingrid is no longer there; they prompt questions, for which Alison has no answer. There is damage to the status quo; Allersmead is not as it should be. And of course Alison is not just on edge, she is overworked, she has too much to do, she has to scamp the cooking, meals are late and substandard, she forgets the washing and there are no clean socks, the dog has fleas because only Ingrid ever remembered to put the flea collar on.

"Why did she go?" says Philip. "Interesting move. But why?"

"Who knows? A whim? A challenge?"

"Challenging who or what?"

"The facts," says Gina. "The situation."

"Of which you were aware? You children."

She nods. "Sort of. Just it was never mentioned."

★ ★ ★

They know. They all know, eventually. They know but the knowledge is tamped down, stowed away somewhere out of sight and out of mind. The house knows, and is silent, locking away what has been done and said and thought. No one quite remembers any more how they know; it is as though the knowledge was not suppressed but arrived through some osmotic process, absorbed from Allersmead daily life, an insidious understanding that seeped from person to person. Not that there were conversations, exchanges, comments. No one has wished to discuss it; if ever the facts of the matter seemed to smoulder dangerously, there would be a concerted move to stamp out the embers, to move away, to find safe territory elsewhere.

"We just didn't talk about it," says Gina. "Best policy, eh?"

Philip says, "But how was Clare's birth explained?"

"Ingrid went and fetched her from some people who were too poor to look after her, so they gave her to us — a lovely present."

"Ah. I see." Philip hears Alison's voice.

"And thereafter the matter was not referred to," says Gina. "She was simply there, and that was all there was to it."

Indeed, no one talks about it. Corinna, to her credit, does not talk about it, except perhaps occasionally to Martin, who is only mildly interested. Corinna is much interested, and will never forget that moment of

135

revelation, at the Allersmead kitchen table. For her it is a seminal moment not just because of the revelation, but because she sees it as a nice instance of a way in which such a revelation changes the entire perception of a scene. Allersmead was reshuffled and rearranged, as she sat there, like the fragments of a kaleidoscope.

It was lunch. Family lunch to which Corinna has come because she was going to be driving this way in any case and she is guiltily aware of not having visited for some while. They are all at the table, children ranged along each side, Alison and Ingrid at one end, serving food, Charles at the other with Corinna beside him. She has not seen the children for some while — 18 months at least — and everyone has grown, naturally enough. Paul is a skinny twelve-year-old, with his father's distinctive bony nose; Gina peers out from under a dark fringe, sharp-eyed; Sandra has a glossy brown ponytail and looks older but Corinna remembers that she is number three. Roger and Katie have both of them Alison's gingery frizzy hair, and a scatter of freckles. Clare — not much more than a baby last time Corinna saw her — has flaxen straight hair and a little pink face. Corinna looks intently at Clare.

Alison is serving up stew from a vast tureen. Ingrid dispenses vegetables — mashed potato and greens. Filled plates are passed down the table, portions neatly matched to size of child; it is a deft operation, well coordinated teamwork.

Corinna stares at Ingrid. Then again at Clare.

I see. Oh, I see.

But who, then, is . . .?

She looks at Charles.

Of course. What au pair girl stays for twelve years? How obtuse one has been. Of course.

She looks at Alison, smiling down the table. Always smiling, Alison.

"Well, quite," says Philip. "No point in harping on it, indeed. Your mother, though, she puzzles me rather . . ."

"My mother was unfathomable."

"You would think she'd feel she was well shot of Ingrid."

"Oh, no. No way."

Alison responds to the postcards. She writes appealing letters to the contact address given by Ingrid, but no postcard ever refers to these. Perhaps Ingrid is no longer at that address; perhaps she has no comment to make.

"I expect Ingrid's got married," says Sandra conversationally.

Alison slams a sauccpan into the sink and tells her to get on and help to clear the table.

And Charles? Charles is writing a book, of course. He keeps to his usual routine, and has the tact (or prudence) not to remark upon the disagreeable household climate — children querulous about late meals and mislaid possessions. Alison's dishevelled mood. He says nothing, and keeps himself to himself, rather more than he would tend to do in any case. You

would think that none of this had anything to do with
him.

"Your father . . ." says Philip.

Gina sighs. She puts her hand on his. "Do you know,
I've had enough of facing down the past. Shall we get
the bill and shoot off? I could do with an early night."

"Of course. Just — your father is inscrutable."

It seems to Gina not so much that people are
unfathomable or inscrutable but that other times, other
circumstances, are unreachable, are no longer available.
That was then, and you cannot go back there, just as
you cannot revisit your own former self, recover the
eleven-year-old Gina of that time when Ingrid went
away. That person is herself, but also someone quite
other, a distant stranger who occasionally signals, and
there is a flash of recognition, but who is for the most
part an alien being.

She remembers that she had a green pencil case with
slots for rubber, sharpener, ruler, individual pens and
pencils. She remembers the splendour of that pencil
case, the soft material of its interior, the pink rubber,
the zip that went round three sides. She remembers
writing a diary that she hid in her pillowcase lest
Sandra should find it. She does not remember
wondering where Ingrid has gone, or what her mother
or her father may feel about this. Just, Ingrid was not
there for a while. So?

It seems to her that your family is at once utterly
familiar and entirely unknown. She knows her parents

intimately — their faces, their voices, the way they walk, smile, laugh, frown, hold a knife and fork, turn their head to speak. And she does not know them at all — why they did as they did, what they experienced, how they saw the world, and one another. As for the rest — Paul, Sandra, Katie, Roger, Clare — the five of them dart through her head like the images in one of those flicker books, every shape and size, and they too are both known and mysterious, she realizes. You thought you had them nailed, but you know now that you did not — they were as slippery as yourself.

And Ingrid?

She tries to remember Ingrid then, to extract her from Ingrid now. Ingrid then was authority of a kind, but secondary authority, not authority on a par with Mum and Dad. You played Ingrid up, you disregarded her, you sometimes obliged her and other times you did not. Ingrid had pale gold satiny hair, and she was good at sewing, she made her own clothes and some of theirs, she could do origami and she didn't like spicy food or coffee. What does this tell you about Ingrid, then? Well, nothing significant, of course. Nothing that throws light on what went on in the grown-up world, that impenetrable world of Mum and Dad and Ingrid, of which they, the children, knew nothing. They were the centre of that world, its focus, but it passed them by.

Alison was in the kitchen, sorting out the wash, when she heard the front door open, and close. It was ten o'clock at night. The Allersmead front door was never

139

locked until Alison and Charles went up to bed. Had Charles gone out, and returned? No, he was in his study, she was sure of that, and even as she rose she heard his door open: he too was wondering who would come in at that time.

So they met in the hall — Alison, Charles and Ingrid, who carried a suitcase in each hand. She set them down as Alison spoke, as Alison opened her mouth in an unconsidered torrent: "You're *back*! But why didn't you let us know, we'd have met you at the station, did you get a taxi? So often there aren't any, oh I wish you'd told me, and have you had anything to eat? There's some cottage pie left, I can heat it up, really, Ingrid, you should have *said* . . ."

And then she dries. She looks at Charles, who has not spoken. He stands there looking at Ingrid, who does not look at him but turns to Alison.

"Yes," she says. "I have come back. That is the way it is, isn't it? And now I am tired. I am going upstairs to sleep."

For Gina, for all of them, there is in recollection simply the revival of Ingrid. She is there once more, and it is as though she never went. Allersmead is complete again; order is restored. If questions are asked, no answers are given. Sandra wonders aloud at breakfast one day if Ingrid went away to meet her boyfriend; Ingrid gazes at Sandra and says that is something that is not very interesting; she does not think that people need to know that. Soon, the whole episode is forgotten, subsumed into Allersmead's history as time marches on, as children grow and develop and mutate, as adults accommodate or fester or rejoice.

"I'll shut up about it, I promise," says Philip, "but I have to say that I find Ingrid enigmatic. There — all three of them. And I think I'm going off the Turkish place. We'll have to find somewhere new."

The German Exchange

Roger has found it difficult to talk about his childhood circumstances to the perfectly sweet Canadian girl who is now his wife. Susan is of Chinese extraction, Canada born, a dermatologist who grew up in a two-bedroom apartment in Markham. Her parents are hardworking, orderly and unfailingly courteous; her only sibling, a brother, is a fledgling investment banker. Both he and Susan have astonished and gratified their parents by so successfully navigating the educational system, and emerging as such significant citizens. When Roger visits, there is a lavish Chinese meal laid on, and the parents sit there smiling and urging him to sample this and that. There is a faint chime of Allersmead here — food as anchor — but otherwise things could not be more different. The parents say little; they beam and nod while Susan and Roger eat and talk of what they have been doing; after a couple of hours or so Susan and Roger leave — the formalities have been observed. Susan says that her parents think Roger eminently satisfactory as a son-in-law. She is a slight, vigorous young woman who enjoys skiing in winter and hiking in summer. Proficient at everything to which she turns her hand, it seems, she has shone in her chosen profession, and in off-duty life is a whiz on the ski slopes and a mean cook (no dim sum or chop suey — spaghetti carbonara, Moroccan chicken, hamburgers). Roger does not find this competence daunting; he respects her and is somehow amused by her and she is the love of his life, at last, thank goodness.

Roger and Susan have succeeded in marrying with minimum fuss, Susan being particularly exercised about avoiding traditional Chinese ceremony of any kind without offending her parents. In the event, this was achieved with the concession of a Chinese meal in a favoured restaurant, the night before, for family and family friends. The wedding itself was a register-office affair, with a party afterwards for a handful of the couple's cronies.

They are now at the tail-end of their honeymoon, which has been spent in taking in as much as possible of the delights of Italy, to which Susan has never been. But a visit to Allersmead is essential, to introduce Susan to her parents-in-law, and this was always written into the itinerary. A few days in London, and then a night at Allersmead. Roger has been a touch apprehensive about this. You could never know how Dad would perform with a visitor. Plus, Roger has never mentioned to Susan the matter of Clare's parentage. He has dithered about this, forgotten about it, dithered again, and indeed has dithered all the way to Allersmead's front door, before which they stand. Too late now.

The arrival goes off well. Alison is effusive, Charles is amiable, Ingrid has baked a cake for tea, in the icing of which a sycamore leaf is embedded. Someone has told

143

her that a maple leaf is the emblem of Canada. Susan is graciously — and genuinely — delighted. Alison beams. She has put on weight, Roger notices, and in the past it would surely have been she who was on cake-baking duty, rather than Ingrid? Is she relinquishing the reins?

Not entirely, it would seem. Dinner is her creation. The Allersmead cuisine has moved with the times; there is no boeuf bourguignon or beef stroganoff, but a fancy sort of salad with rocket and goat's cheese for starters, followed by sea bass and some tricksy accompaniments, rounded off with a lemon sorbet. Susan is again all appreciation; she and Alison get into a cooking conversation, which Roger knows will earn Susan much credit.

Charles has become rather silent. It is at this stage that he breaks into the cookery exchange to ask Susan if she comes from Hong Kong or Taiwan. Susan, Canadian to her toenails, takes this on the chin and replies that she comes from Toronto, while Roger cringes. He suspects that Charles understands Susan's status perfectly well, and is merely being provocative. Alison, unaware of the loaded moment, is keen to get back to cookery, and asks Susan if she does filo pastry. Susan says that she has never been much good at it, and wonders if Alison is fond of waffles. Clearly there is going to be some trading of recipes in due course. Roger sighs with relief and makes a mental note to tell Susan, later on, that she was a real trooper with his father.

144

Roger finds it very strange to be here without his siblings. The place feels both empty and full of ghostly presences — a cacophony of voices from the past, everyone at every age. Gina holds forth about the Falklands War, aged 13; Katie comes banging into the kitchen, dropping her satchel on the floor; a teenage Clare pirouettes in the hall. He says as much, to Alison, which provokes a storm of reminiscence, followed by a frenzy of updating: Gina was in *Iraq*, if you please — on the news night after night, Sandra is managing a boutique in Rome, Clare's dance company is touring Germany — she sent a lovely photo, I'll show you later, Katie you've seen not too long ago, I know, such a shame about no baby.

"And Paul?"

Alison says that Paul is away at the moment. She does not elaborate.

Later, over coffee in the sitting room Alison will display Sandra's postcards from Ischia, where she was staying with a friend, and Clare's publicity photo — caught in mid-flight with male partner, ethereally thin, impossibly supple, her straight flaxen hair smoothed back in a chignon. Susan looks at this with interest.

Eventually, the evening is over. Roger and Susan retire to the spare bedroom and climb thankfully into bed. Roger is relaxed — it has not been too bad; it could have been worse. Made comfortable by food and wine, he talks: this is the moment maybe to explain the little glitch in Allersmead life.

★ ★ ★

"You mean your father fucked the au pair?"

Roger blinks. He has never heard it put like that. He has never put it like that himself. It is too brash, too coarse, too . . . well, true. He says nothing.

Susan is not insensitive. She sees that she has boobed, and scolds herself. She turns to Roger, pulls a face, puts all this into her expression, and the bad moment passes.

"It must have been a tricky time," she says.

Roger shrugs. "Well, I don't remember, do I? I was two. So I don't remember Clare not being there."

Susan is wondering how it was done. Did Alison stuff a cushion down her front? Was Ingrid consigned to a convent for a discreet interval? She keeps these thoughts to herself but is not surprised when Roger speaks: they have reached that point at which mind-reading goes on, in a couple.

"Paul once told me that he remembers Ingrid went away, and when she came back there was somehow this baby too. But it was always our baby, and Mum and Dad were her mum and dad. Something about her real parents not being able to look after her so they'd given her to us as a present."

"And later?"

"Later one sort of realized. Much later. And by then it was simply a part of family life. A fact — but a submerged one."

"Your family is so much more interesting than mine," says Susan.

Roger looks at her, startled. He has found a Chinese immigrant family pretty interesting, and says so.

Susan laughs. "Oh no. We are standard, all over North America. Striving, aspiring parents — achieving children."

Roger protests. He points out the significance of cultural diversity — the value of growing up in one culture but having that other ancestral culture in your bones.

Susan again laughs at this. "My mom's dim sum, and fire crackers at our birthday parties?"

And your face, he wants to say. Your fascinating face that remembers the other side of the world. Instead, he is disparaging about his own origins.

"We were middle England, to the core. There are thousands and thousands of households like Allersmead." Except that, having spoken, he realizes that this is perhaps not entirely so: he thinks of his father's opinions, which were maverick; he thinks of his mother, who seems to have stepped rather from some bohemian milieu of the 1920s, with her errant hairstyle and defiance of fashion; he thinks of Allersmead itself, which also defied the requirements of polite society — middle England is not so shabby, its loos are not Edwardian, its kitchens have been done over since the 1950s.

"Actually," says Susan, "any family is intriguing, if you look closely. I suppose it's just that yours seems exotic in every way, to me."

Exotic? Roger is taken aback. He sees suddenly the chasm between himself and Susan — his beloved Susan — that unbridgeable gulf between any two people which is the product of their early years. Childhood —

which sets the scene, the determining scene, which establishes the norm, which has you observing other people's arrangements with surprise. Childhood — which you do not remember except in cinematic fragments, which was simply accepted and is forever the foundation on which you stand. What is exotic about Allersmead?

It is past midnight. One of the joys of marriage, thinks Roger, is this late night dissection of events in the privacy of bed, this glorious intimacy, when the rest of the world is locked out, and only you and she exist. It is odd to have this take place in the spare room at Allersmead, but the flavour is the same. He tells Susan she was brilliant with his father, some would have got mad; he tells her that she was a star to talk cooking with his mother, she didn't *have* to.

"Look, I wanted to," says Susan. "I'm interested in cooking. Haven't you noticed?"

Roger agrees that he has, indeed he has. He lays a hand on her hip. "Just, you were terrific with them. Mum really liked you."

"And your dad?" He can feel her smile, in the darkness.

"Dad sort of doesn't go in for liking people. At least, not so you'd notice."

"But you'd notice if he didn't?"

Roger agrees, with some emphasis, that you would.

"Then I've kind of squeezed through the middle, I guess," says Susan. She yawns. "I need to pee. Will I wake people if I go to the bathroom?"

148

"No. Their room's at the far end of the house. And Ingrid's up in the attic."

She pads out of the room, without turning on the light. He hears the bathroom door close and then the muffled sound of the antique cistern emptying. Susan returns and snuggles up against him. "I just love that toilet. The ball and chain. Can we have one like that fitted? You can get them from reclamation places."

"No," says Roger. After a moment he speaks again. "When I was thirteen, my parents proposed to exchange me for a German boy of the same age."

"Permanently?" exclaims Susan, amazed.

"No, no. For a month or so. It was a thing that was much done then. To improve your German or French or whatever, and vice versa. And to experience another culture."

"Not a bad idea."

"In this instance it didn't work. The German boy went home after a week. He found the English way of life insupportable — at least as exemplified at Allersmead. And his parents let it be known, as politely as possible, that they were no longer keen to receive me."

"Too bad."

"Oh, I was hugely relieved. I tell this tale, though, simply to demonstrate that not all visitors find my family interestingly exotic. Some are merely dismayed."

"What happened?" says Susan, yawning again. "What went wrong?"

"Never mind that. And don't go to sleep." He pushes up her T-shirt, runs a hand over her thigh. She makes a little sound of protest that is not a protest. Presently they discover, as did Gina and Philip, that the Allersmead spare room bed has the most vociferous springs.

The German exchange was smaller than Roger; he was dark, with large eyes that clearly took in everything, and then some more. He stepped off the train, immaculate despite a journey that had involved several changes, and greeted Alison in equally spruce English. The travel had been good, thank you — his parents had told him what to do; he showed Alison two closely typed sheets of paper. No, he was not hungry at the moment, thank you — his mother's provisions for the travel were only just finished. He shook Roger by the hand and said that they would be good friends. Roger shook back, limply, less certain about this.

"He is charming," said Ingrid, later. Roger, who doubted that anyone had ever said *he* was charming, stared out of the window. Stefan was being shown the garden by Alison, and was conspicuously responsive. From time to time he pointed at something, enquiringly, or gazed at a tree. Stefan had adults sewn up, Roger could see; he didn't even need to be speaking his own language. He seemed to be not 13, but about 30, or a 130. He was unfailingly polite; he leapt to attention whenever Alison or Ingrid entered the room; he asked Charles his advice about English books that he should read.

"Who's this little creep you've brought?" said Paul, returning from college.

"I didn't bring him," muttered Roger. "And *shut up*. He speaks English better than we do."

Stefan was to share Roger's room. On the first evening he stood in the doorway staring at the mounds of jeans, sweaters, T-shirts, the foetid heaps of trainers, the windowsill on which Roger's caterpillar collection heaved in glass jars, the poster of Life on the Seashore, the torn wallpaper, the carpet which had gamely absorbed Ribena, milk, Coke and other substances over the years. In fact, goaded by Alison, Roger had tidied the room. He thought it looked pretty OK, but, glancing at Stefan, he saw it afresh for a moment, and saw it fall short. Stefan's expression was complex: it registered dismay rapidly tamped down and succeeded by resignation. He eyed the bunk beds.

"You can have the top if you like," said Roger.

Stefan smiled. "*Danke schön. Das ist ja sehr freundlich. Vielen Dank.*"

Roger looked at him in horror. His last German exam mark had been B minus. Conversation was not on the cards.

Stefan made a gesture of apology. "I thought perhaps you should practise. Another time. Thank you for the top." He unpacked his bag, from which came meticulously folded garments, and a washbag full of mysterious toiletries. Roger showed him the bathroom, and again had that moment of fresh and disturbing vision: he saw the rail festooned with towels, the ripped shower curtain, the shelf crammed with Sandra's cosmetics, the holder that sprouted a forest of toothbrushes, the flannels draped over the side of the bath, the plastic ducks behind the taps (and who played with those now, for heaven's sake?). The loo. Oh God, the loo. He smelt an awful smell of ancestral damp, and saw Stefan smell it too. "This is the bathroom," said Roger glumly.

It emerged over supper that Stefan was an only child.

"Lucky sod," said Paul.

"Really!" cried Alison. "He doesn't mean that," she told Stefan. "It's a joke."

Stefan nodded politely. "Sod?" he enquired. "That is a word I do not know."

Charles put down his knife and fork. "A colloquialism. Generally regarded as coarse or derisive. My son's conversation will afford you a rich opportunity to study the baser forms of our language."

Stefan nodded again, his expression inscrutable.

Paul said, "Thanks, Dad. It's good to know one's useful."

Alison frowned and addressed herself to Stefan. "You'll find life in a big family a bit different. We all learn to make allowances, don't we?" She looked round the table.

"Not so that you'd notice," said Sandra. "Is there any more, Mum?"

Alison got up. "That's not very nice, dear. Pass your plate. But first see if Stefan would like some."

Stefan said that he had had enough, thank you.

Clare said, "Can't we ever having *thinning* food? Toad-in-the-hole is just stuffed with carbohydrates."

Gina said, "At the age of ten you shouldn't even know what a carbohydrate *is*."

152

Clare said, "Look, I'm getting so fat I can't even do a handstand."

Paul told Gina that he was going to the pub later and she might want to come along and buy him a drink.

Katie wondered if anyone had seen her red purse, it was on the dresser, I'm sure . . .

Stefan said, "Toad-in-the-hole?" but no one heard him.

Roger looked at Stefan and saw a dark, intense, observing presence. He looked at his family and saw everyone talking at once, Ingrid telling Mum that there was no hot water again, Dad asking who had removed the paper from the hall table and would they kindly put it back. He knew, with an awful certainty, that Alison was going to suggest that he and Stefan have a game of Scrabble after supper.

Roger stared at the board. He had four letters left, and the only word that he could make was "fuck". Allersmead house rules prohibited obscenities but Stefan did not know about Allersmead house rules. Stefan was winning — he probably had won — but "fuck" would give Roger 27 and might just possibly put him ahead. Roger was not unduly competitive but Scrabble can bring out the worst in anyone; he did not like being trounced by someone for whom English was not even his own language — it was humiliating. His hand hovered over the pieces; he picked them up one by one and set them down.

Stefan studied the result. He had already mentioned that at home he and his parents sometimes played

Scrabble in English, just for fun (*Fun?* thought Roger, aghast). He said, "With my family we don't allow that word. It is different here, I suppose."

There was just the faintest criticism implied, and Roger saw that he was scuppered. Either he came clean about Allersmead house rules and admitted cheating but retrieved the family honour, or he kept quiet and allowed the family to be tarnished in comparison with Stefan's decent and superior home lifestyle. Or — a possible third way occurred to him — he gave a little snort of amusement at this priggish scenario, as one accustomed to a climate of liberal self-expression.

He stared hopelessly at the board, avoiding Stefan's eye.

The door opened. "What about bed, boys?" said Alison. "Stefan must be more than ready, after that journey. Or do you want to finish the game?"

Roger swept up the pieces. "Oh, we just about have," he said. "Stefan's won, anyway."

Much later, lying awake, it came to him that if Stefan's family was so clean-living, then "fuck" shouldn't be a part of their English vocabulary. After all, Stefan had apparently been baffled by "sod".

The next day Roger and Stefan took a football to the local park, at Alison's suggestion. Roger had not quite reckoned with this enforced twinning by the cultural exchange programme: whatever you did, you did together. You and he were an artificial unit, for the duration of his stay. You slept together, you played together, you ate, drank and communed.

There was no escape, it seemed. "What are you boys going to do now?" Alison would enquire brightly.

They played football, obedient to requirements. For Roger, this was no penance; it was clear that Stefan was less keen, but he kicked the ball around gamely for an hour or so, somewhat inept, which was an embarrassment to both. Eventually, by mutual consent, they trailed back to the house. The day yawned ahead.

Left to himself, Roger would have luxuriated in holidays boredom; he would have mooched, idled, done nothing in particular for many constructive hours. This was now not an option: he must be seen to be doing something in order that Stefan should do it with him. Monopoly, badminton in the garden, Demon Patience, quoits in the garden, Snakes and Ladders, why not get out the table tennis things and set them up in the garden? It was exhausting.

Stefan appeared to be all compliance. Except, Roger realized, that his good manners were so ingrained that it was virtually impossible for him not to comply. "Yes," he would say. "I would like that. You must teach me this game — I do not know it." He played with awful determination; he played for the honour of his country, one felt. At night, he was haggard with fatigue.

Thirteen-year-olds are not strong on empathy. Roger was not strong on empathy, but just occasionally he glimpsed in Stefan a sort of shuttered anguish. He saw it when Stefan awaited his turn for the bathroom, he saw it when Stefan so evidently tried and failed to follow the exchanges over the Allersmead kitchen table, at mealtimes, he saw it when Stefan faced a plateful of corned beef hash ("No, we do not have this at home.").

It was during one of those quick-fire, competitive, coded Allersmead mealtimes that Alison began to explain to Stefan the treat in store.

"It's such fun that you're here for it, Stefan — one of our big family events. It's my *birthday*, you see, and since it happens so nicely in the school holidays — so sensible of me to have been born in August — we always have a family picnic. The birthday picnic. Now — quiet, everybody, please! — we haven't decided yet where it's going to be this year, and it's only two days away, so I want some ideas."

"Alton Towers theme park," said Clare.

"Oxford Street," said Sandra. "With shopping opportunities for those who wish."

"That green bit outside the Houses of Parliament," said Paul. "With placards extolling the sanctity of family life."

Alison frowned. "*Sensible* suggestions, please." She turned to Charles. "What about you, dear? Anywhere you'd particularly like to go?"

Charles had appeared to be lost in some private reverie. Now he surfaced. "Ah, yes, the annual celebration." He glanced at Stefan. "Perhaps our visitor should be allowed to choose the destination?"

Stefan looked panic-stricken. "I do not think . . ." he began.

Katie came to his rescue. "Actually, why don't we go to Whipsnade?"

Groans. "Oh, puh-leeze," said Sandra.

Charles again addressed Stefan. "You will note a certain absence of agreement in this family. A tradition that a ritual should also be a matter of dissension. It's always a challenge to see for how long it can go on." He looked round the table expectantly.

"That's right, Dad," muttered Paul. "Muddy the waters."

Gina went to kick him, and found Stefan's leg instead. "Sorry," she mouthed.

"Perhaps a beach would be nice," said Ingrid. "For the swimming."

Alison waved her arms. "Hush, all of you. In fact, I've had an inspiration. Maiden Castle — nice and grassy for the picnic, and we can have a wander around Dorchester before."

There was a silence. "*What* castle?" said Sandra.

"You know Maiden Castle," said Paul. "Famous for the ritual sacrifice of maidens in — um — the twelfth century."

Charles spoke. "A neat choice, if I may say so. A combination of historical and literary contexts for our visitor. The Iron Age meets the sage of Wessex." He surveyed the table. "Hands up anyone who knows what I'm talking about?"

His children sat in silence, stony-eyed. "That's it, then," cried Alison merrily. "Maiden Castle it is. Fingers crossed for the weather."

The days of the Volkswagen were long gone. There were now two cars — an elderly Volvo estate, which was mainly Alison's, and an equally mature Vauxhall which

157

was perhaps mainly Charles's except that Charles was not a man to have any sort of relationship with a car. He used it from time to time, but was unsure where the keys were kept and did not know how you would check the oil or the tyre pressures. These two vehicles would accommodate the entire family for occasions such as this (fewer and further between, these days) — five in one and four in the other, with room to squeeze in an extra such as Stefan.

There was argument about who should go in which car for the drive to Dorchester, which would take an hour and a half or so. Charles and Alison would both appreciate a navigator, and the only volunteer map-readers were Paul and Gina. Clare would feel sick in the Vauxhall. The Vauxhall being the smaller car, the two other smaller people — Roger and Stefan — would have to go in that, or there would be a squash. Eventually, the two parties were sorted out thus: Gina, Ingrid, Katie and Clare in the Volvo, driven by Alison; Sandra, Paul, Stefan and Roger in the Vauxhall, with Charles driving. The picnic — several baskets, boxes and hampers — was loaded into the back of the Volvo, along with rugs and a few folding chairs. The weather was looking a little dubious, but Alison was all optimism: "It'll clear up — you'll see."

In the Vauxhall, Paul sat next to Charles in the front, with the map; Sandra, Roger and Stefan occupied the back seat. Initially they tailed the Volvo, but soon lost it at a roundabout. Charles and Paul bickered over Paul's map-reading after one wrong turn was taken, landing them in a housing estate. "I thought we'd do the scenic route," said Paul cheerfully. Charles was not amused: "I understood you to be competent with a map."

After a further half hour they went wrong again. "I meant left," said Paul. "Sorry about that." Charles was silent for a few moments. Then, "You'll notice, Stefan, that my son seems unable to distinguish left and right, a failing that would make him ineligible even for army recruitment."

"I don't think Stefan quite heard that, Dad," said Paul. "Don't worry — if the army won't have me, I dare say something else will turn up."

Stefan stared rigidly out of the window.

They stopped for petrol. Paul left the car while Charles was filling up and returned from the shop with a six-pack of lager.

"Are you going to *drink* that?" said Sandra.

Paul sat down and stowed the lager alongside his seat. "No, I'm going to pour it down the slopes of Maiden Castle as a libation."

Charles returned. They set off once more. Stefan, who, along with Roger, had bought a bar of chocolate and seemed to rally a little, said, "The place we are going to . . . it is very old?"

"Maiden Castle," said Paul, "is the site of the annual slaughter of a dozen nubile maidens in a ritual designed to ensure national productivity. Interestingly, this practice continues . . ."

Sandra leaned forward. "Shut *up*. This is *so* boring. Plus, it's contemptuous of women."

Roger looked nervously at Stefan, whose expression was blank.

Charles drove in silence. Presently, he said, "For our visitor's sake, I should remind you all that Dorchester, where we shall meet up with the rest of the party, is Thomas Hardy's Casterbridge. As in *The Mayor of . . .* We are now in Wessex, scene of most if not all of the novels."

"I've seen a film," said Sandra. "Alan Bates. *So* sexy. Fantastic."

Paul broached one of the cans of lager. His father glanced sideways. "Would you mind applying yourself to the map. I think we should be turning off soon."

In the car park at Dorchester they met up with the rest of the party. Alison was in high spirits: "We've got plenty of time before the picnic. What shall we head for?"

"Topshop?" said Sandra. "French Connection? Next?"

"Does it have a swimming pool?" said Clare.

Roger knew where they would go. That was where they always went, in any new place. Dad would announce that that was where they were going, and Mum would agree, to avoid argument and to be seen to be supportive.

"The museum is apparently worth a visit," said Charles. "I believe they have Thomas Hardy's study, recreated."

"Good idea!" cried Alison.

They moved off into the town. From time to time Charles spoke about Thomas Hardy, or the Iron Age, but nobody paid any attention, except Stefan, who trailed dutifully alongside. He would be no stranger to museums, Roger reckoned; his family probably took in a museum before breakfast. Clare was still bleating about swimming pools. Paul brought up the rear, occasionally swigging lager.

In front of Thomas Hardy's recreated study Charles fell silent; the desk, the pen, the papers evidently struck a chord. Probably he felt like getting in there, thought Roger. His natural habitat.

"I don't believe I've read any of his books," said Alison brightly.

Charles sighed. He told Stefan that Thomas Hardy was a novelist who had chronicled the lost way of life of rural England in the late nineteenth century.

"We did him for A level," said Gina. "A girl who has a baby and gets hanged in the end; heavy going but it had its moments."

Charles sighed again. "A neat synopsis, I suppose, but short on literary appreciation." He turned away. "I suggest the archaeological section next, as briefing for Maiden Castle."

In Iron Age Wessex, Sandra established herself on a bench and began a meticulous reapplication of make-up. Paul sought the reinforcement of the lager can. Clare's plait had come undone and required some remedial work from Ingrid. The rest drifted from case to case. Roger stared at an array of gangrenous metal weapons and thought that archaeology was mainly about killing people, when you got down to it. Charles was telling Stefan about the Roman invasions.

Alison leapt to her feet. "It's past twelve. Lunch, everybody! Picnic-time!"

They straggled back to the car park, into the cars. "Now for the assault on Everest," said Paul. He seemed more animated, for some reason. Charles, on the other hand, had become morose. He snapped at Paul to look out for the signs.

"Don't worry," said Paul. "You can *see* it."

You could indeed. This great hill with grassy ramparts and a path snaking up from the car park. Roger eyed it with a flicker of interest; you could roll down those.

The cars were parked, the Volvo unpacked and its contents distributed by Alison. "You carry this . . . Paul, take the chairs . . . Be *careful* of that — it's got the bottles in it . . ." The party wound upwards along the path, everyone laden, like refugees in flight from some disaster, or a troop bearing votive offerings. "Keep those bottles the right way *up*," called Alison. "Has someone got the big rug?" She veered off the path, gesturing: "Along here is best. I remember from when we came years ago. Away from other people and a lovely view."

Her chosen spot, the ridge of one of the ramparts, turned out to command a fine view of a courting couple busy in the dip below, who broke off to glare indignantly. Katie said, "Mum, I think maybe we should go a bit further along."

"It's perfect here, dear. A nice flat bit, and no thistles. Paul, the chairs over there, and whoever's got the rug *here*."

A settlement was established, strewn with open baskets and boxes, a phalanx of bottles arranged on a

162

folding table (wine for adults, soft drinks for the rest), an area designated for sitting. The courting couple got up and departed, with resentful glances. "How to spoil someone's day . . ." murmured Katie.

Alison had excelled herself. There were quiches, sausages on sticks, salads, cold roast chicken, home-made strawberry ice cream, raspberry tarts. Roger perked up further. The group settled — some people sprawled on rugs, the three adults on chairs, and Sandra, who did not want to risk messing up her skirt. Alison distributed food: "Paper napkins over here, plus bowls and spoons for the ice cream. Charles, will you open the wine?"

Charles poured wine for Ingrid, Alison and himself. He drank some immediately, which seemed to put him in better humour. He raised his glass: "Here's to the birthday!"

Beakers of lemonade and Coke, and a can of lager, were raised. "Cheers, Mum," said Sandra. Stefan said, "I wish you a happy birthday," and then sank into mortified embarrassment.

Ingrid said, "So many birthdays. But perhaps not so many more."

"Thanks, everyone!" Alison was complacent. "What *do* you mean, Ingrid dear? Oh — people growing up. But they'll come *back*, won't you all? Family traditions are sacred" — a merry laugh — "and, anyway, that's ages off. Roger, pass round the sausages and the chicken — I want it all eaten up. Do you have traditions in your family, Stefan? So important. I mean, everyone has Christmas and birthdays, but it's making them special, isn't it?"

"Personalized," said Sandra.

"What, dear? The thing is, in this family I've always made sure we had our little ceremonies. When everyone was younger, we had the treasure hunts at birthday parties, and we always have a special lunch when anyone has something particular to celebrate. Lots of GCSEs — that sort of thing."

"Or few, in one case," said Charles.

Paul hurled an empty lager can down the side of the rampart with great force.

"Oh, Paul, *don't* do that," cried Alison. "*Litter*. Naughty boy. Go and pick it up later. Now, that salad wants finishing and there's masses of quiche still. The thing about a tradition is that you have all these memories. There was the time we had the treasure hunt in Kew Gardens — Katie's day, that was. Kew Gardens are famous . . . well, gardens, Stefan."

"I remember," says Katie. "I fell and cut my knee."

"But mostly of course at home — the treasure hunts. All over the house, if wet."

"In the garden was best," said Ingrid. "Except the time Gina . . . fell."

Alison was halted. "Well, such a pity, but accidents will happen."

"And really the scar does not much show," Ingrid continued.

Gina closed her eyes for a moment, reopened them and said, "Thanks, Ingrid. Thanks ever so."

Sandra was lost in examination of her fingernails.

164

"Ah, such happy times," said Paul.

Alison beamed at him. "Of course they were. Now *you* had the best birthday of all. The first. All to yourself."

"Quite. It's been downhill ever since."

"I made you a little cake, with your name in blue icing. Talking of which . . ."

Alison got up, bent over an as yet unopened box, and produced, with a flourish, the birthday cake. "Chocolate walnut, with you in mind, Clare — I know you love it. Now, where's the knife got to?"

"Happy birthday!" sang Paul. "Happy birthday, dear Mother . . ."

They all sang. Stefan sang, looking around nervously. Roger sang, and as he did so he seemed to see the others with detachment — this group sitting on the side of a hill, singing: his parents and his brother and his sisters, those infinitely familiar people, who could not be otherwise, and yet, it occurred to him, they could, they had been, they would be once more. They had been younger (a smaller Clare floated suddenly into his head) and would be older. As would he. Grown-ups, eventually.

Except that that was impossible. Unimaginable. Out of the question.

Cake was eaten.

"Ceremonial feasting," said Charles. "Plenty of that done up here in Celtic times." He poured himself another glass of wine.

"What did people eat in those days?" asked Stefan valiantly.

165

He was told, at some length. ". . . emmer wheat," Roger heard, with half an ear. ". . . fermented barley . . ." He eyed the slope of the hill, and wondered about rolling down it. "That is most interesting," Stefan was saying, and Roger felt a twinge of sympathy. It came to him with horror that in due course he would have to converse with Stefan's father, only it would be all in German so he wouldn't understand a word.

"Who did the cooking?" said Sandra, looking up suddenly. It had not been apparent that she was listening.

"The women, of course." Charles smiled benignly. "It was a patriarchal society."

"I don't know what that means."

"It means — men rule, OK," said Paul.

Ingrid, packing rubbish into one of the boxes, turned her head. "I think it is not so different now."

"Wow, Ingrid!" said Sandra. "Go on."

Ingrid shrugged. "Just . . . it is not so different now." She was disconcertingly emphatic. People looked at her.

Gina weighed in. "Soon will be. Next generation, gender discrimination will be a thing of the past. It'll be the post-feminist age. Sexual egalitarianism."

"I could do with a bit of women rule, first," said Sandra.

Charles drank, inspected the wine bottle and poured the last couple of inches into his glass. "Don't they now?" A sardonic glance around.

Ingrid stood up. She spoke, apparently, to the sky. "I do not think so."

"I don't know *what* you're all talking about," said Alison. "Ingrid dear, make sure what's left of the quiche gets wrapped up."

"Dad does, don't you, Dad?" Paul, *sotto voce*, to another lager can.

"I beg your pardon, Paul?" Charles, loudly.

"Nothing, nothing . . ."

"Women are doing rather well in contemporary western society. One would be ill-advised to tangle with them." Charles chuckled; a private joke, it would seem.

Paul got up. "Who's talking about contemporary western society?" He glared at Charles, threw his lager can into an open box and walked off along the rampart.

There was a silence. Alison stared for a moment at Charles and then became busy packing up. Charles gazed out over Dorset, impassive. Ingrid had sat down once more and was expressionless. Roger wanted to say something, to crash into this silence, but nothing came. He felt as though some dark and alien presence had crept into their midst. As though there were someone else there, whom he did not know.

It was time to go, Alison said. "But where *is* Paul? Tiresome boy — we'll have to send out a search party."

Charles was reading the paper. Sandra was stretched out on the rug in the sun. Ingrid sat a little apart. Katie was immersed in a book.

"I'll go," said Gina.

Roger leapt to his feet. "I'm coming too."

They set off along the rampart, Stefan a few paces behind. "The thing is to start at the highest point," said Gina. "Where we can see most. And work down."

There were fewer people around now. They circled the hill once, to no avail. "Ho, hum," said Gina. "Easy to miss him, with all these lumps and bumps." They tried calling. Their voices sank into the hillside, floated off into Dorset. "I feel silly," said Gina. " 'Please, have you seen my brother?' He's not exactly a toddler."

They found him in a hollow, flat on his face, empty lager cans beside him.

"Oh, dear," said Gina.

"He is asleep?" said Stefan helpfully.

"You could say that." Gina bent down. "Hey! Come on — up!" Paul grunted. "Come on, Paul. On your feet."

"Fuck off," said Paul.

"No way. It's home now, and just shut up, right?" Gina draped Paul's arm round her neck. "OK — quick march."

They stumbled along the hill. Stefan followed, wide-eyed. "I think your brother is perhaps . . ."

"Yes," said Roger glumly, "He is."

Little was said, back at the encampment. Charles gave Paul one look, folded his newspaper and got to his feet. Alison too looked, for rather longer, and then said, briskly and artificially, "*There* you are. Let's get off, then."

In the car, Paul slept in the back and Roger discovered that he could read a map. It was a heady moment, akin to sudden fluent mastery of a foreign language. Charles said, "Pretty good, Roger. In fact, remarkably good." Roger sailed into the evening on the rip tide of this new skill, and failed to notice that Stefan had asked if he might please telephone his parents. Indeed, he barely took things in when it emerged that actually Stefan was going home tomorrow, and a few days later, following the receipt of a letter from Stefan's parents, that he himself would not be completing the exchange. He was too busy thinking about how long he would have to save his pocket money before he could buy some Ordnance Survey maps.

"Just because your brother was pissed?" says Susan. "Most boys get pissed from time to time."

"Not just that. It was the whole package, I reckon. We were too much for a delicately nurtured lad from Freiburg. A case of cultural revulsion."

Nightwaves

"Hi! Where are you?"

"I'm at home," says Gina. "Paul, it's nearly midnight. You *never* ring at a civilized hour."

"Because you don't answer then, do you? And you're too busy in pursuit of news to call back. Or you're on the other side of the world. OK — I'll go."

"Don't," says Gina. "As it happens, I'm not in bed yet. And Philip's away. Where are *you*?"

"Where do you think I am? At Allersmead. As per usual. As so often. Where a guy of my age should not be — in the parental home."

"Listen, Paul . . ."

"In fact, I'm applying for a job at Wisley. Seeing that I've got all this horticultural experience. D'you think they'll take me? I've written ever such a persuasive letter. And sent my credentials."

"Ah," says Gina. "What credentials exactly?"

"My CV demonstrates flexibility, if nothing else. Bar hand, hospital porter, school groundsman, motorbike courier, fruit picker, car-park attendant. Wide experience of living circumstances: several squats, various sofas and put-u-ups, share of a flat with — um — five others, agricultural workers' hostels, shared room at rehab centre. One-night stands in police cells."

"I'd scrub that last item," says Gina. "If I were you."

"I'm going for honesty, aren't I? And those were pure oppression, anyway. Instances of under-occupied coppers picking on someone enjoying a pleasant night out. Over-reaction."

"Suit yourself," says Gina. "If relentless honesty is your concept of a CV."

"I'm offering the whole man. Adaptable, wide-ranging and not unflawed. The shrinks at the rehab place were most interested in flaws. Know thyself. We mulled over my flaws in many a productive session. I bet they could find a flaw or two for you, if they really worked you over."

"Dozens," says Gina. "Philip will be glad to list them."

"Nice guy, I thought. Is he a fixture?"

"Do you mind?"

"Sorry, sorry. Only asking. Concerned for my sister's welfare. Let's get back to me — a far more precarious subject. Where were we? Oh — the CV. Dog walker, Dodgem-car operator — have I mentioned that one?"

"No," says Gina. "I don't know about that."

"Probably best not to. Let's just say my advice is never get mixed up with fairground folk. A pretty unsavoury lot even by my standards, and I've learned not to be fussy. That's how I lost a front tooth. There was a girl I used to chat to and her boyfriend had an issue with that. Taught me to be more wary where women are concerned."

"Always advisable when they're someone else's," says Gina.

"We'll leave her off the CV. In fact all women are off the CV, including live-in ones. Or will that make me look . . ."

"Gay?" suggests Gina.

"That wouldn't be a problem. I'm thinking more . . . undesirable. Unappealing. Reject material. Maybe we'll have women as a footnote. The usual emotional attachments — that sort of thing."

"You do realize this is becoming a rather odd sort of CV."

"Maverick, let's call it. Individual. We're trying to reflect my personality. You could call that quite individual, couldn't you?"

"I'm afraid so," says Gina.

"Is this criticism? Oh well, I'm inured to that. From schooldays onwards. 'Paul has once again failed to realize his potential.' You, of course, were always off the scale, achievement-wise."

"It was a crap school," says Gina.

"Quite. But Dad's divvies were never going to run to private education for six."

"We should have hanged ourselves in the scary cupboard," says Gina. "'. . . we are too menny'."

"Come again?"

"Literary reference."

"You know perfectly well I can barely read. No need to show off. Now, back to the CV. We've done work experience, pretty well, though there's plenty of bits and pieces I've left off. We've touched on the itinerary, as it were — the geographical progress — though that

172

could do with some filling out. We've agreed that the emotional life is on a back burner."

"Tell me," says Gina, "exactly what is this CV for? Not Wisley, I think."

"Ah, good point. Shall we call it more a kind of stock-taking? An assessment exercise. We're always doing that at the garden centre. What have we got, and what do we need more of? Incidentally, I'm a plant wizard these days. I can rattle off miscanthus and verbena bonariensis and whatever. Maybe I've missed my vocation. Why didn't they send me to horticultural college? I am charmingly helpful to little old ladies in search of a nice climber for the trellis."

"Paul," says Gina, "what is all this about?"

"I've told you. Self-scrutiny. Candid evaluation of the record so far." (Pause.) "I don't know whether to laugh or cry. Remind me how old I am?"

Gina does not reply.

"No, don't, on second thoughts. It's something I try to forget."

"Enough of this," says Gina.

"Enough of what?"

"Self-flagellation."

"I've heard that term before. Maybe it's one the shrinks used. I tended to shut my ears to the long words. The questions too, in so far as that was possible. Very persistent, shrinks. 'Would you like to talk to me about your childhood, Paul?' No, thanks. And then you have to, to keep them quiet. I told them about the cellar game, once."

Gina laughs.

"Very interested, they were. 'And what was your role, Paul?' James Bond. Chief pirate. Shrink nods understandingly."

"What else did you tell them?"

"Nothing much. None of their business." (Pause.) "Anyway, you can't tell people, can you? It doesn't exactly translate into words. It's in the mind, and there it stays. Done with. Or not, as the case may be."

"The general view is — not. Hence your shrinks."

"Huh . . ." (Pause.) "Shall I tell you something?"

"Feel free," says Gina.

"She once told me I was her favourite. She shouldn't have done that, should she? True or not. That wasn't good mother stuff. Good mothers don't have favourites, or at least they don't say so. Was it true?"

"Yes," says Gina.

(Pause.) "Did everyone know?"

"Yes."

(Pause.) "Did you mind?"

"Me? Not specially. I thought it a rather perverse choice, I remember."

"Thanks very much."

"Listen, are you OK?" says Gina.

"Of course I'm OK. When have I not been OK?"

"Well . . ." murmurs Gina.

(Pause.) "Let's not go there, shall we?" (Pause.) "I'm fine, except for backache from heaving compost bags. It's we manual workers who really keep the world on the move, never mind strutting around in front of a television camera."

"Be that as it may," says Gina, "we both have to work tomorrow, and it's past midnight."

"Is that a hint? OK — I'll let you go. Bye, then."

Paul is lying on the bed. He puts his phone down and stares at the ceiling, a ceiling he has known all his life. Those cracks — like a river with tributaries. The discolouration — Allersmead does not go in for new décor. After each absence — months, a year or so — he returns to contemplation of this ceiling, and he is both resigned and maddened. Such is his relationship with the ceiling. It is his personal ceiling — a comfort and a mockery.

It mocks him now. That pattern of cracks in the plaster resolves itself into a face in profile, and the face becomes that of a girl he knew once, and he is sitting beside her on the low wall of the esplanade, and he is happy. Actually, he cannot now, at Allersmead, staring up at the ceiling and back to that moment, see her very well, except for the line of that profile, but oddly he can hear her, and he can hear seagulls, and the swish-wash of the sea on the pebbles. And he knows about the happiness; it occurs to him that he did not know then that he was happy, that only now can he identify the flavour of that moment.

She laughs at him for being a barman. Not derisive laughter — amused laughter. That is *such* a fun thing to be. She is younger than he is and she works in a florist's shop along the road from the hotel, which is not much of a fun thing, she says. In fact it's a dead end but she's just marking time while she looks around. She may go to the States — she has some cousins there. She lives with her parents in one of those big houses on the edge of the town, but she can't wait to get away somewhere and in the meantime she is ready and willing to meet up with Paul when they both have time off. They have kissed on the beach and behind the hedge in front of her parents' house, and here on the seafront they hold hands and Paul is happy, happy. There have been other girls — of course there have — but she is of a different order. She is berry brown and dark-eyed and she has this rich laugh that thrills him each time he hears it.

They have sex on the bed in Paul's cramped room in the attic of the hotel, after he has talked his room-mate, the other barman — a student doing vacation work — into staying away. She is less amused by this slightly foetid setting (niffy sheets, discarded clothes) — a girl used to band-box suburban hygiene — but she is responsive, innovative, indeed, and afterwards they have dinner at the Turkish restaurant, which costs Paul most of his weekly pay packet. She asks Paul what his plans are in terms of a *real* job, eventually, and Paul has to do some ducking and weaving; he does not mention the string of other temporary occupations, nor does he mention the spell at the rehab centre. He avoids much mention of anything, and aims at giving the impression of one who is enviably footloose and uncommitted, at least for so long as he wishes to be thus.

He is not invited into her house, which is reminiscent of Allersmead — same expansive presence amid neighbours similarly kitted out with trees and grass and the sweep of gravelled driveway. He knows where she comes from, because he comes from there himself, and presumably she senses that, which is why she is amused

176

by this masquerade as a barman. He is really a solid citizen, even if he is leaving it a tad late to solidify.

Why is he not invited in, presented to her parents? Perhaps because she knows that her parents would not be so entertained by the idea of a barman as boyfriend to their daughter, albeit an amateur barman, albeit that she herself has never bestowed on him boyfriend status. This is a seasonal romance, so far as she is concerned, and it is played out on the beach, on the cliffs beyond the town, in cafés and pubs and — when Paul can persuade her — up in that attic bedroom at the hotel.

That is her view of the situation. The trouble is that Paul's is veering off in a different direction. In the past, girls had come and gone and no regrets, but this time he cannot bear the idea of letting her go. She matters. He is besotted. All right, he is in love, he has finally joined the human race. He has not told her of his condition, because he senses that she might run for cover. He tries to keep up the pretence of airy involvement, of a summer spree, of casual alliance.

And then one day she is abstracted, irritable, and the next day she fails to turn up at the appointed time. She does not return his phone calls. Her mother answers the phone and says that she will pass on the message; her tone is cool.

A week, and they have not met. Ten days. Two weeks. He has walked past the florist's shop a dozen times, seen her within; twice he has steeled himself and gone in — she has frowned and told him she can't talk now, she'll be in touch.

★   ★   ★

At Allersmead, all these years later, the girl tumbles in Paul's head along with other stuff, so much stuff. Mostly, it is shadows that tumble, her shadowy figure, and above all the shadows of feelings, of what he felt when she . . .

When she told him she was pregnant. For an instant he was shocked, and then there surged up this euphoria. Pregnant. Pregnant means a baby. A baby means a couple. A home. Somewhere to be, someone to be with. He tells her they should get married. He wants to marry her. He longs to marry her.

And she says, "Are you mad?"

She does not want to marry him. She has not the slightest intention of marrying him. This is a mess, this shouldn't have happened, but no way does it mean they are staying together. It was going nowhere, can't he see that? Actually, she had been going to tell him they should maybe stop seeing each other.

There is ice in his stomach. From euphoria to ice. He stares at her. Then he pleads, he implores, he tells her he will get a proper job, they'll have a place to live, a baby will be . . . (he searches for the right word, a word to suit her) . . . fun.

She hears him out, expressionless. Then she says, "No way, Paul."

She is implacable. Cold, detached. She has become someone else; that delicious laugh is heard no more. She has withdrawn into her situation and there is no place there for him. He is sidelined, discarded. He is

178

devastated, he is confused; it seems to him that he does have some kind of status here, some claim even, but he cannot think how to present it. He has an appalling sense of loss: for a moment he had glimpsed some utopian future, and then she had snatched it away.

In his confusion, his dismay, his inability to think clearly, he says that he would like to see the baby, when it comes.

She looks at him with a kind of tired contempt. "There won't be any baby," she says. "I'm going to have to fix that, aren't I?"

Occasionally, over the years, Paul has thought of this nonchild, just as occasionally he remembers the girl. It is a long time ago; he was quite young. He is a good bit older now, and possibly not much wiser but well able to look back clear-eyed. Mostly, he does not like what he sees, and that of course is the problem. If only he had . . . If only he hadn't . . . And the summer of that girl seems to him a point at which things might have swerved in a new direction, if only she . . .

But she didn't. And she has vanished now, into that morass of people once known, who from time to time are still heard, mostly telling him things he would rather not hear. Authoritarian figures accuse him of lacking motivation, employers wonder if he is really cut out for this job, girls tell him they just don't feel they can count on him, people at the rehab place echo again and again about perseverance and application and giving himself a chance.

He hasn't done drugs for years, in fact. Just once in a while. Booze — well, booze fairly frequently but not to excess, not compared with some people, for heaven's sake.

Each time he fetches up back here at Allersmead, in his old room, his old bed — whether it is for days, or weeks, or months — he gets this eerie feeling that he has never really left. It is as though his life beyond was just some kind of imaginary excursion, and really he has always been here. His present persona seems an anachronism — this hulking man; an *alter ego* lurks — the child, the boy.

"You must think of Allersmead as the safety net," she said. Once. Years ago. "It's always here for you. We're always here."

Dad has not said that, or anything like it. He has said other things, from time to time.

Stock-taking. Assessment exercise. Fancy terms for this involuntary process, this thing that happens each time he is back at Allersmead, this arrival of figures who stand around the bed, requiring that he remember them, that he reconsider what happened.

Tonight, it is the turn of that guy who ran the couriers — Speedbikes. He sits behind the dishevelled desk in that greasy cubbyhole of an office in the mews from which he operates, and tells Paul that he is letting him go. They no longer require his services. He is fired, in short. And Paul, who has been expecting this, sees the man's florid face, always in need of a shave, which has hung in his head ever since, though his name has evaporated. He sees this now so familiar face, and the sandy eyebrows, the reddened broken veins, the thick ridged neck, and is glad that he won't be seeing it any more (except that he will, he will), and never mind about the job; he'll find something else and he was fed up with it anyway. The man is holding out his hand for the bike keys and saying some more, which seems to be that there will be no pay due for this week on account of the compensation demanded by the confectionery shop. This will make things a bit tricky — Paul will have to borrow off someone, or see if the bank will oblige, but it is clear that arguing will get him nowhere, and all he wants now is out. Enough of this guy, enough of hurtling through the traffic, enough of sitting in a jam drinking exhaust fumes.

Something genteel next time, indoors. Newspaper editor; brain surgeon; member of Parliament.

Courier had been good, at first. Black leather from top to toe, slipping like a seal between a bus and a lorry, revving away at the lights, winding through the city streets, the back ways, the rat runs. Heady stuff — oh, this was the life. Handing in the goods with a smile to pretty receptionists behind glass desks in marble halls amid jungle greenery; waiting for a consignment and sometimes there's a coffee and a chat. Mostly he is transporting paper — large envelopes and small envelopes and Jiffy bags and packets. He whisks a cargo of paper around the city; goodness knows what it is all about — that is not his business; he is merely the conduit for all this paper, the means whereby it flies from one address to another. Occasionally there is different freight — reels of film, mysterious packages. It

181

is all one to Paul: get the stuff from A to B, and wait for the next set of crackling instructions from that guy in the office. Mostly, it is pretty plain sailing, just the odd hitch when you can't find the place you're looking for, or the traffic holds you up and you get an earful for not getting the job done on time.

Occasionally, there's worse. The first time he came off the bike — taking a corner too fast — the taxi driver who pulled up to help him out of the gutter said, "A short life and a merry one, eh?" Having checked that Paul was unhurt, he added, "I've yet to see one of you lot aged over twenty-five." Paul grinned.

There were other falls, subsequently. The leather gear saves you from tarmac grazing — that's half the point of it — and you learn to roll away from the bike, hoping there's not a car behind you. Main thing — have you still got the consignment? He always had, until that last day.

Well, not quite always. Once, he nearly lost a big flat folder — architectural drawings, it turned out. Strapped to the pillion, it was, but the strap broke when the bike tipped over — hit the kerb, that time — and the folder split open and shed stuff all over the road and some was damaged. There was a hell of a row about that. Fat Face in the office threw a proper tantrum.

Fat Face had one eye on the clock, always. He knew how long it should take between any two points, A to Z; much longer, and you had to account for it. And if there was one thing that really got him going, it was the suspicion you'd stopped off at a pub. Paul kept the Amplex in his jacket pocket.

That day, that last day, he'd stopped off a couple of times for a beer. It was hot, and the traffic was diabolical, and twice he found the best route for a particular job took him past one of his favourite pubs — surprise, surprise. He hadn't been long each time — just long enough to put away a pint, and feel all the more efficient for it. And then after the second stop the phone was crackling with the next job, which was a bit of an odd one; pick up a birthday cake from this confectioner's to take up to Hampstead, one of those mansions by the Heath — and get a move on, they want it for a kid's party *now*.

The woman at the confectioner's was a bit put out: "Why haven't they sent the van? It's normally the van for a cake." Paul explained that the van was off the road at the moment: "It'll be fine." The case was in a box. "Look, the box'll go in my carrier." As it would, just, though he couldn't quite close the lid. "Be fine — not to worry."

The lorry slammed its brakes on as they were going up Haverstock Hill — a dog ran out. Paul went into the back of the lorry, came off the bike, skidded across the road, the carrier burst open, so did the cake box, and that was that. You could see it had been a class act, that cake, even when broken up all over the tarmac: white icing and pink icing and rosettes and piped writing. Shame.

So that was it, at Speedbikes. "Just once too often, mate," said Fat Face. And now here he is beside the bed at Allersmead, saying it again. But you can get rid of such people, with an effort. You concentrate on something else, someone else, and tell them to shove off.

They never surface in the right order, these people in the head. Charlie from the rehab place comes way before Fat Face at Speedbikes, but here he is now, staking a claim.

Paul and Charlie shared a room. The first time they met Paul said, "You've got the same name as my dad." He said it for something to say, but also because he was struck by the incongruity. Charlie was a chirpy south London wide boy, about as far from Dad as you could get. And Charlie replied — assuming the tone of a concerned shrink — "Tell me about your relationship with your father, Paul." After which they both rolled on their beds laughing, and knew that they could get by here, with a bit of mutual support.

Charlie was thin and jumpy and seldom stopped talking; he had been helping out on his father's market stall since he was six and he'd truanted from school as a matter of policy and of course he'd done drugs. He had three sisters and his mum had died when he was nine and he'd been nicked for shoplifting when he was ten and he'd been knocked off his bike when he was twelve and was on life support for a week. Or had he? Charlie had many life stories, customized for different occasions. He was the most willing and fruitful contributor to those group therapy sessions when a bunch of them sat around with one of the rehab people and confessional utterances of some kind were required

184

of everyone. "The breast-beating binges," Charlie called them, and he could always outdo everyone in submitting some hitherto unmentioned instance of personal deficiency, abuse or suppressed distress. Fired by his example, Paul presented Allersmead as a Sartrean hell, in which the six of them vied for a crumb of parental attention. He tried to strip it of middle-class attributes, giving his father a chronic disability in place of a tendency to write books, airbrushing Ingrid and replacing his mother with a self-obsessed termagant. The guilt that he felt about this was quite opportune, since it made him deliver in a hangdog, hesitant way, which went down well. He earned much sympathy and understanding advice from other members of the group.

Even Charlie was impressed. He took it for granted that Paul wasn't telling the truth, and displayed little interest in the reality of Paul's circumstances. The only point was to manipulate the system here, give them what they wanted and ingratiate yourself in so doing. He would sit on the edge of his bed, hugging his knees, a small, febrile figure, and instruct Paul on how to take control of any situation in which you found yourself: "You take a good look, right? And then you play it your way but so they don't realize." He was popular with both the staff and other inmates, and would no doubt leave the centre an apparently reformed character. There were hints that he was already familiar with such places. But he was coming off drugs this time, he told Paul earnestly, that was for definite, no question. Drugging was a mug's game.

At such moments, you believed Charlie. Paul found himself envying his kind of innate self-confidence that allowed him to pursue this course of guile and persuasion. It took both energy and imaginative drive. Paul was well aware that he himself lacked this quality of motivation — figures in authority had been telling him that for years — and he studied Charlie hopefully, wondering if some of his method might rub off. There was a consistency to Charlie; he might offer conflicting versions of himself but it was done with unswerving intent. He had a plan, and he stuck to it. And the plan, roughly, was to live as he chose to live and not as other people might choose for him.

Paul envied the plan. He had no plan, and he knew that he did not. He had not intended to flunk his exams at college, to drift from one dead-end job to another, to get into drugs — these were simply things that happened and the more they happened the more they seemed to become a self-perpetuating process. This was not the way that other people saw it, of course; he had lost count of the number of times he had been told to get a grip on himself or (a general favourite, this) that he was his own worst enemy.

The enemy theory rather appealed to him. It suggested an insuperable internal conflict, one's own two warring personalities: good, achieving Paul forever scuppered by bad, obstructive Paul. And if that was the way you were made, then there wasn't much you could do about it, was there?

Paul now no longer knew how long he had been at the rehab place; that period was reduced to a collection

186

of images that would flash up from time to time, featuring shrinks and fellow inmates and, above all, Charlie. "You take it from me," Charlie would say. "Once you let them see you're giving in, they've got you where they want you." Paul was not clear what was implied by giving in, but Charlie's conviction was charismatic, and it seemed a good idea to line up behind him in subverting authority. Accordingly, Paul told the rehab people whatever he thought they would like to hear, and tried to absorb from Charlie some kind of personal direction. A plan.

Charlie finished his rehab shortly before Paul did, swearing eternal friendship. He wrote down a phone number; "Give us a bell, right? We'll get together — go out on the town."

Paul never saw him again. When he called that number the person at the other end had never heard of Charlie. Only now does he occasionally visit, grinning away beside the bed at Allersmead. "Remember me?"

Sometimes it is Dad who appears beside the bed. Dad of course is asleep in the bedroom along the corridor; this is another Dad, the Dad who refused to cough up for you to go to Amsterdam with your mates, once upon a time, the Dad who appeared grim-faced at Bude police station, with Mum bleating behind him. That Dad is terse, sardonic; the tone is infinitely familiar and indeed it is still to be heard from Dad of today, but it carries less weight now, it is bleached with repetition, it has become a kind of white noise — irritating but without the power it once had. Paul looks at Dad these days and sees a man who is getting old, and that seems somehow pathetic. Even him, even Dad.

But that Dad carried weight, way back. Oh dear me, yes. His tongue could scorch; he could make you feel more inadequate than you already knew that you were. The way he always won an argument, produced the definitive put-down. His scrutiny of a school report, handed back in meaningful silence.

When we played the cellar game, thinks Paul, and I was always the father, the idea was to be as absolutely un-Dad as possible. Shooting buffalo. Captain of the ship. Turning into James Bond if I felt so inclined. But a kind of shadow Dad crept in, I seem to remember — I'd make everyone else toe the line, boss them around. My turn now, down here.

From time to time a sibling pops up. Sandra opens her clenched fist and puts a spider in her mouth — or does she? Roger takes a clinical interest in Paul's gashed finger: "I need to see how much it's bleeding." Clare wants him to watch her doing handstands. Katie looks worriedly at him — he is ill with flu or something and Mum has sent her up with a glass of lemonade. "Are you going to die?" she says.

Gina tells him to sort himself out. She is fierce. "You can't go on like this," she says. "One dud job after another." It is years ago — the hospital porter period. They meet for a drink; she is hot from some TV studio, he is off-duty from trundling fodder to the operating theatres. She talks about training schemes, about City and Guilds. She is trying to send him back to college, it sounds like, and he veers away. This is just to fill in for

188

a bit, he assures her; he's going to look around for something serious when he's ready, a real job. She frowns at him. "You cannot go on like this, Paul."

It is only Gina to whom he talks now, in the world of today. Odd, the way all the others are so far flung. Roger in Canada, Katie in the States, Sandra — where? Italy, is it? Clare hither and thither with that dance company. He hasn't spoken to any of them in ages. Time was, you were all on top of one another, every day of the year, their faces and voices were as intimate as your own, and then — whoosh! Blown away. Allersmead is a dandelion clock, its seeds dispersed.

Except him. And Gina is still local, as it were — but she goes global half the time. Did everyone want to get as far away as possible?

Mum speaks. Frequently. Of course. She speaks in torrents, as she ever did, and most of it is just atmospheric crackle, but every now and then a snatch is loud and clear. She is telling him that Dad won't see that terrible school report: "I'll sort of lose it, dear." She weeps, at Crackington Haven: "It was those wretched other boys, wasn't it? On your own you wouldn't have done it, would you?" She beseeches: "Give us a *phone* number. I never know where you are." From a tempest of her recollections, he hears only this: "Of course you were always my favourite."

These days, at the garden centre, he never lets on where it is that he lives. "Actually, I live with my parents and their — er — au pair girl." Definitely not. He attracts inquisitive interest, inevitably — too old for this sort of job. Why's he doing it? What's the problem?

He fends off enquiry, his policy for years now; he is adept at striking up cheery temporary acquaintance without ever letting anyone close enough to probe. The landscape is littered with people who have known Paul quite well — have chatted with him, drunk with him, slept with him — but who have subsequently realized that they know nothing of him. They would say that he appeared to have no past.

Lying in bed at Allersmead, with that inescapable and populous past reverberating, Paul sorts through those who offer themselves and allows Sophie to step forward, the teacher from that school where he was caretaker for — oh, a couple of years. Commitment, that was, and Sophie was responsible to a large degree. They shared a flat, eventually; they were a couple — the head teacher knew and smiled benignly.

Sophie teaches the infants — the reception class. She is delightful — a small, smiling, sociable girl, and it is thus that he likes to think of her, rather than the other Sophie who will surface in due course. He sees her laughing at him across a table in a pub, he sees her striding beside him on a walk in the park, he sees her in bed, rapturous. But once he has let her appear, then inevitably that other Sophie will muscle in, talking differently.

"Shouldn't I meet your parents?"

"*Where* was it you were at college, Paul?"

"The trouble is, school caretaking doesn't really lead anywhere."

Sophie becomes someone else. She finds a voice that is tediously familiar to Paul, first heard long ago at

Allersmead, and subsequently from one authority figure after another — the voice that tells him what he ought to be doing rather than what he is doing, that questions and criticizes and recommends. He had thought better of her.

She hints at a long-term arrangement. Marriage. A baby.

Once, a while ago now, when confronted with the prospect of an unanticipated baby, Paul had seized upon the notion of another kind of life. But that was then, that was a different girl, she who had him on the ropes. This is not like that. This is becoming another of those occasions when he may have to take evasive action.

Marriage, Paul considered then and thinks now, is for others — not for him. How do people endure that proximity, that having to consider the other person, that fetter? Well, with difficulty; witness the divorce rate, witness the marriages one has known.

Them. Mum and Dad. Dad does not do much considering, on the whole; his study door has saved him from excessive proximity; he has not always felt fettered, it would seem. For Mum, marriage is her profession, or, rather, the by-products of marriage have been. Allersmead; us.

Paul thinks of his mother, asleep along the corridor. She too is now on the brink of old age, of course, but somehow in her case this is less unexpected; when he flicks back through his images of her he sees a mutation: she has always been getting a bit stouter, and a bit more grey. And what she says was always just the background music of Allersmead — wallpaper music, a domestic form of Vivaldi, the accompaniment to childhood, to growing up. It pattered around one's head, both heard and not heard. And does so today.

Paul takes evasive action. He ignores Sophie's hints. He absents himself more and more. Sophie objects. And then one day he is simply not there any more. He has given in his notice at the school, and, as Sophie will bitterly tell all and sundry, scarpered. All and sundry remark that he was a bit of an odd sort of guy and maybe she is best off the way things are. Sophie is not entirely sure about this but she appreciates the sympathy and, being a sensible sort of girl, she sets about expunging Paul and looking around for a fresh interest. She might derive a certain satisfaction did she know that, in years to come, she will occasionally put in a brief appearance at Paul's bedside.

The members of this nocturnal troop chart Paul's life — a higgledly-piggledy assortment of people, some of them crucial, others incidental. Sometimes, they crowd in; other times a person will sneak up, unexpected, and require that Paul revisit a particular site. Sophie sits on the sofa of that shared flat and scolds him for disappearing all evening, *and* yesterday. Fat Face holds out his hand for the key to the bike. The shrink at the rehab place wants to know how he feels about himself.

That policeman leans out of the window, saying, "Paul, let's have a talk."

Let's not, says Paul, years later. Just clear off, do you mind? I know you mean well, but let's not go there.

★   ★   ★

The room is at the top of this tall building, this office building in which there has been a fire. He is alone in the room, the smoke-blackened walls of which he must clean. The contract cleaning company is perhaps the furthest down that he has got — a job that mops up those who have failed to find more congenial employment. His fellow workers are as motley as they come — a polyglot crew many of whom do not speak much English. No matter — a cleaner can be briefed by gesture and exhortation. Paul is amongst them because this is a time when he does not care about anything, he does not care what he does or where he is, he would prefer not to be anywhere at all, he would prefer not to be. He is simply moving through days, one pointless painful day after another; he is without anticipation — except for a fix when he can achieve that — without expectation, without will. What will he has is addressed to the operation of cleaning machinery, because otherwise the supervisor will be on his back.

He has been alone in this room for quite a while. It is his room, his task. It is largely empty; furniture and carpets have been removed. There is just one large desk, which is water-damaged, and those black and oily walls to which he has addressed himself for an hour or so. The door is open, and he can hear the voices of others from rooms along the corridor. The supervisor was in five minutes ago; he will not be back for quite a while now.

Paul goes to the window, which is flung wide and opens onto a narrow balcony shared with other rooms on this floor. The balcony runs the width of the building, and has a parapet. Paul stares at this, and then he puts a leg out of the window, then the other, and stands on the balcony.

He looks over the parapet. It is a long way down to the street below, a good long way. Not a busy street — parked cars, a few people walking by, a man going into the newsagent opposite, a waiter smoking a cigarette outside the bistro next door to it.

Paul looks. He stands looking for some while. For a minute, for five minutes, for a quarter of an hour? Goodness knows — time has not much meaning any more.

The parapet is fairly high, but not too high. He moves a few paces to his left, away from the window, until he is at a point between that and the next window. He gets one leg over, then the other, and he is sitting on the parapet, legs dangling over the edge, over the street. He is feeling dizzy now, which actually makes things easier. Go on, he tells himself.

The waiter looks up. He drops his cigarette and shouts. Paul cannot hear what he says. Another waiter comes out, and someone who is perhaps the proprietor, in shirtsleeves. The three of them look up, as does a woman who was passing and now stops. The man who went into the newsagent comes out and he too joins the staring group. He gesticulates, and shouts.

Paul looks down at them. They seem very far away, and nothing at all to do with him. Go on. Go *on*.

194

Another passer-by has stopped. And another. There is conversation going on, consultation. The proprietor of the bistro goes back inside.

Everything is entirely real, and also quite unreal. Paul hears a car horn, an aeroplane, the slam of a car door. He sees a face at a window of the building opposite, he sees two pigeons sidling down the roof, he sees a gull floating overhead. When he looks down, he feels dizzy again, everything swings a little, the street ripples. He hears a police car's banshee siren.

The police car rounds the corner into this street, and pulls up below, silent now, its blue light flashing. Two policemen get out. Paul sees them, but also does not see them. Go on. Now.

The policemen are not there any more, and the little crowd on the pavement has grown. A woman has her hand to her mouth.

Paul watches an aeroplane crawl across the sky above the roofline. So slowly. How do they stay up? He will put out his arms and be an aeroplane.

Someone is talking to him. There is a head at the window a couple of yards away. The head speaks. It says one thing, and then another, and then another, and then something else. Sometimes Paul answers.

"What's your name?" says the policeman.

"Paul," says Paul. "Just don't come near me, OK? Just keep away."

"Listen, Paul," says the policeman. "Let's have a talk. Come inside and we can have a talk."

"No," says Paul.

"Have you got family?" says the policeman. "Is there anyone you'd like us to get hold of?"

"I don't have family," says Paul.

"Anyone else?" says the policeman.

Paul does not reply. The policeman is outside the window now, standing. Paul edges along the parapet away from him, and then he sees that there is another policeman at the further window.

Paul says, "Don't come near me."

The pigeons on the opposite roof take off. Go on. *Now.*

The policeman says, "I'm going to the Arsenal match this afternoon. Are you an Arsenal fan, Paul?"

There is no traffic going below any more. There is another police car slewed across the end of the street.

"Hot out here," says the policeman. "Would you like a drink, Paul? Bottle of water?"

Paul looks down. He looks into the upturned faces of the people below. His stomach seems to liquefy and he has to look up, across at the roof opposite, where a fresh pigeon has arrived. He studies this pigeon, its iridescent breast, its bobbing head.

The policeman shifts his feet, a little scraping sound.

"Don't come near me," says Paul. "Or . . ." He looks down again.

And now the other policeman speaks. He too is out of the window and standing on the balcony. When did he do that? "Paul," he says, "why don't you get inside and we can have a chat."

Paul turns his head towards him. "Don't come . . ."

196

Strong arms grab him round the waist and pull him backwards off the parapet. The two policemen converge and between them they heave him through the window and into the room. He is helpless.

"Good lad, Paul," says the first policeman. "Well done."

He goes, the policeman. Both of them go; they melt back into that morass of people in the head, and Paul is relieved. He does not care for that particular site; he would like to junk it but you don't choose what gets junked and what does not, do you?

"And the first thing to do," said Gina, "is to quit that bloody contract cleaning company. Of all duff jobs . . . Now listen, I've got a plan . . ."

"Don't tell her," said Paul. "Don't tell them. About . . . that. Swear?"

Gina sighed. "I'm trying to tell *you* about my plan. All right. Though personally I think they should know."

"*Swear.*"

"I've said all right. Now *listen* . . . I've found this training scheme."

Paul does not care to revisit that site, either. Training schemes were never his thing. They went on and on, you couldn't ever see to the end of them, you were bored with whatever it was you were being trained for after a few months, or weeks. The thing was to hop off the conveyor belt before it was too late, before you were processed into being something you didn't want to be.

He stares up at the Allersmead ceiling, and it seems to him that Allersmead itself had been a kind of training scheme. Growing up. Growing up here, thus. But six of them had undergone it, and look at us, he thought. Not exactly consistent, as products.

Allersmead settles itself around him — those familiar nocturnal creaks. He is six again, or ten, or 16.

The Farmer Wants a Wife

Gina is 39. You are supposed to be in a slight panic at 39, about to hit the buffers at 40, but as it happens she is pretty contented, perhaps more so than ever before. She can cock a snook at 40; work is going well, and there is Philip.

Gina has always regarded relationships as shifty business: count on nothing, nothing is for ever. Some early mistakes and betrayals taught her this. She knows that she herself has been at fault, as often as not. The six years of David have been her record, and that alliance foundered in due course, as she had always glumly anticipated.

But now there is Philip.

She finds herself thinking that perhaps this time. She finds herself hoping that perhaps this time.

Gina recognizes something of herself in Philip. He too is restless, quickly bored or irritated, hard-working, curious. These qualities can lead to the occasional spat, but more often they mean enjoyment, appreciation, the satisfaction of shared responses and reactions. And she likes the way he looks, his thin face with that expressive mouth — the set of his lips is eloquent — those intent brown eyes. She loves his roaming interest, his furious concentration. She loves him in bed.

Philip's life is not like hers. He is not for ever poised to catch a flight on order. He's got more sense, he says. He is a producer, a desk man for long stretches of time, a planner and contriver for the most part, with occasional bursts of action. He is amiably derisive of Gina's globe-trotting existence: out of your minds the lot of you, he says, drama addicts. But she knows that this masks respect and, frequently, concern. She is on the phone home more often than ever before, seeking the comfort of his voice from hotel rooms in some other continent. She knows that this existence does not foster abiding relationships. For the first time, she has considered giving up foreign assignments. Back to the dog shows and centenarian interviews, in some more elevated form: party conferences, outbreaks of foot-and-mouth disease. When she floated this with Philip, he smiled: "You'd be manic within a month, lusting for Heathrow. It's habitual now — you're branded. I know why you're suggesting this, and I'm flattered. But don't do it." She was relieved, and grateful. All the same, she noted that her colleagues on the road were many of them without the tether of a partner. Some of the men had a wife and children tucked away in Surrey; the women were for the most part unhampered. Or unhappy?

They had talked only once of children. Briefly. Something we should get sorted, he had said. I'm up for it if you really want to. Otherwise . . . Otherwise? said Gina. Otherwise I'll pass. Well, me too, she had said. And anyway I'm 39. So that had been that.

He had no children from his marriage. The ex-wife had dithered, busy with a compelling job, until children were no longer a sensible idea, with the marriage on its last legs. Just as well, said Philip. No collateral damage.

Gina knew that she might one day regret this decision, if decision it has been. As it is, ironically, her life is full of children. When disaster is afoot, the world over, it is children who are in the front line, who furnish the story, the camera shot, who will hang around thereafter in Gina's head — mute, wide-eyed with stick limbs and swollen bellies, ulcerated, malformed, with a stump for a hand or a leg. She confronts these children because it is her job, they are why she is there, the world must know about them. She sends them into a million comfortable homes, to prompt unease.

Gina leads two lives. There is life in London, at home in the flat with Philip, the tube journey to work, the Saturday supermarket shop, the lunches or suppers with friends, the jaunts to a film or a gallery. A life in which distresses are minor ones and rapidly addressed: toothache (pick up the phone to the dentist), a bout of bronchitis (antibiotics), a leaking pipe (plumber). The bandages are all to hand, in Gina's life, and in the lives of everyone she knows. Once in a while, something awful happens to someone — the car crash, the cancer diagnosis — but these are exceptional events, so removed from the norm that you are shocked and startled, outraged even at this intrusion, this malign reminder.

In Gina's other life everyone lives on the cusp. She parachutes into worlds in which all is awry, worlds where people are routinely starving, or are shot at as a matter of course, are diseased, HIV-positive, mangled by landmines, beaten up by the henchmen of despotic rulers. People for whom some toothache or a plumbing problem would pass unnoticed. Gina and her camera crew move amongst these people, face their situation but know that they do so from behind an invisible screen, distanced from them by the flight tickets in their baggage, by their passports to a place where things are done differently. They are voyeurs, she sometimes uncomfortably feels, and has to remind herself that this voyeurism is benign, it may lead to something, someone may help.

The children of these distorted worlds have never known anything else, for the most part. Distress is the norm, and that is all. It is not that they accept starvation and brutality, simply, they are not aware that there is an alternative.

Gina thinks of childhood at Allersmead. Sheltered, privileged. But sharing that universal attribute of childhood: the Allersmead world being the only one they knew, they could not conceive of an existence that was otherwise. Until, of course, they grew up a bit and looked around and saw that families come in other sizes and shapes, that not all homes have a cellar and a kitchen table that seats twelve, that other parents are different but still recognizable as parents.

She remembers these perceptions as a revelation. She remembers — suddenly? gradually? — finding that she could stand beyond Allersmead and look at it with a kind of detachment, as though she were someone else.

202

She looked at her parents, and saw them with fresh eyes: a cool, appraising stare.

Gina sometimes wonders if it was this early exercise in scrutiny and assessment, in questioning, that directed her into her present trade. Journalists ask questions. Gina questioned her own circumstances, early on. She then began to question many circumstances, as a matter of course.

Gina tells the Minister for Education that the government's handling of the miners' strike has been a disgrace. The Minister for Education says a little tartly that he has not come to the college to discuss the miners' strike, though he notes her views; he is here to meet sixth form students and to explain the government's education policy. Gina has plenty of questions about that; the Minister leaves feeling a trifle ragged. You do not expect to be grilled by a kid at some college out in the sticks. He bares his teeth politely at the head teacher and says that it has been an edifying experience, some interesting points made by that lass who had so much to say, she'll go far that girl, no doubt. Just so long as it's as far as possible from me, he thinks.

Gina enjoys the sixth form college. It is satisfyingly different from school, you feel grown-up, there are more like-minded people than there had been at school, the work is more challenging.

But she had had to fight to get there.

★ ★ ★

"You were never my favourite child," she says. Mum says. And Gina is thrown. She is thrown in a way that is entirely uncharacteristic. She is the one who is capable, self-sufficient, independent, who takes what comes her way and deals with it.

She stares at her mother, who is now once more in full flow. ". . . Well, if you must go, I suppose you must go, but I do find it *odd*, I mean here you are with a lovely family home, everything done for you, lovely home-cooked meals — you do realize you'll have to take your clothes to a launderette and goodness knows how you'll manage for eating — I simply can't see the point, for a different sort of teaching, you say, I mean you've been doing fine at the school . . ."

Had she said that? Did those words spill out, now washed away? You were never . . .

". . . you were always like that, getting some idea in your head and can't leave it alone, writing to the Prime Minister if you please I remember, got to have a typewriter last year, months of pocket money, cash only for birthday and Christmas, talk about obsession, and now it's bolting off to some sixth form college forty *miles* away and a bed-sit during the week . . ."

Never my favourite child. Well, one hadn't thought that one was, and does it matter?

Somewhere, in some deep tender unsuspected crevice, it does.

People get labelled in a large family. Sandra was the pretty one, Roger was clever, Clare was athletic, Paul was the eldest — primogeniture counts for a lot —

Katie was helpful. I was difficult, thinks Gina. I was "Gina, don't be so *difficult*."

Difficult meant arguing, questioning an instruction or a decision. Being rational, to my mind.

Dad wasn't so averse to difficultness — he welcomed discussion. Argument on some neutral matter was welcomed. Mum thought this being silly at best, being cheeky at worst.

Gina had realized by the time she was twelve that they were at a crap school. By 16, she had found out about sixth form colleges and that there was one in a town some way away. She applied, was accepted, got hold of the town's local paper and tracked down a bed-sit in the home of an elderly widow and then took the proposal to her mother. She had already squared matters with the college, who clearly approved of her powers of initiative.

And so it all began. Partial flight from Allersmead at 16, full flight to university at 18. Detachment thereafter.

"You have an extremely skimpy past," says Philip. "Or should one say an embargoed past? Do you realize that?"

"I've had too much of other people's," she replies.

"Oh, indeed — we all have. But you're the opposite extreme. Information has to be extracted with pincers."

Gina smiles.

"I'd known you for a couple of months before it became apparent that you had a family. I was beginning to think orphan status, or care of the local council."

She laughs. "As if . . ."

"And thereafter is not exactly an open book," he continues. "Radio Swindon has been mentioned — the early days. Some significant assignments since."

"It's all in the CV," says Gina.

"I know. I've read it. It's between the lines I'm interested in."

"You know about David. You know about my various run-ins with my editors."

"Indeed. All in the public domain, so to speak. It's the defining moments I'm after."

"Oh, those," says Gina.

They are in the French bistro, which has supplanted the Turkish place. Gina is off to South Africa next week. Both are aware of looming separation.

"The thing is," she says, "does one recognize them? Not at the time, that's for sure."

"But they surface, don't they?"

"So does a whole lot of rubbish. Stuff you remember that's neither here nor there."

"Ah, that's not for you to say. Deeply revealing, perhaps."

Gina reflects. Then: "We're walking to school and there is a caterpillar with a green stripe down its back on a fence, and Roger puts it in his pencil case. Revealing of what?"

Philip shrugs. "You'd have to take that to a professional."

Further reflection. "I'm in Bosnia, I think, and our cameraman is sitting by the side of the road eating a slab of bread and cheese. He puts it down for a moment, and a stray dog sneaks up and scoffs it."

"You're cheating," says Philip. "You're deliberately serving up the junk."

Possibly. Probably. Gina knows that she is perhaps economical with self-exposure. Why? Well, that too is presumably a matter for the professionals. Suffice it that she prefers not to release too much of all those retrospective moments, even to Philip, whom she loves. One's interior life is murky enough, in its way; no need to display it to others.

Different kinds of murk, there are. The murk of moments you would prefer to obliterate, when you did something stupid, unpleasant, regrettable. That camera-man: the coda to the dog-and-slab-of-bread moment is that she slept with the man that night, a guy she hardly knew, might not see again, didn't much care for, and why the hell did she do that? Murk.

But there is that other kind of murk — the times that have slid away into a sort of mist, stretches of time into which you peer, when you see some of what happened, and grope for the rest.

She is in the hall, messing about, pulling faces at herself in the mirror above the table. There is no one else around, which is exceptional; at Allersmead there is always someone else around. She can hear voices from upstairs — Roger and Katie, with Clare piping up from time to time. The others are maybe out. Ingrid went off somewhere, earlier on, which is unusual also. Ingrid has been peculiar lately.

207

The door to Dad's study is slightly ajar, and now she hears voices from within. Dad says something, and Mum breaks in, audible, with the pitch that means she is in a state.

"You have to talk to her."

Dad's reply cannot be heard.

Mum again, shrill: "If she goes, goodness knows what . . . She *mustn't* take Clare."

Gina is idly interested. Take Clare where, and why?

Dad says, "I doubt if we have any right to prevent her."

Mum, at danger level: "Don't you *care*?"

Nothing from Dad. Silence.

Mum, quieter now, dangerous in a different way: "This is a family. Clare is part of it. And the situation is all your responsibility. Is it not?"

Dad says, "I am hardly likely to forget."

Mum is now inaudible. There is a brief flow of sound from which there lifts the occasional words: ". . . hurt . . . shock . . . young . . ."

A silence. Then Dad says, "Indeed. An aberration for which I have paid dearly."

A what? What has Dad paid for? Gina is now quite attentive, alert to tension, to adults behaving oddly as much as to what is being said. Why are they talking to each other like this?

A floorboard creaks. Someone is moving in the room. As her father opens the door, Gina shoots into the kitchen, just in time.

★　★　★

Radio Swindon seems very far away. Gina today is not exactly a household name, but her face would seem vaguely familiar to very many people. In the Radio Swindon days she was a girl with a microphone, waylaying town councillors and businessmen and people in the street, politely insistent; now, she has the authority of her network, her attendant crew — she is not so easily brushed aside. But she doesn't feel much different; the game is the same. You muscle in where you may not be wanted, you ask people questions that they may not wish to answer but, also, you inform, you reveal, you communicate. It's a perverse way to earn a living, she sometimes thinks.

She was programmed from an early age, that is how it now feels: the need to question, to investigate, a certain relish for argument. She cut her teeth on that Minister for Education, perhaps. She remembers an enjoyable *frisson* of indignation at this patronizing figure, empowered by status, hectoring the impotent young. I may be young, she had thought, but I can field an opinion or two.

She had considered politics as a career, and then veered away, seeing politicians as self-serving, professionally glib and versatile. Either you bludgeoned your way to the top, or you served time as a quacking back-bencher.

Radio Swindon may be far away, but Gina sees that time as climactic. That was when she realized what she wanted to do, what she was going to do. She loved the wayward nature of an interview, its unpredictability. The centenarian who would suddenly erupt into

209

blasphemy, giving pause for thought to the studio editor; the dangerous shoals of vox pop — even in Swindon they could startle you.

Outside a primary school she seeks views on family size from waiting mothers. A parenting guru has advocated two as the ideal extent of a family — three at a pinch; there has been much press comment. Gina feeds some leading questions, hoping to get someone to say that this is the first step towards mandatory limitation, along Chinese lines. The mothers are for the most part uncooperative and their opinions anodyne: it's nice if you get one of each, then you feel you can stop; of course there's always the accident, isn't there? (A giggle.)

Then a woman says, "How old are you, love?"

Gina smiles, trying to deflect. The interviewee does not do the questioning.

"Younger than most of us, anyway. No kids?"

This won't do. "Well, no," says Gina. "Tell me, do you think people should be limited to two children?"

The woman says, "You wait, my dear. When you get started, you won't be counting them out. They happen or they don't. How many in your family — brothers and sisters?"

Gina smiles again, parrying. "Suppose there were legislation limiting family size — would you go along with that?"

"How many?" insists the woman.

"Six," says Gina crossly.

"Catholics, were you?"

This is getting out of hand. "No," says Gina. "Would you personally be prepared to . . ."

"Six and not Catholics," says the woman. "Then either your mum was put upon or she was a glutton for punishment. So how was it for you, in a family that size?"

Gina is on the back foot now. "Actually, that's not really quite the point," she says.

"Come on," pursues the woman. "Don't tell me you weren't at each other's throats half the time. Boys or girls, were they?"

Enough. Gina knows when she is outmanoeuvred. Close the interview, as gracefully as possible, and move on.

Now she is 39 and then she was . . . what? 22 or — three. She cannot see that other self — cub reporter harassing older women who became justifiably resistant. You do not see yourself in those earlier incarnations; you remain the observer, the centre of the action, the person for whom something is happening. Each slide is suspended, it hangs in the head — over and done with but going on for ever.

And what about this one? Earlier? Later? All she knows is that she is — was — in the Allersmead kitchen with Sandra, and Ingrid, who is ironing. What have they been talking about that led up to this? Gina does not know, only that what was said next has crystallized in her head, just this exchange.

* * *

Ingrid looks up from her ironing. She addresses Sandra: "It was Gina's birthday party. Of course, you did not mean to push her. Not so as to hurt her. Just, you pushed a bit."

They stare at her.

"How do you know?" says Gina.

Ingrid shrugs. "I saw."

Gina turns to Sandra. "Do you remember?"

Sandra looks away. "Not really. I remember . . . the fuss. I was *seven*."

She probably did, thinks Gina. It fits. Did Mum know? Does Mum know?

Gina turns to Ingrid. "Does Mum know?"

"She did not see," says Ingrid. "Only I saw." She sounds distinctly smug.

Gina laughs, startling all three of them. "And all this time you've kept shtum. Why?"

Ingrid is intent upon the ironing. She spreads a sleeve upon the board, smoothes it. She shrugs. "It was something that only I would know. I liked that."

Gina addresses Sandra. "I forgive you. It was an inexcusable act of aggression but I forgive you."

Alison walks into the room. "Forgive her for what, dear?"

Ingrid looks as though she may be about to speak.

"For helping herself to my shampoo," says Gina. "How magnanimous can you get? Eh, Ingrid?" She beams upon Sandra (upstaged, wrong-footed) and sweeps from the room.

★　★　★

A family is a coherent mass, a set of people united because that is the way it is, progressing thus from day to day, year by year, and who is to question the matter? The component parts of this mass may make their individual sorties into the outer world — they may go to school, go to work, go shopping — but they always roll back into that self-contained unit. Until, in the nature of things, fission takes place — but at Allersmead that was a long way off, unthinkable even, for what now seems to Gina an eternal present. There was Allersmead, and its inhabitants, except that now and again there might come a moment of observation, of evaluation.

She watches Clare one day and sees that Clare looks like Ingrid, very like Ingrid. Has she never seen this before? Well, yes — but she has never *thought* about it before.

She thinks.

Roger and Katie look like Mum. Paul looks like Dad. Sandra and I have a bit of each. Whereas Clare . . .

People do not get to look like each other because they live in the same house. It is to do with genes.

She nurtures these thoughts for a while. Eventually, she mentions them to Paul, who just looks puzzled. When she raises the matter with Sandra, in a rare confiding moment, Sandra is not puzzled; she is brisk. "Yeah," she says. "I know. I've noticed too."

But Ingrid has no boyfriends. Ingrid has no life beyond Allersmead, so far as anyone knows. That Jan who came to Crackington Haven is in the future still. I was five when Clare arrived, thinks Gina. Sandra was four. That was well before Ingrid went away that time. Ingrid had been here all along, and nowhere else. And she has always stayed. They are both thinking this, but neither comments. Merely, Sandra's eyebrows lift.

"So why did she stay?" says Philip. "Why didn't she just take Clare and go? It doesn't look as though she and your father were exactly . . ."

"A unit?" says Gina coolly. "Oh no. If they ever had been."

"So why?"

"We were a family, weren't we? Families are indissoluble."

Philip is interested. Allersmead interests him. Gina is amused rather than irritated by this interest, knowing that this is the way he is. He enquires, he is programmed to pursue. And she likes that quality. Moreover, she can glimpse through his eyes — she can see Allersmead as he sees it, as a baffling, intriguing phenomenon. Whereas for her it is just the immutable fact from which she has arisen.

Indeed, these days she does not much think about family, and Allersmead. From time to time, she touches base with Paul. Occasionally her mother will ring. And of course that eternal present drifts back, reminding her that a person is forever hitched to an elsewhere, to the other time and place.

Today, she is everywhere — in the flat, in the office, out and about in London, on a plane, stepping off a

214

plane into one of those alternative worlds that make up the globe. She has been everywhere for years now, miles and miles from Allersmead. Allersmead lies submerged beneath many layers of subsequent experience, some of which has revealed to her something about Allersmead.

Gina considers marriage to be a curious institution. Nowadays people do not so much bother with it. Perhaps in due course it will wither away entirely. It would seem to survive because it has a legal significance, and a religious one for some, and a fair number of young women still like to dress up and be the centre of attention for one ecstatic day. And of course it has been replaced by something very similar, if not so legally hazardous. Living with someone is marriage without the red tape. The pleasures and perils are the same.

Around the world, Gina has seen and noted the subservient role of married women in many societies. Women cook and mind the children. Ring any bells, does that? She sees Alison in the kitchen at Allersmead, serving up meal upon meal upon meal. She does not have to fetch the water from a well, or grind the corn, or milk the goat, but her life's work has been the provision of food. How lucky that she actually enjoys cooking, thinks Gina.

Subservient. Subservience implies inferior status, doing what you are told, or what is expected of you. But Mum did what she did because that is what she wanted to do. Dad was fed and watered like the rest of us, and no doubt would have spoken up if service had ceased, but he did not instruct.

What *did* he say to her, indeed? Listening, Gina finds the airwaves rather silent here. They didn't say much to each other, she finds. Mostly, Mum is addressing everyone, or attending to a particular child. Dad is making some comment, very likely sardonic, or is silent, or is simply absent, segregated in his study. She does not hear her parents discuss the state of the nation, or even what to do at the weekend.

She thinks of the dialogue between Philip and herself — the daily, ongoing dialogue. She sees her parents afresh. She wonders about this strange, required system that sets two people alongside one another, in bed and out of it, this precarious conjunction.

She is young — seven perhaps, or eight. They are on a beach, it is the summer holiday, and she is paddling in the surf. She turns and looks back, and sees her parents quite small and far away, sitting side by side on a rug. Dad is reading. Mum is putting sun cream on Katie and Roger. All around are other groups, other families. She sees that the world is made up of families; everyone is thus hitched, thus identified. The beach is composed of these units — self-sufficient, self-contained, alien one from another: the only known faces are those of her mother and her father and her brother and sisters.

David once said to her, "You don't need me. You like me — possibly you love me — but you don't need me." She heard this as a reproach, a criticism, but knew that he was right, and saw the end of their time together, like a bank of cloud on the horizon.

David is with someone else today. They have a child. Gina sees now that he had needed her, and that this imbalance was at the heart of the difficulties into which they had fallen. Perhaps need is the crucial element in any relationship, the necessary bonding material. Sexual need; emotional need; material need. But both parties must be needy, in one way or another, or things will run amok.

She does not care to assess the levels of need, where she and Philip are concerned. Occasionally, gingerly, she squints at her own need and sees it quite emphatic — healthily so, perhaps. Him too? No, let's not go there. Fingers crossed.

"The farmer wants a wife, the farmer wants a wife." She hears that nursery song; you played that game at birthday parties, in a circle, one person in the middle, Mum chivvying people into position, the wind-up gramophone wheezing out the tune (they were the only family still to have a wind-up gramophone; visiting children gawped). "Everybody sing now," cries Mum. "The farmer wants a wife, the farmer wants a wife . . ."

The farmer needs a wife to cook and wash and milk the cow and to provide him with strong farming sons. But the wife doesn't want him, or so Gina seems to remember, she wants a child — the primordial urge. But actually the wife would have needed him, even if she didn't want him, because in the early modern period and beyond (Gina's history module at university prompts her) the position of an unmarried woman was dodgy — you needed a man to supply food and shelter, to give you social status. See Jane Austen, see the plight

217

of girls in the man-deprived years after the First World War.

That kind of need is not much around in Gina's circle, but it certainly obtains elsewhere. Gina has recorded the dire circumstances of women whose husbands have been slaughtered in Rwanda, in Sudan — women left with a clutch of children to feed and no provider. It obtains indeed in Glasgow or in Brixton. Forget social status, the wife needs a man for sound practical reasons. Only in the clear blue air of well-paid jobs for the girls is that need eliminated.

Gina needs Philip, she finds, but she does not need a child, want a child. Not particularly. If a baby arrived — well, then one would make the best of it, no doubt — end up rejoicing, perhaps. But as it is she'll pass quite happily, like Philip. Her own mother's evident lust for children is therefore mysterious to her; she simply cannot imagine feeling like that. She remembers the evident distaste of Corinna — Aunt Corinna — each time she visited Allersmead and had to wade through the mêlée of nephews and nieces. She didn't care for children and made no bones about it, thinks Gina. Does that make me like Corinna? Perish the thought. Dried-up academic Corinna — surely I'm more human than that? Corinna was my patron — the Allersmead term for godparent — but her patronage was limited to a book token at birthdays and Christmas, and the occasional display of benign interest since. Journalism is barely on Corinna's radar — she is impressed only by achievements within her own rarefied sphere. I don't write studies of nineteenth-century poets so I am beyond her remit. She gave me her own book about Christina Rossetti for a birthday present when I was 16: "I feel you're perhaps old enough for it now, Gina."

Gina remembers Corinna's ill-disguised contempt for Alison. Women like Alison were throwbacks, retards, stuck with the mindset of another age, mired in childcare and cookery, not even conscious of the fresh air beyond — that was Corinna's view. She ignored Mum, thinks Gina. She let Mum wash over her without listening. And, thinking this, she can conjure them up, both of them; they are in her head, clear as clear, she sees and hears them. Extraordinary, she thinks, the way we are stuffed with other people, all milling around in the mind, their faces, their voices, preserved like wraiths, incorporate but unquenchable.

Alison is at the head of the kitchen table, pouring tea from the big blue pot. She is wearing something made of brown needlecord, one of those waistless garments that she favours; Ingrid makes them for her, from a worn-out Butterick pattern. Her hair flies out in wisps from the bun into which it is unsuccessfully twisted. "Milk, Corinna?" she says. "Do take a slice of the walnut cake."

Corinna wears a crisp white shirt under a blue jacket; there is a silver brooch on her lapel, a celtic knot that matches her earrings. Her short straight hair has been cleverly cut. She is talking to Charles, holds out her hand for the tea but does not take any cake. She is telling Charles about her new project on Swinburne: "So underrated, don't you agree? I'm going to put him back on the map." She has to raise her voice to compete with the chatter around the table; the family is assembled. Charles is apparently studying his teacup.

Alison breaks in from behind the teapot. "Is he someone one learned by heart at school? I'm hopeless at names. Roger, don't do that with your feet — we can't hear ourselves speak. Of course, they don't learn by heart now but I do think there was a point, I've got yards in my head, 'The boy stood on the burning deck . . .', 'Lars Porsena of Clusium, by the nine gods he swore . . .', — now who was *that* by? You'd know, Corinna. Clare, not sandwich and cake both at once. I do think poetry is so important. You know they write it now in school instead of learning it. Gina did a lovely poem for homework last week, she had to read it out in class. Gina, get it to show Corinna."

Charles speaks. He says, "No sadism at the tea table, for heaven's sake."

Alison frowns. "I don't understand, dear. Gina, wouldn't you like to . . ."

Gina glares at her.

"Macaulay," says Corinna, without looking at Alison, turned still to Charles. "I'm thinking of trying the OUP with this one. Have you published with them? Or maybe they aren't commercial enough for you?" — a roguish smile — "Mercifully one doesn't have to think about that too much, the priority is a well-produced book, and of course the academic library subscription is guaranteed."

220

Charles sends his empty teacup down the table to Alison. "How fortunate. Though those of us dependent on a readership still quite like our books to look nice."

He is wearing a black sweater over a grey shirt with frayed collar. One arm of his glasses is held on with a piece of sticking plaster.

He floats thus still in Gina's head. So does everyone.

Gina has not seen Sandra for years. Nor Katie, nor Roger. She talks to Paul quite often, and has always done so. She sees him at Allersmead now, and before that whenever he turned up and suggested meeting for a drink.

When Clare's dance company — based in Paris — comes to London, Clare too will call. Gina has seen Clare dance a number of times, and is always startled by the lithe professional who has sprung from child Clare, from teenage Clare doing the splits in the Allersmead sitting room. She is startled also by the young woman who talks in a matter-of-fact way of retirement before long. Clare is 32. You burn out around then, in her trade. Clare's dance company is not that of tutus and Tchaikovsky; hers is the world of modern dance, all shape and style, as far a cry from Diaghilev as James Joyce from George Eliot, thinks Gina, as Picasso from Stubbs. Gina has watched with appreciation, though this would not be her chosen art form. But she likes the grace and athleticism, the inventiveness, the element of shock and surprise. When she spots Clare on stage, she sees her as a creature quite unrelated to that once-Clare, that child in her

221

head. And again, over coffee or lunch, that child will be there again, subsumed within this elegant, delicate woman at whom people glance. Thin as string, and that corn-coloured hair still, swept into a coil on her neck. Ingrid's hair, but that is never mentioned, not even now; nobody goes there, the matter is sealed up, tamped down out of harm's way.

"Retire?" says Gina. "Christ! Then what?"

"Teach probably," says Clare with a shrug. "Retrain as a probation officer?" She laughs. "Go rural, maybe. Pierre fancies a vineyard in Languedoc." Clare's partner is an IT consultant. She eyes Gina. "Do you people just go on for ever?"

"Dear me, no," says Gina. "Plenty of ageism in my business. You go on until shouldered aside by the young turks coming up behind."

"You're so clever to do what you do."

"I think you're pretty smart," says Gina. They grin at one another.

Clare has just been down to Allersmead. "I can't believe I was there for years and years. It seems like a foreign country now. They're just the same, aren't they? Except a bit kind of . . . faded. Mum kept hinting about grandchildren."

Gina considers Clare. It is hard to see how a baby could fit into that sparse body. "Will you oblige?"

Clare shakes her head. "Probably not."

"Genetic drive seems to have died out with our generation," says Gina.

"Actually, I really don't much like children. Is that awful?"

"I used to feel the same myself, back at Allersmead."
They laugh.

"We're a pretty assorted lot, aren't we?" says Clare. "Flown off in all directions. All doing quite different stuff."

"True. It doesn't say much for our nurture."

They consider one another, across the table; two women operating in vastly different worlds, but sprung from the same source.

"None of us having kids," says Gina. "Except possibly Rog, I imagine, in time. Most of us gone global, except for Paul."

"How is Paul?"

Gina pulls a face. "OK. In so far as he's ever going to be."

Clare sighs. "What happened there?"

A small silence. "Who can say? Nurture, nature? Mum smothered him, didn't she? The favourite. And he's — well, feckless, I suppose. And the rest of us are not. And he wound Dad up, so Dad practised sarcasm on him. Recipe for — well, loss of self-respect?"

Clare nods. "And he ends up the only one still kind of tethered to Allersmead. So are we others flung far and wide because of Allersmead?"

"No. You're where you are because you're a brilliant dancer. I'm doing what I do because I stick at things and I'm fairly pushy and I love foreign assignments, and Rog is a career doctor and" — Gina spreads her hands — "we are what we are."

"All the same, we've rather — gone away, haven't we? So much for family. Mum's iconic family."

Mum.

"Mum," says Clare, lifting an elegant eyebrow. Smiling. "I know. But what else would I say?"

Gina is taken aback. That of which we do not speak. She is silenced, for a moment. Then: "Should we all have sat down and talked about it, years ago? Sat *them* down — made them confront it?"

Clare shakes her head. "No. Muddle was better, to my mind."

"You must have felt . . ." Gina trails into further silence. She has not much idea how Clare must have felt, she realizes.

"Muddled? Oh yes, indeed. I remember asking you if our father was my father. After a carol service. You assured me that he was."

"Did I? I remember . . . sort of realizing . . . way back. Then putting it aside, not knowing where else to put it."

"Exactly," says Clare. "As we all did. Them too. All three of them."

"Ah, them. And there they still are. What's left of the family. Ironic, or what?"

They stare at each other. "Whew!" says Gina. "We should have done this before. But you . . . are you *all right*?"

Clare smiles. "I'm probably more all right than one would expect."

"And . . . Ingrid? Do you . . .?"

"No. Never. She doesn't do emotion. You may have noticed."

224

Gina nods. And then, before more can be said, the waiter arrives, there is discussion of who wants coffee, and what kind, Clare remembers that she is meeting Pierre in half an hour, she starts to talk about her company's new production, they are off on another tack.

"This new dance sounds intriguing," says Gina. "A geometrical theme ... And what are you? Definitely not a square."

"I have been reading one of your father's books," says Philip.

"They're out of print, I'd have thought."

"What is the internet for? Three fifty, slightly scuffed, minus the wrapper."

"Which one?"

"The study of youth. Adolescent rites in Namibia, and all that. I can see that you would have been horrified, peeking at his typescript that time."

"I wonder why my father intrigues you so?"

"Probably because he's so unlike mine."

Philip's father is a retired accountant, a man whose inoffensive days are marked out by dog walking and the crossword. He and his wife do the washing-up together in a silence so companionable that speech would seem superfluous. Gina has been struck by this; it was silence of a special quality.

"Do you feel that you know your parents?" she says.

"Of course not. I assume you ask this because you are thinking of your own?"

"I suppose so."

225

"People from different planets. My parents would be astonished by yours."

"Aghast, I should think."

"Oh, come on," says Philip. "They can be seen as a trifle eccentric, perhaps. Hardly outrageous."

"I believe they've given me a distorted view of marriage."

"Ah," he says.

On the flight to Johannesburg Gina works. She goes through the briefing papers that she has been given; she discusses a schedule with the camera crew. They are doing a series of reports on the incidence of AIDS in the townships. When she has finished all that she needs to do, she settles down to sleep, but, unusually, sleep does not come. Gina is adept at snatching a kip whenever and wherever, so what is the problem?

Somewhere, subliminally, Philip is the problem, but she is not allowing herself to think about this. Why has he been so quiet, this last day or two? Distracted, in some way, offhand, almost. Is he . . .? Are they . . .? No, no.

So she is not thinking about Philip, she mustn't. It is association that is the problem; she can't sleep because while flicking through the duty-free magazine her eye fell upon a perfume advertisement — a full-page, free-floating bottle of Miss Dior — and at once she is at Allersmead, that Christmas. Which is of course absurd — the juxtaposition of Allersmead and a bottle of perfume. But there you go — that's how memory works.

★ ★ ★

Alison unwraps the bottle and stares at it. "Oh, goodness," she cries. "*Scent*. But I never really . . . How lovely — scent. Who . . .? Where's the label? Oh, it's you, Sandra. But I don't know, dear, really, that I'd ever . . ."

"If you don't want it," says Sandra. "I'll take it back and change it for a five-year supply of washing-up liquid."

"Can I smell?" says Clare. "Ooh — *gorgeous*. I'll have it."

The Allersmead sitting room is awash with people, with crumpled wrapping paper, with each person's stash of unopened presents. The Christmas tree presides over the depleted pile of parcels; it drips tinsel, its branches glint with balls and bells, the angel leans from the top, as she has done for years and years. The dog has keeled over in front of the fire, its fur all but scorching. The family is complete. Dispersal has taken place; all are gone, even Clare, now at dance school, but the departures are not finalized; everyone still comes back for Christmas. Through the open door, from across the hall, comes a blast of roasting turkey.

Gina eyes the bottle of Miss Dior, which Alison is now gingerly sniffing. A loaded present, suggesting what Mum might be instead of what Mum is. But then many presents are loaded, are they not? Alison has given Charles a Black and Decker drill ("I just thought, you never know, he might find it *fun* to put up shelves or something"); Charles has given Alison a nineteenth-century edition of Mrs Beeton, at which Alison has

227

gazed in bewilderment: "Oh, old-fashioned cooking, isn't that interesting?"

This is the only present that Charles has acquired and wrapped for himself. The rest of his giving is subsumed into Alison's — a swathe of gifts chosen by her: "Happy Christmas from Mum and Dad". And ". . . from Alison and Charles": a Shetland sweater for Ingrid.

The Shetland sweater does not seem particularly loaded. Ingrid puts it on immediately.

"Lovely," says Alison. "The colour's just right for you — I thought it would be. I havered a bit — there was a green as well, but no, the blue is right. Roger dear, if those socks are too small . . . I still can't believe you're *man* size. Gina, have you opened yours yet?"

Gina's present is a tea set: pretty pink patterned china, cups and saucers, teapot, milk jug. "I thought, for your flat. I know you're sharing with another girl so keep it for yourself, it can be the beginning of your bottom drawer." A merry laugh.

I see, thinks Gina. My trousseau, which people no longer have — Mum is a trifle out of touch. Definitely a loaded present; one that says, settle down and get married, attend to the essentials.

Sandra has a fluffy white angora cardigan. "I couldn't resist it," beams Alison. "It's the sort of thing I longed for at your age, but no such luck." Sandra and Gina exchange glances, momentarily at one.

The sheepskin slippers allocated to Katie and Clare seem unexceptional, but Paul stares in perplexity at his tennis racket. "You were really rather good when you were at school, dear, and I thought — he should take it up again, join a local club or something, so good for you and you'd meet nice people."

Paul is not much heard from these days. There is concern and complaint from Allersmead, from Alison.

"Thanks," says Paul. "That's great. Thanks." He gets up and tries a forehand drive.

Alison glows. "I knew you'd like it. And you know you could always come home at weekends and go to the Country Club — we'd pay for membership, wouldn't we?" She turns to Charles.

Charles inclines his head. "I'm sure Paul would be an asset to the Country Club. Just the kind of member they're after."

Paul studies his father. "That wouldn't be sarcasm, would it, Dad?"

Some rogue element has tiptoed into the room, bringing silence. Alison laughs: "Don't be silly, dear. Dad's just joking."

"He does not make jokes," says Ingrid. "Not so much." Everyone looks at her. She rises: "Shall I bring coffee?"

Alison's voice is a notch higher, always a bad sign. "Yes, please do, dear. And could you have a look at the turkey? I must take it out soon." She reaches for a parcel. "Now who's this from? Oh — Corinna and Martin. I sent them a nice little garlic press. I thought Corinna would find it handy. Roger and Katie, I don't know why that's so funny."

"Sorry, Mum," says Katie. "It's just the thought of . . ."

"Corinna savaging garlic cloves," says Roger. "Pull yourself together, Katie."

Gina dives into the pile of parcels. "Here's yours from me, Dad."

Charles unwraps an ivory-handled Victorian paper-knife. "Ah. To stab my enemies with, is that?"

"It's for opening letters," says Gina.

"As he well knows. I believe that really was a joke," says Paul.

"*Stop* it!" cries Alison. "Paul, go and help Ingrid with the coffee. She can't carry everything."

Gina watches Alison. She knows the signs. Alison is revved up, primed. Christmas is the very peak of family life, after all, the signature day, the moment of ultimate cohesion; it is Alison's greatest challenge — the food, the décor, the presents, the ceremonies. Fridge and freezer are stuffed; the house is rampant with holly and ivy; they sang carols last night, even though Paul hadn't yet arrived, Sandra was busy washing her hair and Charles had gone out, for some reason. Alison is at pitch point, tight-wound. This is the culmination of her year, of the family year, everyone is here; this should be her moment, instead of which she is on edge, at risk, volatile.

Ingrid and Paul return, and hand out mugs of coffee.

"Actually, I'd thought the good cups and saucers, for Christmas," says Alison. "But never mind. Do you all remember that Christmas when Roger claimed he'd swallowed the sixpence from the pudding but of course he hadn't really, wretched boy. And that time that Sandra fell off the stepladder, putting up paperchains, such a bruise on her leg. And when I forgot to take the bird out of the freezer and we had to thaw it in the bath. Oh, you know I can remember all the Christmases, right back to when everyone was small and some of you weren't even here, back to when there was just Paul, just Dad and me." She appeals to Charles. "Doesn't that seem a funny time now?"

"Indeed," says Charles. "An age of innocence. Prelapsarian. Eden, I suppose."

Sandra looks up from a parcel she is opening. "So who's the snake, Dad?"

"Me, presumably," says Paul. "The shape of things to come."

Clare laughs. "All of us. One snake after another. Maybe he never wanted children." She has put the sheepskin slippers onto her narrow feet and inspects them with a tiny frown; perhaps they are not quite her.

"I think in the Bible there is only one snake," says Ingrid. "Also Adam and Eve have just boys, no girls, I think."

"Dead right, Ingrid," says Paul. "And one bumps off the other — isn't that right? So watch it, Roger."

Alison bangs her coffee mug down on the table. "Stop being so silly, all of you. I don't know what you're all talking about but it's just too stupid. And of course Dad wanted children, Clare, that's a silly thing to say, everyone does, I mean I suppose a few funny people don't but it's not something I can imagine, I always, ever since I can remember, and thank goodness ... we've been so lucky and Dad feels that way too ..."

Alison's voice soars. Possible meltdown, thinks Gina. She breaks in: "Absolutely, Mum — I say, look, here's another you haven't opened." She thrusts a parcel at Alison.

Alison stares at the parcel, puts it down. "I mean, it's the natural and normal thing, wanting children, I always, a real family life is such a privilege, you're still too young to realize I suppose, I mean can you imagine *not* growing up at Allersmead, with all of you, and when Dad and I got married naturally the assumption was . . ."

Gina glances at Charles. Impassive. Impervious?

". . . and whatever happened, I mean *whatever*, as far as I was concerned family life came first, that was what really mattered, family, and of course Dad felt the same, didn't you, the important thing was for people to grow up in this lovely big family and a lovely home, and that always came first, *whatever*, one's own concerns were neither here nor there, well of course they were but I never . . . what mattered was the family, always, when you're a parent that's how you feel, one day you'll understand that when you have your own children, Dad knows what I'm talking about, and of course he's always felt, haven't you . . .?"

She is pink-faced, has run herself into the ground. She stares at Charles.

He does not look at her. He puts the ivory-handled paper knife on the table. "Any contribution would be superfluous. You apparently know how I feel."

It is said quietly, courteously even. He gets up, walks out of the room. No one speaks. Seconds later they hear the slam of the front door.

Down in the cellar there was a different Mum, thinks Gina. In the cellar game. Me. I reinvented her. I made a person who never cooked anything but somehow bangers and mash simply appeared, who told stories, who turned old bedsteads into boats and a cindery floor into the Antarctic. I made a kind of archetypal ur-mother who did nothing but around whom everything revolved. And Paul, now I come to think of it — he had his own concept of what a father is. Well, well.

In Johannesburg, Gina checks her emails. There is one from Philip.

He says: "I seem to have been unable to say this over the last few days. Don't know why. Attack of nerves. Stupid. Anyway, here it is.

"I would very much like it if we got married. An early reply would be appreciated."

Clare

My mother was not my mother, says Clare. And the person who was my mother wasn't, if you see what I mean. Well, no — how could you? My father was my father, so that at least is straightforward enough. And my brothers and sisters were apparently my brothers and sisters, as indeed they were, or half were.

I don't know why I'm telling you about all this. I don't talk about it. Pierre knows. He's been to Allersmead a couple of times. He finds it all rather peculiar but he just shrugs; well, he's French.

I'm a bit French myself by now. Ten years based in Paris. And a bit Spanish and a bit Dutch and a bit Chinese — we're multicultural, in the company. And of course a bit Scandinavian by birth. Which bit, I wonder? The hair, certainly. The hair was always a giveaway.

My not-mother has rather frizzy hair — brown once, grey-brown now. I remember stealing Mum's hairpins when I was small, to play with. My father — goodness, I can't see his hair, somehow. Nondescript male hair, no particular colour, thin on top.

Ingrid's hair is mine. Dead ringer. I like it, I'm glad I've got it, but it can be a pain to do — it's so fine and slippery.

234

There were six of us, six children in that great big house. Allersmead. It was one of the first words I learned, I'm told, taught by Roger and Katie. "Where do you live, Clare?" "Allersmead."

Paul, Gina, Sandra, Katie, Roger and me at the end — that's the age order.

Do you really want me to go on?

All right, then — you can always go to sleep.

Ingrid? Well, yes — you've got it. Ingrid was — is — my mother. The au pair. So you see it's an unusual family background, to put it delicately.

Clare is in bed with a man not her husband. She does not make a habit of this; indeed, this seldom happens, just once in a while, like now. In fact, strictly speaking, she is not in bed with him, but sleeping with him. Alex is in a separate bed, this being a twin-bed hotel room, and a somewhat Spartan hotel at that.

Alex is just about her best friend in the company. Alex is gay. The hotel — or the company manager — has cocked-up and there are not enough rooms to go round, so some people must share. Clare and Alex are happy enough to oblige. They are both still a bit hyper after the performance and not ready to sleep, so they lie there talking. Alex tells Clare about his parents' divorce, when he was 17, which he found quite upsetting, and now his mother has a new man, and Alex, who is 25, hasn't yet come to terms with this but guesses he will have to. People don't much talk family stuff in the company, perhaps because the company itself becomes family in some odd way — a new family.

235

Clare is older than practically everyone, and she goes back ten years with the company, so she is a veteran and when people want to tease her they call her the den mother.

Alex says, "Are your parents divorced? You never talk about them."

"Don't I?" Clare is vague. "No, I don't, do I? They're a rather odd set-up, as parents go. My mother was not my mother . . ."

How do I feel about Ingrid? says Clare. Well, she's Ingrid and always has been, she's always been there, one can't imagine Allersmead without her. I don't think mother, if that's what you mean, I just think Ingrid. I'm fond of her. I'm fond of them all, but they seem so far away now. So long ago.

Yes, she's always been at Allersmead — except one time, apparently, when she went off for a few months, but she came back. And of course one wonders how it's been for her. She'd never say. Ingrid's quite — buttoned-up. She doesn't do emotion. You couldn't have a heart-to-heart with Ingrid.

No.

No, really — I know it seems odd. I've never talked about it with her. Never. Or with the others. We all kind of stashed it away and left it at that.

Well, yes, I suppose there was a point when I somehow realized . . . but it's very cloudy now, I can't exactly remember . . . just somehow cottoned on, sort of saw things differently but it didn't really change anything, things went on the same, they were the same people, just there was this new slant, only one didn't too much think about it, preferred not to go there, I suppose, and anyway by then all I cared about was dancing, how to be a dancer, how to get to dance school, I was already moving away from Allersmead as it were, it was getting less relevant . . .

Clare sees that Alex is asleep, one hand under his cheek, like a child.

Bless. He's such a lovely guy.

Here and there, the clouds get thinner, and there is clarity, of a kind.

The hair, of course. She is trying to get it into a coil — it is quite long now — and she says to Sandra: "My hair's just like Ingrid's — isn't that funny?"

What does Sandra say? From far away and long ago Sandra says something about people often looking like their mother.

Their mother?

Clarity, of a kind, Allersmead seems to swing a little, and reassemble itself differently. Clare cannot now remember what she said in reply, if anything. Perhaps Sandra has simply confirmed something that has floated in her head, that has shiftily been there maybe always.

There is another rent in the clouds, at some other point. This time Gina is involved, the other big sister, knowledgeable, confident. They have been to church. Allersmead is atheist, so this is unusual, but an exception is made for the school carol service. The

Lord's Prayer is in Clare's head: "Our Father, which art in Heaven." Our father. She says to Gina: "Is our father my father?"

Gina looks at her. Gina's look knows everything, understands everything. "Yep. He is. All of us's father. Forget it, right?"

So she forgets. Sort of.

She forgets but she also knows. This knowledge is tucked away somewhere deep in the mind, digested, received perhaps rather than accepted, seldom taken out for examination.

I suppose some people would have rushed screaming to an analyst long ago, she says to sleeping Alex. But I've never been that way inclined. I think when I first began to realize I just pushed the whole thing away, it was too confusing, too much of a challenge, maybe that's partly why dancing became such an obsession. Wanting to be a dancer shoved anything else aside. And since — with adult eyes — I just see it as all pretty weird; what were they thinking of? How was it for them? One has no idea, none at all. They're like some other species, when you think about them that way. But also they're exactly the same. Mum and Dad and Ingrid.

Ingrid knows that I know. Don't ask me how I know that — I just do. She knows and she doesn't propose to talk about it, that's been the message. Ingrid's come up with surprising things, occasionally, but never anything touching *that* — the main issue. Other things, once in a while. Sudden revelations. I was complaining about

Dad — it was just her and me in the kitchen at Allersmead, when I was back once from dance school, and there was some fuss with Dad about the money I needed for my flat-share. We all used to complain about Dad being tight-fisted — actually now I just see him as a man with rather a lot of children.

"He's so *mean*," she complains.

Ingrid makes no comment. Her face, as ever, registers little but there is perhaps the hint of a smile.

"You cut up his book that time," says Ingrid.

Clare gasps in astonishment. The destruction of Dad's typescript is family legend. "I did? I don't remember anything. How do you know?"

"I saw you. I saw you come out of the room, with the scissors. You were not allowed to use scissors. You were six."

Clare laughs. "Wow! Did I really!" She is struck by a thought. "Did he ever know? Does he know?"

Ingrid shakes her head. "Only I knew," she says with satisfaction. "And now you."

When I look back at them — look back in a grown-up, detached way — what you can't work out is who was the sufferer, who was exploited. All of them? Nobody?

Ingrid

Ingrid no longer thinks in her own language. Somewhere within, she has this other resource, this speech that she could call on at any point if she so wished, and that does sometimes well up spontaneously — in a dream, or making some comment — but it is shut away, set aside; it refers to pre-Allersmead days, which are now very long ago. It refers to young Ingrid, girl Ingrid.

Ingrid today is far from that other Ingrid, who seems indeed like a person who speaks a different tongue. And that person is succeeded by yet another — an Allersmead Ingrid who is still bilingual, just, but subsumed within Allersmead culture, gone native. Ingrid today is still in touch with that alter ego; from time to time that other Ingrid surfaces and bears witness.

I was amazed, when I saw Allersmead first. I did not know there were such homes. I had no home then, my mother was dead more than a year, I was living in a hostel, doing waitress work by day.

And before that there were the different places with my mother, the bedsits and the flats, here and there wherever she decided to be, and sometimes the man who was my father coming for a bit but not much, and in the end he went. My mother had men friends, different ones, many, and they would be there, and then go again. I remember faces, the one with the beard and the one with tattoos. I remember being in bed, and noises of drinking and shouting next door. Often my mother was drunk. She was drunk I think when she walked into the road that night and a car got her.

I came to England I think because I did not know what to do next, and that agency offered jobs, and you would learn to speak better English. I had English from school but not so good then.

The agency sent me to Allersmead, and there was Alison; she was young too but very much a mother, as though that was what she was always meant to be, and there was just Paul then but Alison said, of course another soon, and more. Laughing. She always laughed a lot, Alison. And it was all so far from what I had known, my mother, and the men, and those not nice flats and bedsits and always moving on, and the next place just as bad. I began to forget all that, and now I can hardly remember; it is like looking at old photographs gone brown. I was not going back there, I knew that, I was at Allersmead now, and Alison saying, Ingrid, you are such a treasure, I couldn't manage without you.

For Alison it was children, children — husband I think was necessary but not so important. Back in the first years, with Paul small, and Gina, and Sandra, I thought it was odd she was not so interested in Charles, odd they talked so little. I thought perhaps that is just how English people are, when they are married. I saw Charles must be very clever, with his books, and Alison is — different.

Six children is many, but for Alison not. For Alison it is family that matters, and more family is better. So there were babies, another and another and Allersmead is a big house so there was space, and for him to go in his study and shut the door and you must not disturb him. I do not know about his books. I have looked but I do not read books like that. So he was writing his books, and Alison was having babies and soon there was the family and always Alison said of course you are part of the family, Ingrid, what would we do without you? And I suppose that is what happened. Only perhaps more than she meant then.

I did not like him so much, in the beginning. Alison, yes. With Alison it is very easy to get along, there is no difficulty — she is always talking, yes, but you do not need to always listen, and we have worked together very well. There was much work then, with all the children young.

Much work, but it was good. For me, Allersmead was what a home should be. I had never known anything like that — the big house, and children, and the garden and the dog and food like Alison makes.

Perhaps it was not so much that I did not like him. I did not know how to relate to him. I did not understand the way he sometimes talks that you think is perhaps to be funny but it is not. You get used to that, it is just his way, it is sarcasm, so there is no need to pay attention. I was very young. It's hard to reach back to

242

when you were young — that person is someone else. I was someone else. I think he too was someone else.

He looked at me. I saw that he began to look at me. I had not had much to do with men. There was a boy before I came to Allersmead, but that was nothing much.

I think now that was a bad time for him, for Charles. He was drinking sometimes — you would see the bottle and the glass on his desk. Alison was busy, busy with the children. Perhaps his work was not going well.

And he saw me in a new way, I suppose. And I saw him, as a man.

We were having sex for a short while only. Some weeks, I think. The first time, I was surprised; I hardly understood what had happened. Then I felt bad. So did he — I know that. He was a little bit crazy then, I think. And I was young, I was confused, I knew he should not, I should not, and then he said this must stop, he was sorry, he had done a bad thing and we must try to forget it, and I suppose that has been done, but there was Clare.

Alison arranged everything. Where I would go and how I would come back after and what would be told to the children. This is a family, she kept saying, and Clare must be in the family, and that was what mattered. So that is how it was, and they were all quite young still so they did not much ask questions not then and not later except that later I think they somehow knew, her too. It would not be good to talk about it with her; it is best left the way it is. Perhaps she knows, I think she knows. To talk would be to open up that time and I do not want that. It is over now, finished, a mistake. Except that there is Clare, and a person cannot be a mistake, she must never think that so it is better never to talk.

I can know what I know without talking. I can feel the things I feel. About Clare, about what happened. Back then, I hated him a bit, because of everything, and then somehow he began not to matter so much; Allersmead was as it has always been, and he was a part of it, and so was I, and so was Clare. But it is always there, what happened, and sometimes if I am annoyed I say something, perhaps I have learned from him to be sarcastic. Anyway, I am a person who says what she likes.

I know everything, in the family. I have always heard, watched. I know things no one else knows, and I like that. I say what I like when I want to, but about some things I say nothing. I know all of them, all the children, from when they were babies. Paul cannot ever stay with anything, he has never known where he was going, he was like that from young. Gina you knew always would go where she wanted, would go high. Sandra was like girls in magazines, even in her school uniform. Katie and Roger were always together, but he did his own things, Roger, he worked hard at school, Katie too, and she never gave trouble.

Clare was the youngest, the baby, people made a fuss of her always, she was a bit spoiled perhaps, and she was athletic, right from quite small, handstands and somersaults, and then later she found dancing, and you could see in the end dancing would take her away, and it has.

I have never danced. I do not know from where it comes, this dancing.

Much later, I went away that time to see how it would be. To see if I could be somewhere else. I had jobs and there was a man for a while. But all the time I felt I was in the wrong place. I told the man about Clare and he said I should go to fetch her, and when he said that I saw that he did not understand. He did not see that that was not possible. I stopped seeing the man and in the end I went back to Allersmead. I knew I had to go back, that was my home now, it was our family, like Alison says. And there was Clare.

Ingrid does not much revisit that time — the time she went away. She remembers working in a café. The man she remembers only vaguely. It is a long time ago now, but she does remember that there had been that sense of deracination, as though she were in the wrong place. And so eventually one night she had walked through the Allersmead front door once more, suitcases in hand, and that was that.

She remembers this, but without great interest. These days, she is interested in vegetables. She will grow curly kale this year, and salsify, and this new kind of carrot that they say does not get the fly. She does not know the word for salsify in her own language.

Black Marble

Sandra sits watching models undulate along a catwalk. She is thinking about bathroom suites and light fittings. When at last the undulations cease, she realizes that she has made no notes, that she has not — to put it bluntly — been involved at all.

Can this be? At 38 can she have entirely lost interest in fashion? Ex-fashion writer, ex-fashion correspondent of a daily newspaper, manageress of a thriving Rome boutique, is she in fact a sham? She rather thinks that she is, and does not care. She will order one or two garments for the boutique, guided by a well-honed instinct, because commerce must continue; she will greet a few acquaintances with exaggerated delight, and then scarper, thinking black marble and rose-tinted uplighters. People want the works, the wow factor. Italians especially.

Property development is so fun. This is her third flat, her third buy low, sell high (you hope). She is fascinated by the numbers, by the elegant conversion of x number of euros into $x + y$ euros, which you then plunge into the next property so that in due course you will have $x + y + z$. She enjoys the juggling of mortgages and builders' quotes, the *pas de deux* with the builder, the site manager, the bank manager. She

246

positively revels in kitchen designs, underfloor heating and precise shades of paint. She has immersed herself in the literature, and is now an expert in cutting-edge Italian interior décor. She knows exactly what will lure the kind of person who will buy this kind of flat: chic, pricey, enviable.

The show dealt with, she is now free, having negotiated herself a four-day week at the boutique. Free to develop property. She has a flat to look at, though in fact she is some way off her next purchase, but you need to keep an eye on the market, and then she must visit the site, to talk black marble and other matters with Luigi, the builder.

The flat that she sees is not especially tempting though the price is informative. She drives to the site — if absorption into the hectic progress of Roman traffic can be called driving — and finds a parking space, by a miracle. The building is an old one, its half-dozen apartments mostly decked out for the twenty-first century, except for Sandra's, which was inhabited until recently by an elderly widow and is ripe for the full treatment. It is now a wasteland of trailing wires, unplastered walls and builders' rubble, through which she picks her way to locate Luigi, who receives her with enthusiasm. She and Luigi get on. This is their second project together. Luigi likes feisty women and knows a sharp lady when he meets one. Sandra's fluent but occasionally deficient Italian is a matter of amusement to him, and he has made it his business to extend her vocabulary into the more arcane regions of builder talk.

247

Together, they pore over some brochures. Luigi approves of black marble; he too knows the market. There is a slight skirmish over door fittings — a question of price and the budget. Then Luigi's mobile goes and he steps over to the window, with an apology.

There is an excited conversation. He returns; his daughter has just been delivered of her baby, a son. A first grandchild. Luigi is exuberant, but then checks his rapture. He is remembering that Sandra is without children — some tact is in order. It would not occur to him that her childlessness might be by choice. He returns sternly to the matter of doorknobs.

Sandra is not fooled. She had noted Luigi's complicated expression of condolence when her lack of *bambini* cropped up, a while ago now. A man — Mario has occasionally answered the phone when Luigi has rung her at home — but no *bambini*. Luigi has five, and has refrained from mentioning them too often, from then on.

Last week, Sandra had an abortion. Her second. The first was twelve years ago and she had thought that couldn't happen again, no way, but evidently it could, and did. So she has had to take an unscheduled holiday, and go to London. No doubt there are ways and means, in a Catholic country, but she hadn't the time to hang around and find out, so it was a matter of some phone calls and a flight booking, and an unpleasant couple of days in London, incognito and incommunicado. You do not really ring up old friends to say: "I'm over briefly for an abortion — let's do lunch."

Luigi would be appalled. Mario is something of a lapsed Catholic but even so he wasn't too happy about it. He and Sandra have been together for two years, and it was clearly understood that Sandra did not intend children, and Mario — who is a few years younger — wasn't bothered either way at the moment. But when it came to Sandra's terse announcement some atavistic response kicked in. There were a few protests, not too convinced, which faded away in the face of Sandra's calm resolve and, perhaps, thoughts of his own about the implications of a baby. Mario is a photographer, and likes the good life.

Sandra changes men about every three to four years. She is not especially proud of this record, but it is the way she is, so what can you do? There comes a moment, always, when he has become a bit irritating, a bit boring, when she knows that their time is up. There has then to be a process of detachment; she tries to minimize damage and complications. The men find that they have been gently distanced rather than discarded and, if realistic, will move on of their own accord. Since Sandra always makes sure that their current shared home is in her name, it is the men who have to go elsewhere, rather than her. Once, there was sufficient fall-out from the break-up to make it a good idea for Sandra to look for a radical change. This brought her to Rome, a few years ago, when the world of London journalism became rather too small a pond for both her and her ex-lover. She had always relished Italy; she had always fancied the idea of running a boutique. So go for it, Sandra.

Sandra tends to succeed, for perfectly good reasons. She is resourceful, she can work hard; she is also personable, shrewd and capable of opportunism. When young, she prospered in fashion magazines, rocketing from tea-girl through copy writer to an editorial chair. But she is also restless; just as men become a touch tedious in time, so also do jobs. When magazines grew stale, she moved into mainstream journalism, purveying fashion for a high-circulation daily. And now there is the boutique, whose owner has found Sandra's skills as a buyer, along with her exotic English charm — and good looks — an irresistible combination to customers. The boutique does not know about Sandra's new interest — none of their business — and so is unaware that perhaps its days are numbered, where she is concerned.

Mario does know about Sandra the property developer, and has remarked that if she goes on at this rate she is on track to becoming a wealthy woman. Sandra points out that you can also come a cropper, in this game, so don't count on it. Mario jokes that nevertheless he will hang in there, in the hopes of becoming a kept man. But he knows Sandra, and is well aware that she does not carry passengers; he appreciates the nature of their relationship, and will probably jump before he is pushed. Sandra's recent visit to London gave pause for thought; he saw that she meant it, about children, and he might in time feel differently himself. He is an Italian male, and has a mother who drops hints. She has made it apparent that she did not think much of Sandra, when he took her to visit: too old, too foreign, undoubtedly deficient in domestic skills.

Sandra has never taken Mario or, indeed, any of her men to visit Allersmead. She does not much go there herself — blows in once in a while with a fistful of expensive presents: classy wine, gastronomic delicacies. The presents, she fully recognizes, denote unease of some kind, or guilt, or the need to compensate, or all three. She sends lavish flowers on her mother's birthdays.

She found herself thinking of Allersmead, of family, over the time of the abortion, and sees this as an indication of weakness, of regression. Abortion is notoriously traumatic. She had remembered a period of weakness on that previous occasion, when she was much younger. She had been caught weeping in the loo by a colleague on the magazine, and had confided. The colleague was all sympathy and worldly wisdom, and advice: "I mean, some people go for counselling, and you may want to think of that but quite honestly I think a long talk with someone close to you . . . Does your mother know?"

And Sandra had cried, "It's because of my mother that I don't want to have children!"

Is it? Sandra today would be more circumspect, more worldly wise herself. She does not want children because they would not be compatible with her preferred lifestyle, she feels no particular affinity with children (luckily) and, yes, because of that bedrock of memory, that place in the mind, which has triggered certain reactions, certain reservations, certain revulsions.

Never, ever, will she live with a bathroom that is infested with plastic bath toys. Never will she spoon gooey slop into a gaping dribbling infant mouth. Never will her home be a shrine decked out with child art, crude clay animals, customized mugs and an acreage of commemorative photography. And all right, that is Allersmead, but how otherwise would she know what she must avoid? She was trained by Allersmead, habituated, and thus she knows what she does not want. Perhaps that is why, right now, she is creating Roman apartments that are as far removed from Allersmead as a penthouse from a beach hut. Though, that said, when she looks at Allersmead with detachment, with new eyes, she can see just what she could do with it: that Edwardian stuff is the business nowadays; you'd beef that up with period features — more stained glass, freestanding baths with claw feet, mahogany-panelled bathrooms — landscaped garden, tennis court, croquet lawn.

But the house was just the backdrop. What went on in it was *her* creation, in every sense. Motherhood was her profession, and I have no idea if she fell into it or planned it from the moment she was a five-year-old with her first doll. Suffice it that that was what she did. My mother — our mother — set out to be the archetypal mother, the universal lap.

Sandra can remember sitting on that lap, just. She can remember trying to push Gina off it. She loved her mother, maybe she still does, but she finds it odd now that that one word covers such a range of feeling. Love of a parent has absolutely nothing in common with love of chocolate, say, or love of nude bathing, let alone — let absolutely and definitely alone — sexual love.

And one must not confuse sexual love with love of sex. Do I, Sandra, love sex? Well, I certainly enjoy it, but not in the abstract, not the activity *perse*; it has to be carried out with the right person, it is an exchange, it involves two of you. Which is where the love aspect comes into it. What you are feeling about the other person conditions the success of the sex.

She remembers that boy at Crackington Haven. Of course: the initiation.

Such a let-down. The disappointment. Life's first climactic moment, one had been led to believe, and, instead, a few minutes of embarrassed probing and grunting. As for climax — forget it. But of course one felt nothing for the boy — liked him well enough, I suppose, but love was still well out of sight. Falling into it, falling out of it. First time *that* happens you're in grown-up country, oh dear me, yes. And the one thing you recognize is that this is entirely unlike anything you've ever felt for another person before. The prefix does help a bit — *in* love. You are not so much engaged in loving someone, you are consumed by the emotion, drowning in it, barely able to surface for long enough to function normally. And one wouldn't really want to go back there, either.

Actually Sandra still falls in love, but it is nowadays a more tempered process, more considered than those untamed onsets of youth; she would be capable of pulling back if she saw that this was going to be a thoroughly bad idea. But she requires that each new man should provoke something of the old fever; if not, this will be nothing but a sexual deal, and Sandra considers that poor taste. Perhaps she is a romantic?

Romantic or not, she finds monogamy hard to understand. Just one relationship, till death you do part?

Allersmead again. Look at them. Mum and Dad. We can't be talking romance, surely? Love? Well, who's to know, who's to have the shred of an idea? Other people are inscrutable, aren't they? Especially those you know best.

But one person? When there is all that variety out there; all those intriguingly different men.

Sandra does indeed have monogamous friends and acquaintances, and they do not seem to be in a state of permanent frustration. She accepts that it is perhaps she who is out of step but is not bothered by this. She has chosen to live thus — a serial partner, if you like — and it has suited her very well. She has even managed to remain on amiable terms with her former men, except for that London journalist who took exceptional umbrage when the curtain fell.

She is thinking of him, with a certain indifference, when she leaves the site after her consultation with Luigi. She had picked up an English paper at a kiosk and saw his byline. *Plus ça change*: same paper, same theme. He is a political commentator, and she is only too ready to agree that politics is an infinitely more compelling subject than fashion, but it is equally driven by winds of change over which you have no control, and it was this feature of journalism that had eventually become tiresome to Sandra — the way in which you were obliged to react to remorseless circumstance. There comes a point when it is hard graft to drum up an enthusiastic commentary on the new season's catwalk offerings.

The political commentator had broached the subject of marriage. That is when alarm bells ring for Sandra, even if everything is still satisfactory. The hint of a permanent commitment has her on the alert; she will begin to notice things about him that had seemed unexceptional — his repetitious jokes, the state in which he leaves the bathroom, that jacket. Sex becomes perfunctory. Time's up.

She throws the English paper into the back of the car, and slots into the traffic. She is meeting an old friend for lunch. She and Mary go way back — they worked together on a magazine. Mary was Beauty Tips; Sandra answered fashion queries. Mary is here for a few days with her husband, who has been sent off to the Sistine Chapel while Mary has a girls' lunch with Sandra. They have not seen each other for several years.

Mary is already seated, at the restaurant. As she rises to wave, Sandra sees at once that she is pregnant. Good grief! Mary is 39, and as firmly into child abstinence as herself, Sandra had thought. Over antipasti, it emerges that Mary and James had been having second thoughts, during the last year or two.

"And with me getting so elderly," says Mary, "it was now or never."

They are indeed elderly, both of them, Mary and Sandra, in their world. The girls on the catwalks are 16, 18 — washed up by 28. The photographers — like Mario — are svelte, black-clad twenty-somethings; Mario himself is a touch long in the tooth at 33. People over forty are either the editors — the queens of the magazine world — or customers at the boutique, who are rich enough to patronize it either because they're high earners or funded by a man, and whose purpose is to grab time by the throat and hold it still, to shave off a few years by being thinner, more elegant, more hollow-cheeked, more wrinkle-free.

And now here is Mary, with a bulge of which she is patently proud, a hint of a double chin, crows' feet and her eyebrows all over the place.

"You look fantastic," Mary says. "That *dress* . . ."

Sandra finds herself oddly discomforted. By the pregnancy? By Mary's evident complacency? One will say nothing about the abortion, that's for sure.

"I know what you're thinking," says Mary. "I was a paid-up member of the child-free brigade, just like you." She pulls a face. "Something changed. Both James and me . . . So there we are." She pats her bulge.

Mary is small, neat and is wearing one of those clinging pregnancy outfits that seem designed to accentuate rather than modify the bulge. Sandra remembers the discreet smocks of yesteryear. Fecundity is to be flaunted, nowadays. She thinks of Alison; perhaps her mother was ahead of her time.

"We'd have liked two," says Mary. "But we'll see how it goes with one, first. I was an only and James says I'm self-centred. You had masses of brothers and sisters, didn't you?"

Sandra smiles. "Indeed. And I'm the soul of generosity and self-sacrifice in consequence. On the contrary — it's in a large family that you learn to fight dirty and look after number one. I pushed my older sister into a pond when I was seven, it seems."

"Really? Is that the one who's on telly sometimes?"

"Gina. Yes."

"Well, she seems to have done all right, despite that."

"And we used to go down into the cellar, among the spiders and black beetles, and fantasize. I used to fight my brother over who was James Bond."

"Bliss," says Mary. "Heaven. Weren't you lucky!"

Was I? Were we? Sandra looks across the table at Mary but is transported back to the Allersmead cellar: the murk, the damp, and that atmosphere of thrill and intensity, removed from reality, disbelief suspended, plunged into other worlds, pretence but also not pretence — nothing since has been so all-consuming. Shark-infested seas, wolves howling on the prairie, hunched shadows of the Daleks in their corner. "Eat a spider!" says Paul. Did I?

Sandra shrugs. "Well, I don't advise six. My mother was . . ." She pauses.

"Frazzled," says Mary. "Laid out, I bet. No, no — I'll stick with one. Two conceivably."

You've got it quite wrong, thinks Sandra, but never mind. Neither frazzled nor laid out. Triumphant, on the whole. Fulfilled. Numbers matter — we were her bank statement. Quantity counts. We were the largest family on the street, in the school — in the town I dare say. She was unchallenged. And of course the little local glitch was a family matter. Who was to know? Who does know? Just us — we've never gone in for spreading the news around. The family closes ranks. She considers felling Mary with a conversational ace: actually, one of us wasn't hers.

"You do that," she says. Suddenly she is bored with all this. She would quite like to describe to Mary the black marble bathroom that she and Luigi have so lovingly designed, but knows better. Property development is not an occupation that impresses others, unless it be other property developers. It is seen as a touch indecent, too commercial, rapacious indeed. As perhaps it is. But she does not feel rapacious. She feels — creative. The bathrooms, the kitchens, the dulcet shades of paint. And the satisfaction when the figures too are creative — when $x + y$ has become $x + y + z$. If this is rapacity, then she could make a case for rapacity as an art form. And the money is, after all, mythical money. You never see it, handle it — it merely ticks away on screens. A market trader is closer to the real thing. Even the boutique, where credit cards are flourished. The boutique is commerce; figures do indeed flower. But they do not flower with such simplicity, such elegance.

So she puts her primary concern to one side and allows the conversation to drift, agreeably enough. The meal over, they embrace, and part. Sandra watches Mary make her way along the street, her bump cheerily emphasized by the skin-tight, wasp-striped top that she

258

is wearing over her jeans. She suspects that she and Mary will see even less of one another in the future.

Few of Sandra's friends have children. They are childless, like her, by inclination, or, frequently, by omission — life has somehow rushed by, too busy, too demanding, and they have never got round to it. In Italy, it is a somewhat unusual position. Children are endemic, here. Well, a Catholic country — most people are at least nominal Catholics. A family of six would be unremarkable. Indeed, you soon realize that Italy is a land of teeming youth — the streets flow with the young, the air rings with their confident voices. The buzz of their scooters deafens you. Youth teems elsewhere. Of course. In Brixton or Bradford or Glasgow. But the young of Italy are more insistent, more pervasive. From the *putti* that gambol on fountains, that float on ceilings, to the streams of today's schoolchildren who occupy the pavements, hold up the traffic, the city seems to be in defiant, flamboyant production, regeneration.

My mother would approve, thinks Sandra, held up in revving traffic as a seemingly endless file of pinafored tots is ushered over a crossing. But of course she never came to Rome. They never travelled, did they? No holidays in the Algarve for us.

And, anyway, was it that she liked children for themselves, or just her own children as validation, as endorsement, as proof of her maternal prowess? Her own children? Clare? Clare was treated just the same as anyone else; I don't remember so much as a flicker of discrimination, ever. And of course the facts of the matter were kept under wraps. We were the family, and that was that.

The tots are safely across the street, and the traffic roars ahead, taking Sandra with it. *La famiglia* is pretty sacrosanct in Italy, which is one good reason to keep the involvement with Mario in check bearing in mind that appalling mother. Don't worry, Mama, I'm not planning to snitch your little boy, and no way would I enter your suffocating embrace. At least my mother doesn't call up to report that she is about to go to the shops, or that the window cleaner has been.

Sandra is still thinking about family, the family, Allersmead, when she climbs the stairs to her apartment — the apartment that she shares with Mario, for now. The apartment has big windows with a wide view over a park and a slice of golden Rome; it has cool stone floors and a huge pale leather sofa and a low glass-topped table on which there are always flowers. It is stylish, tranquil, there is no mess, no clutter, pictures are precisely hung, the paintwork is in mint condition. It is a million miles from Allersmead.

When Sandra was still at Allersmead, still a child, she had glimpsed such alternative worlds in magazines. The dentist's waiting room had been a revelation. She had scrutinized these amazing interiors: so this was how people could live. And had known that she would do so herself, in due course.

But the apartment, this afternoon, is overlaid by Allersmead. She wanders around that virtual reality place, so intimately known — the sitting room with its shabby chintz-covered sofas and chairs, the faded blue curtains, the kelim rug in front of the fireplace, the kitchen with that great battered table, scene of a thousand family meals. She wanders — not in the spirit of nostalgia but of curiosity, of surprise, even. It seems odd that she was ever here, was here for so long, without, as it were, noticing.

But I probably noticed first, she thinks. I remember thinking — we are not like other families, we are not a normal family. Mum and Dad hardly ever talk to one another, and there is Ingrid who is family but is not, and there is Clare. Gina did a bit of thinking too, but we didn't much exchange views. And by the time I was — 17 or so — I noticed all the time. Oh, not the decor, the general Allersmead ambience, that was neither here nor there by then — I noticed that this was a pretty weird sort of family, a seriously odd family, a screwball family.

What did I feel? Well, kind of exasperated. I felt sorry for Clare. I thought someone should sit down and talk it through with her. And with the rest of us, for that matter.

Now, I see it all differently. I see three people for whom things had gone dramatically wrong, who probably should never have been together anyway. I see them muddling on, because no one could face up to doing otherwise. Condemned to cohabitation.

The phone rings, and virtual reality Allersmead evaporates, along with Sandra's thoughts. That was then, this is now, and now is on the line. Sandra's deputy at the boutique is unable to mollify a customer whose ordered garment has not arrived when promised.

261

Sandra knows this customer well — the wife of a wealthy industrialist, a woman for whom shopping is a career; you do not offend such customers. She speaks to the woman herself, assures her of immediate, violent action; she is placatory, flattering, unctuous even, and afterwards she is contemptuous — of herself. That woman is a vapid parasite; Sandra despises her, and her like. But the fashion world is full of them — it is for them that the fashion world exists.

That is the problem with fashion. Sandra spotted this long ago, when first fascinated by clothes and what could be done with them. The products of fashion are intriguing and entrancing — the fabrics, the styles, the ingenuity of design. They are craft of a high order, and a craft furthermore that determines what the woman on the high street will look like this year, or next. This manipulation is itself remarkable — that an idea, a concept, a sketch can blossom, can send tentacles worldwide, can decide the contents of a million wardrobes. The whole edifice of fashion is impressive — the way in which a catwalk garment priced for plutocrats will reappear, modified and made accessible to the populace. Fashion percolates downwards, until it becomes relevant to anyone. What a clever trick, and how nicely it thus contrives to make lots of money for lots of people.

And that is the trouble — the people. The consumers on the front line, like the patrons of the boutique, the lettuce-leaf ladies with no thoughts but of self-gratification, and the entire frenetic army of those who cater for them, the task force of designers, and *vendeuses*, and PR girls and buyers, all of them stupefied by the glamour and significance of their calling.

Such as Sandra? She would admit readily that this was perhaps the case way back, when first she found herself in the heady world of magazines, awed by the brittle, assertive older women and those who danced attendance — the slick photographers, the other besotted acolyte girls. Disillusion set in long ago — it was all right to be a part of all this so long as you stayed sane, and saw it as a sort of lunatic circus, playing to an audience of turnip heads. And the clothes could be mesmerizing — the hang of a skirt, the elegant conceit of a trimming. Plus you have to earn a living somehow.

But today even the clothes are losing something of their charm. Sandra still loves (ah, that laboured word) — enjoys — the glorious touch of silk, the pleasure of some new unfamiliar weave, the interest of a clever cut or a challenging design. The fascination persists, if a touch diluted, but there is increasingly the sense of déjà vu, the catwalks have become a yawn, the entourage more and more of a pain. Luigi is better company, marble bathrooms more inspiring.

Well, it is not too late to jump ship. If this current project works out, sells well, and the next — then maybe she'll say goodbye to the boutique, go all out for . . . marble bathrooms. One might well go back home, to England — rumour has it that you can do well there in the housing market, and she has never seen Rome as more than a phase.

Sandra believes in following her nose. If things become stale, in love or in work, then sniff the air and move on. 20 years in fashion is perhaps enough. The determined eighteen-year-old who got a foot in the door is someone else; a different Sandra is ready now for change. She remembers her father's curled lip when she announced that she had a job with this magazine and would be leaving home.

"A *fashion* magazine?" cries Alison. "Well, my goodness, I suppose if that's what you want . . . But why not go to university, like Gina?"

Because — Sandra thinks but does not say — because that takes three years and I haven't got the time. And that's what Gina's doing, so I am not.

Charles says nothing. He simply looks, which is enough.

Dad would never have seen a magazine in his life, whether it was *Vogue* or *Country Life* or *Yachting News*. That is, he would have laid eyes on them, in the newsagent or wherever, but he would not have seen them because they were not within his sphere of interest. Dad did not notice TV sit-coms, rock music (unless from Paul's room), our clothes, our friends, much of our conversation. And that was just Allersmead. Beyond Allersmead, he was unaware of football league tables, bingo halls, horse racing, coarse fishing — anything indeed that was irrelevant to his concerns. Which were? Well, the books — whatever he was writing at that particular time. So, mostly, Dad let the world pass him by — he looked the other way.

Sandra has inspected the books. She has stalked into his study in his absence; she has eyed titles,

264

browsed within. If she put her mind to it, sat down and gave her full attention, she could follow well enough. She is not stupid. She got good marks at school, when she wanted to. When she wanted to show that she could match Gina, if she felt so inclined. "Sandra has a good mind . . ." school reports used to say — teacher-talk for not stupid, ". . . but does not always choose to apply herself." School was a pain; one was simply enduring, waiting for release.

A fair number of people must have read Dad's books — bought them, taken them out of libraries. He got money for them. Sandra glimpses suddenly a host of strangers — a kind of person she does not know, people who seek the sort of book she does not read. There is something oddly tantalizing about this — you do not like to think that you are shut off from a whole section of society, even if people you perhaps couldn't be doing with anyway. Dad's customers. Unlike the boutique customers, that's for sure. But one can't abide the lettuce leaf ladies.

Have I missed out? she wonders. If I had got down to it and read Dad's books, and similar books, would I be someone else, consorting with unimaginable strangers?

People like him? No, no, there can't be a whole horde of Dad clones. And if there are, he never knew them. Dad didn't have friends, colleagues, people who dropped in, rang up.

She sees in detachment this solitary figure, and feels a kind of compunction. There he was, one lived with him all those years, and one knows nothing of him.

He tells her that if she were an African girl of twelve she would have scars on her cheeks. He makes some comment about her green fingernails, so Mum notices.

He comes into the kitchen with ribbons of paper streaming from his hands. "Who did this?" he roars.

Who did, by the way?

Gina has given him a paper-knife for Christmas, and he asks if he is to stab his enemies with this?

He walks that cliff path at Crackington Haven, alone, staring at the sea. He does not see them.

His physical presence is eminently retrievable. That slight stoop, the strong, rather beaky nose, the way he wrinkles it to hunch up his glasses. Oh yes, the glasses — always opaque, in desperate need of a wipe. His clothes — vivid still, item by item. Those shirts with button-down collars (frayed) — the blue denim ones and the red one and the green checked one. The brown cardigan thing with suede front. The grey sweater and the black one. The tweed jacket with elbow patches. The fawn belted raincoat.

Actually he was — is — rather good-looking. Strong features. Women — some women — are said to seek a man in the image of their father. Surveying her own men, Sandra sees no one bearing even the faintest resemblance. So much for that. Rejection? Tell me about your relationship with your father, Sandra.

What relationship? When she tries to isolate herself and Charles, to find a connection that is personal, specific, she is unable to do so. Of course, there is presumably a finite amount of paternal attention, and

266

in his case you have to divide by six. One-sixth of maybe rather cursory paternal attention. Sandra trawls back, in search of the flavour of her personal sixth. When, and in what way, did one feel that he was *my* father rather than *our* father? What little jokes did we have, just him and me? What chats? Oh, come on, you know he neither joked nor chatted. What conversations, then? But Allersmead conversations tended to be collective, a free-for-all around the kitchen table at mealtimes; when Dad spoke, he spoke to — or at — everyone, on the whole. We argued with him, oh yes — Gina most of all — but his end of argument seems oddly dispassionate, in recollection, neutral — a general response, not customized, not now, Sandra, you and I must have a good talk about this.

So even the one-sixth of Dad is somewhat impersonal, one sixth of this father figure, our father, our father who art in his study and do not disturb, a father type who nevertheless defines what a father is, must be, how could they be otherwise? A father is Dad, because that is what one has known.

What did I feel about him? Awe? Respect? Well, not really — you took care not to provoke him because you didn't like the way he would respond. Sarcasm — though you didn't then know the word. Mostly, you skirted him, ignored him as though here were some inconvenient feature of the landscape.

And now? When Sandra returns to Allersmead today, she seems to be visiting some historic site, which is entirely strange, entirely surprising, and yet at another level infinitely familiar. Both Charles and Alison are startling — is this really how they are? How they speak and behave? — but also disconcertingly normal. Of course, this is how it was, how it is; the shock is that it still goes on, parallel to the world of today, the life of now.

Enough, she thinks. She has been lying on the sofa in the Rome flat, flicking through a kitchen installation brochure, with Allersmead swirling all around. Enough of this, there is work to be done, phone calls to make, messages to check. She gets the laptop, starts to go through the emails and stares in shock.

There is an email from Ingrid. When Allersmead chooses to communicate in this way, it is Ingrid who does so. Alison has never got the hang of the computer; Charles probably does not know what it is.

Ingrid is brief. Brief and bald — a statement. Sandra reads and rereads, frowning.

Mothercraft

Alison is a little disappointed that the Mothercraft class does not seem to be catching on. It is an offshoot of her cookery classes, which have been going strong for nearly 20 years now, over-subscribed; you can't sensibly have more than seven or eight under instruction in the Allersmead kitchen so there is often a waiting-list. She had thought Mothercraft such a brilliant idea, so much what young mothers need, surely, but so far only five have turned up, and she finds them oddly unresponsive. They want to know how to stop their babies crying at night and what to do about two-year-old tantrums, and sit impassive while she tells them that the important thing, the really crucial thing, is a real family life with lots of love and attention for everyone, all the time, and plenty of family rituals, birthday parties and everyone *belonging*, and of course lovely home-cooked meals. On the first occasion, a girl had interrupted: "Actually, if you don't mind my saying, Mothercraft sounds a bit odd; it's Parenting now, really." When Alison had pointed out that it's *mothering* that counts, I mean that's the really central thing, isn't it, the *mother's* role, there had been a ripple of dissent. Apparently they don't see it quite like that. Someone else said, "One's not on call twenty-four seven, I've got a job, and it's

269

turn and turn about with my partner." They bring their babies and toddlers, of course, and the idea had been that Ingrid would run a sort of creche, but Ingrid hasn't seemed all that enthusiastic, and Alison had rather forgotten how chaotic it can get with a few little ones around.

She may have to cancel the Mothercraft class, but possibly it was going to be a bit too much anyway, with the Basic Cookery course on Tuesday afternoons and the Advanced on Thursdays. When she started out, Alison had imagined that she would be catering for young brides, for Basic at least, and had looked forward to starry-eyed biddable girls, but in the event most of the punters, for both classes, are older women, quite a lot of them her own age, and they are neither starry-eyed nor biddable. She had installed a new cooker, even larger than the one that had done duty for so many family meals, but even so there were — and are — undisguised reactions to the Allersmead kitchen, ranging from merriment to downright scorn. She had not realized it was so unusual; it was other people's kitchens that had always seemed odd to her — so shiny and small. When people are being kindly they say, "How lovely and old-fashioned — my *mother* had a dresser like that." Other remarks are not quite so restrained. She has caught mutterings about the potential of a place like this, in the right hands, and once overheard one woman, putting her coat on in the hall, announce: "God, that kitchen . . . but, face it, she's a fantastic cook."

There lay her authority. Those who were initially unimpressed by Alison's lack of chic ("Where does she *get* those sack things she wears?") and the individuality of the Allersmead ambience soon changed their tune after exposure to Alison's skills. A casual interest would soon become keen ambition: they too could turn out those elegant dishes, impress their friends, confound their menfolk. Those who had come along just for the fun of it were soon the most ardent acolytes, progressing from Basic to Advanced, from essential salad ideas to Italian, Middle Eastern and Thai cuisine. Alison's cookery persona is a surprise, they discover; her house may be crying out for a makeover, she may be dressed by Butterwick 1975, but when it comes to cooking she is on the cutting edge. She has availed herself of all the pundits, and added her own twists and amendments — she has outspiced Claudia Roden, trumped Nigella, improved on Jamie Oliver, revived and reinvented Elizabeth David. The members of her classes, women who thought they knew a thing or two themselves, are silenced in the presence of achievement of another order. They watch Alison chop, whisk, stir. They marvel at what comes out of her ovens. They submit meekly, deferentially, to instruction — chopping and stirring alongside in the Allersmead kitchen, vying for her attention: "Alison, is this thick enough?"; "Alison, *why* can't I get my pastry like yours?" Alison has taken wing, floating masterly in her own element, untouchable. The women know that they will never achieve her finesse, they recognize that she has some sort of culinary sixth sense not available to them, but they see that something will rub off, they can raise their game, cookery is all the rage nowadays, it is well worth an afternoon and a few quid.

For Alison, the cookery classes have been affirmation, and a small personal income. They have given her a new status, now that the children are no longer there, and some money to spend as she wishes. She has never particularly felt the need of money; Charles has always left management of the household finances to her, and has never asked to see the accounts. There has always been just about enough, so long as one was careful, though what comes into the bank from his dividends does seem to have been getting less and less lately, for some reason. There has never been extravagance at Allersmead, but even so the little bit of spending money from the classes has been a source of satisfaction. Over the years Alison has treated herself — has treated Allersmead — to the latest in blenders and microwaves; she has had a Dyson vacuum cleaner, and a proper wash-basin for the downstairs loo instead of that ancient sink. Remarks had been made about the sink, by cookery-class women.

Charles remains in his study on cookery-class days. Most of the women have never set eyes on him; sometimes there is vague murmured speculation, Alison being so obviously and productively married (the family photos everywhere, those named mugs). Ingrid is supportive, if enigmatic; she comes in and out of the kitchen, sometimes does a bit of brisk clearing up, and is referred to by Alison as "my PA". Alison is not clear what the term means; Ingrid suggested it, and they both rather like the sound. The women are a bit puzzled by Ingrid, who is unforthcoming when discreetly probed ("You must be Scandinavian . . . let me guess — Swedish?") and makes it clear that her role is strictly professional: "I am working with Alison for some time now."

Ingrid has moved down from her bedroom in the attics to Gina's old room. The attic room has developed a tiresome ceiling leak that means a bucket when it rains. A builder came to look at the roof; there was much shaking of his head when he descended, and a subsequent estimate that was patently ridiculous, all those noughts. Alison assumed there was some mistake, but apparently not. Charles simply stared at it and shrugged, and of course he hasn't been up to the attic floor for ten years or so. Buckets are now arranged up there as fixtures, and that seems to do the trick.

Allersmead appears somehow isolated these days, clinging on in a neighbourhood that has subtly changed. There is a different kind of neighbourhood now; huge sleek cars are parked in driveways, one Allersmead-sized house on the street has become a nursing home, another is divided into flats. The people next door sold their garden to a developer, and a bungalow sprang up, much to Alison's indignation. The neighbours are younger and more distracted — they whisk off in the sleek cars at crack of dawn, and reappear late at night, wives and husbands both; their children are shepherded around by young nannies. Ingrid claims that there are children who do not recognize their parents.

Letters from house agents drop through the front door, saying that the house agents have clients who are anxious to acquire a property in the area, similar to Allersmead, or, indeed, by implication, Allersmead itself. Alison bins these. She is aware from the comments of the cookery-class women that Allersmead is perceived as a curious marriage of archaic and highly desirable ("I mean, what one could *do* with it . . ."). The women themselves tend to come from the leafy roads of detached four-bedroom new and newish houses on the outskirts of town, from the villages round about or from the old warehouses down by the canal that have been converted into lofts. They exclaim at the Allersmead stained glass, and the black and white marble of the hall floor. Alison is irritated by this; she does not like to have Allersmead seen as some kind of anachronism, a survival. "This has always been a home," she says. "A real family home."

It is so long since Alison lived anywhere other than Allersmead that she can no longer remember what other houses are like. She left her parents' home to marry when quite young. Her own childhood memories are of that north London Edwardian semi — roomy but not expansive, and anyway there were only the two children. When she thinks about the place, it is inevitably set beside Allersmead and does now seem, well, a bit poky.

She recognized Allersmead, when first they saw it. She stared at it — the steps up to the big front door, the many windows indicating many rooms, the solidity of it, its assurance — set there amongst big trees with

274

the quarter acre of garden spreading away behind (so said the agent's particulars). She stared — and before her eyes the place became populated. Little faces peered from the windows; a small figure rode a bike round the gravelled circle of the driveway. She hurried forward, with Charles a few steps behind.

He said, it's rather *big*, isn't it? She was busy allocating space and hardly heard. He said, what would one want all that garden for? She had marked out the croquet lawn and hung some swings. He said, that's an industrial-size kitchen. She had tracked down a great scrubbed table and the removal men were edging it through the hall. He said, there's another floor, up those stairs, it really is *very* big. She was installing Ingrid, or someone like her. He said, it's rather beyond the budget, in fact. She said, that big room off the hall, the one opposite the sitting room, the one with the panelling and that funny old tiled fireplace, that could be your study. He took another look; he began to measure up for bookshelves.

Allersmead — ownership of Allersmead — rests on Vim and Dettol and Brasso and Harpic and Robin starch. There had to be an erosion of Charles's inheritance from his godfather, that blessed sustaining lump of money derived from the prinking and polishing of a million homes. The chunk taken to buy Allersmead meant that there would be some diminishment of income in the future, but Alison reckoned that they could manage perfectly well. In fact, Allersmead, though not cheap, was nothing like as desirable then as it apparently is today. People didn't want such large, cumbersome old houses. How would you heat it? How would you keep it clean?

Charles did not ask these questions. He did wonder, aloud, from time to time, how on earth they were going to use all this space. Alison merely beamed. Smiled and smiled. Oh, you'll see, she cried, you'll see, it'll be fine. As for the heating and the cleaning — simple. Good thick sweaters in the winter, and one just won't be too fussy about a bit of dust. And, in the event, that was how it worked out. Allersmead children were amongst the last to experience that fine aesthetic thrill of frost patterns on the inside of the windows; a monthly blitz of the place by Alison, and, in due course, Ingrid, saw to the worst of the dirt.

Allersmead children. Of course, that was the object of the exercise, and if Charles had not realized this, well, he was at the start of his writing career, he had other things to think about, one book out, another simmering. Alison had happened to him, and things had rather rushed ahead, and one has to live somewhere and perhaps preferably no longer in a rented flat, eating at the café round the corner.

Or had Charles happened to Alison?

I wanted to get married, of course. I mean, girls did then — I know it's different now, most of those Mothercraft people weren't, but you took it for granted back then. You got married, and children *of course*, unless you were someone like Corinna, and really one does wonder what her life can be like, but she always seems pretty satisfied with it, makes that clear enough.

I knew I wanted lots. Growing up in a family of two always seemed not quite right, somehow. Two is not a family. Not that it wasn't a happy childhood, blissful, I've no complaints, goodness no, it was a golden time, just what childhood should be, but I always wanted little brothers and sisters — doll-mad of course when I was small. So I assumed children, right from early on — children were obvious, sooner rather than later. And I suppose I was thinking about marriage too. Well, you had to, back then, didn't you?

I wasn't *looking* for someone to marry, goodness no, I was very young, there was no hurry, just I suppose it was in the back of one's mind. When I met Charles at that Highgate library, I never for one moment thought of marrying him. Mummy had sent me to get some books, and he was there and he helped me to find a book she wanted, and then we had a coffee and I rather liked him so I asked him to a drinks party my parents were having, and things just sort of went on from there.

I didn't know anything *about* birth control, one didn't in those days, and of course later after we were married I didn't bother with it, and then eventually there was no need. And anyway I never liked the idea — it's killing babies, isn't it, in a way; one does sort of sympathize with the Catholics. So I just didn't worry and I suppose it's not surprising that — well, that Paul was started a bit early as it were.

We'd have got married anyway. Oh, yes.

I knew Allersmead would be perfect as soon as I saw it. A lovely, lovely family home, just waiting. Yes, of course it was a bit expensive but not *that* much, and it wasn't as though we were going to live expensively, not like they do nowadays, those cars you see parked outside, and Ingrid says they all go to the West Indies or the Seychelles for their holidays, no question of Devon or Cornwall. Ingrid talks to the nannies sometimes — they get paid the earth apparently.

And Allersmead *has* been perfect. Plenty of room for everyone and the garden to play in — and so good later for Ingrid and her vegetables — Charles had his study and the kitchen was ideal for so many children, and then for years it's been just right for the cookery classes. We rattle about a bit today, I suppose, but one of them visits every now and then, and of course the whole place is full of *memories*. They're still here, as far as I'm concerned.

Paul actually is here, of course, like he often has been. Things so often haven't worked out for him and then he comes home, well, to sort of take a break and look around. The garden centre work is just to tide him over for the moment while he thinks about what he really wants to do. Eventually Paul's going to hit on what he's really good at — he's had such a lot of bad luck, fetching up with the wrong work and, frankly, the wrong people sometimes, from way back when he was very young and got led astray into that drug business — left to himself he'd never have got involved. He's always been a bit of a worry, Paul, and of course he's the eldest, and I suppose one's had a special feeling . . . yes, he was rather my favourite.

But you love them all, and if there are six you don't spread it more thinly, somehow there's just more of it.

278

When they're small, they love you back, but of course later even if they still do it doesn't much show, and you just have to reckon with that, you can't expect demonstrations of affection from sixteen-year-old boys, not that Roger wasn't always a perfectly *nice* boy. And girls go their own way, nothing you say is going to make a blind bit of difference, Gina rushing off to that college place, Sandra so sure of herself, clothes mad when she was eight, and Clare just dance, dance, dance.

One did one's best, and at least one was always there for them, they had a mother, and a home, and that's what matters. I mean, so many children don't — one wonders actually about the people round here now, with the cars and the nannies. Allersmead was a real home, I was always here, I'd be waiting for them after school, and there'd be a cake for tea. Children need security, don't they?

Those Mothercraft girls went on about their partners and shared duties. I never expected Charles to do much if anything, and of course that's how he saw it too, just a bit of help with homework sometimes when they were older — and arguing with Gina, I suppose that would be called parenting now. Though I won't say there weren't times when . . . well, when I wanted to break down the study door. But of course one laughed it off, obviously everything's not going to be plain sailing with a household like ours, there are going to be points when things get on top of you.

It was just a wretched accident, the Limoges plates. Paul didn't *mean* to, he just wasn't quite himself that evening.

Charles had his work, the books, and one respected that. I know I'm not much of a reader myself but Charles knew I don't read a lot — though always bedtime stories with the children, always — and you don't marry someone because of what they've read or not, do you? Well, I dare say you do if you're people like Corinna and Martin, not that they *are* married, and no doubt they do talk about Shakespeare at breakfast, and rather them than me, frankly.

Charles wouldn't have *wanted* to talk about the books. His books.

In a family like this everyone was talking, all the time, children's chatter to begin with, and of course there's so much practical stuff, someone needing this or that, but later it gets more grown-up, a bit too much so sometimes I found, Gina and her opinions, and Charles would have his say then, not always in a way that people liked — Dad being sarky, they used to call it.

But the thing about Allersmead was that people could escape from one another if they wanted to. Charles with his study, and Ingrid had her room up at the top, and the times when no one was to bother her. And the children had the garden and sometimes they all used to go down into the cellar, if you please — the big ones were reading to the younger ones, apparently. Isn't that rather sweet?

Other people's houses felt so small. And other families seemed — *thin*. Just a couple of children or three at the most. I used to feel so lucky, by comparison. Oh, there were comments — "Your delightful Victorian family, Alison," and Corinna

280

saying, "My sister-in-law is doing her valiant best to prop up the declining birthrate," — saying that to Martin, I remember, when she first brought him here, she didn't know I'd heard.

I never had any problems, getting pregnant. It would just happen. I even used to feel maybe you didn't need to — make love. That perhaps I just got pregnant anyway. It's called having sex now, isn't it — not making love. That sounds so — basic. I was a bit horrified, the first time, but it's surprising how quickly you get used to it, and eventually it's just routine.

If cross-examined on the matter — something that has not happened, and just as well — Alison would probably admit that she never much cared for sex. She agreed to it willingly enough for procreative reasons — virgin conception was a romantic idea but Alison knew well enough that its only record is biblical. The Allersmead four-poster bed thus saw a standard amount of marital sex during the early years; the bed itself, an untypically flamboyant gesture, had belonged to an aunt of Alison's who was going to send it to a sale — Alison pounced and it was reprieved. Paul, Gina and Sandra were born in it: Katie and Roger had to make do with the local hospital because by then home deliveries were not so popular with doctors and Charles had made it clear that he shared their reservations, though probably not for the same reasons.

Alison enjoyed giving birth. She couldn't understand why some people made such a fuss about it. All right, it hurt a bit but not *that* much, none of hers had taken long, just a final hour or so of ouch! and heave, and there you were, with the dear little bundle. She had loved sitting up in the Allersmead bed, displaying the bundle to its siblings, and to Charles. There had been such a sense of achievement, and being the centre of a wonderful primal ritual, the woman in the home having a baby; the house around her was grateful, she used to feel, as though she had adorned it, made the one superb addition to its furnishings. Hospital was a fearful let-down: strangers all around you, other women with their bundles and their noisy relatives, nurses clattering up and down, clamping the baby to your breast as though plugging an appliance to a socket, the assembly line doctors and midwives, hauling babies out, so many per day.

There is no record of total Allersmead births, but it must be assumed that small Edwardians let out their first yell here, in the age of innocence before 1914, and later there must have been infants of the 1920s and 30s, and then perhaps on into the war years, adding up to a collective howl of outrage, the universal greeting to a cold and dazzling world. These cries are buried in the walls, along with everything else that the house has heard and witnessed; the babies have grown up, and gone, and some of them are dead, but somewhere there may be a pair of elderly eyes for which the first sight was an Allersmead ceiling, and which first blinked at the light through Allersmead windows.

Allersmead fathers of times past no doubt did the traditional thing and paced up and down while people busied themselves boiling kettles, and the doctor

282

hurried up the stairs with his black bag. Charles did not pace; he got on with some work, distracted by the comings and goings and the generally portentous atmosphere. He felt uncomfortably aware of having the supporting role, of being inevitably involved, but also at this point superfluous. Exasperating midwives would refer to him as Daddy, inadequate meals were perfunctorily flung together by Ingrid, the existing children roared around the place quite out of hand. When the drama had reached its conclusion, he would go upstairs ("Someone's ready to see their Daddy now,") and do duty at the bedside, while Alison beamed, and the bundle squirmed and snuffled, and seemed to him quite remarkably inhuman. He always thought of the pig baby in *Alice*, while trying not to.

Alison looks back with nostalgia at those halcyon early years. You had babies, and there were small children and a baby for ever, it seemed, and just those manageable problems — teething and croup and a spot of sibling jealousy — except that it was not for ever, not at all; there was this unruly race up the measurement wall, and suddenly no more pliable little figures but instead an entourage of wayward people who are both deeply familiar but also dismayingly unknown. Allersmead has been fingered by some alien outside force, mutation has taken place, and Alison is helpless.

Alison responds. She reinvents herself. She sees that she is now the guardian of their security. They still need Allersmead, they still need her; they are not fledged, just flapping.

So the halcyon years are succeeded by those more challenging times. Alison finds that she can adapt, and Allersmead does the same. The babies' high chair goes up to the junk room on the attic floor. Tricycles give way to bikes flung down by the front steps; the nursery gramophone ("The farmer wants a wife, the farmer wants a wife . . .") is overtaken by Paul's stereo, Sandra's Walkman. The garden swings grow moss; the sandpit is buried in dead leaves. It is all right, it is fine, everything is as it ever was, except different. Alison has faced down the passage of time, and emerged, if not triumphant, then afloat, on course.

And there is more. Much more. There has been white water; she has navigated, and come through. She has kept her head and been sensible and firm, however difficult, however much she felt let down, betrayed; she has kept her sights fixed on the one thing that matters: this is a family, this shall always be a family.

I said, this is what we are going to do. This is what I have arranged. I told her. I told him.

Well, I said more than that, quite a lot more. I can't remember exactly now. I know I talked a lot, because it helped somehow, and nobody else did — there wasn't much for others to say, was there? And of course the children mustn't know, not then, not ever, so the talking had to be done when they weren't around, which wasn't often in those days. Roger was only two.

I talked mostly to Charles — well, at Charles is more what it was, I suppose. Charles didn't say much. He'd sit there staring sort of through one in that way he

284

does, and you're not sure if he's listening or not. I told him that however hurt I was and however he'd let us down all that mattered was the family. The children. *All* of them — the one that was to come just as much. And Ingrid. Her too. I never for one moment wanted her to go — I told him that straight off. That was out of the question, I said. I told him it was a silly, stupid mistake and I realized that — now we all had to live with it, for always. And the only way, the best way for everyone, was to live with it together, as a family. Except of course that the children didn't have to know, they mustn't know, none of them, not even . . . Clare. I'd thought of what to tell them, and they'd be told, and that would be that. They could just forget about it, and there'd be six of them then, and that would be fine. And there need be no more talking about it, ever again, we were talked out now, at least I was, everything was settled and we were just going to make the best of it. Do you see? I said to him. You understand? And he went on staring and I don't remember what he said. Nothing much.

It was the only way. The only way to deal with it. They've never known, the children. I'm sure they haven't. Sometimes I almost forget about it myself. Sometimes.

And it is all a long time ago now. Alison is someone else; she is no longer a young mother in flowing Laura Ashley with mousy brown hair that tumbles from restraining grips but a sixty-five-year-old mother in cord shift dresses with grey-brown hair that does the same. She is still first and foremost a mother, but motherhood is emblematic now; therein resides her status but it is no longer her occupation. Her days are busy with Allersmead — Allersmead is still demanding, it still requires servicing, policing — and with the kitchen. There are still people to be fed; twice a week there are the cookery-class women, who can be taught how to feed others. Women have come and gone — indeed, over the years they have merged, for Alison, into a sort of conglomerate kitchen greenhorn who keeps on bungling her hollandaise and collapsing her soufflé. There have been high-flyers, graduating with honours. And there have been those whose personalities have left a permanent impression, whose comments and glances are stored, much as she would like to wipe them. These women wear choice clothes, their hair has received attention, they have waistlines and good complexions and, by implication, well-appointed homes and attentive husbands. Alison has been made aware that if she were not the cook that she is, they would not notice her, that, for them, she is some kind of subspecies. They have made her wonder if she really likes other women.

Alison has fewer friends these days. In the past, when the children were at school, she had a circle of neighbourhood friends, the other mothers with whom she consorted, who delivered offspring to play at Allersmead, before whom she could not resist preening herself. No one else had *six*. From no other house came such a rich procession each school day; no other house so rang with child life, was so redolent of family.

Back then, Alison felt that she queened it — graciously, tactfully — over friends and acquaintances less well endowed.

But they seem all to have evaporated now, those other mothers.

Old familiar faces have vanished (their offspring grown, the house too big) and been replaced by the hobbling inhabitants of the nursing home, the fly-by-day owners of the expensive cars. There is no pausing for a chat in the street, these days.

Alison is not bothered, on the whole. Allersmead was always self-sufficient; it is indeed diminished now, with the children gone, but it remains the unit that it ever was. And it is populated by all those winsome ghosts — perpetually happy, harmonious, the ideal family; they swing on the swings, they dig in the sandpit, the nursery gramophone croons away upstairs: "The farmer wants a wife . . ."

Charles is grey, more stooped, but otherwise unaffected by the years, or so it would seem. He still spends most of the time in his study, but no book has emerged for some while now. He has found publishers unenthusiastic. Old contacts have been replaced by very young men and women who politely reject his proposals — they find themselves unable to get behind this idea, interesting as it is. Charles is still working on a book — of course he is, what else would he do? — but he finds that his relationship with this book is different from that with other books: not much is written as yet, he feels little urgency or compulsion, the book is like some comfortable garment that he puts on when it

287

suits him to do so. He doesn't really care if it is published or not. Suffice it that he has reason to be occupied in his study as he ever has been. Sometimes he does not feel too well these days.

Ingrid has gone entrepreneurial. During the growing months she sells surplus produce from the vegetable garden to the cookery-course women. She has branched out into cut flowers, and has turned a further area of the garden into a permanent border from which she can harvest a steady supply of blooms. Alison has insisted that she keep the income thus generated, but Ingrid, equally, insists on putting it into the household kitty. She is aware of a certain cashflow problem, perhaps rather more than either Alison or Charles, who prefer to ignore this difficulty.

Ingrid has thickened — she no longer has that girlish willowy look. But her hair — that betraying hair — is still corn-golden, without a thread of grey. She has still that impassive, enigmatic gaze, she is still inclined to slightly disconcerting conversational intrusions. The cookery-class women are baffled by her; they can't work out her role, and her stonewall response to their advances makes them feel put in their place; Alison is blank when probed: "Oh, Ingrid is *such* a support — what would we do without her?" That "we" seems to draw in the seldom visible Charles, the husband about whom the women are mildly curious. Those who have glimpsed him, and have even tried to exchange a word, report a vaguely distinguished-looking guy in *the* most ancient tweed jacket you ever saw, not what you'd call

288

forthcoming, polite enough but dived straight back into that room of his; what does he *do*, one wonders.

Allersmead provokes a certain curiosity. Perhaps it always did, but back in the days of full occupation, when the place ran with children, the response was also vaguely critical — what were people doing with a family that size, in this day and age, not even Catholics apparently, and what an odd mismatched couple, him so reserved, barely says hello, but her all smiles and chatter. Today the interest is focused on the inhabitants — this trio so out of kilter with the times (except where gastronomy is concerned), and what exactly is the Ingrid person for? — but equally on the place. Most neighbours are very property-conscious — either they're sitting on a goldmine or they've mortgaged themselves silly in order to buy one — and they note that Allersmead is far from up to scratch these days. The roof is visibly in need of repair, gutters are sagging, the paintwork is flaking and there is a zigzag crack up the brickwork by the porch. Does this suggest apathy or lack of funds?

Ingrid acquired a computer a few years ago, having explained email to Alison, who at once saw its potential: this was the way to keep track of everyone. Ingrid has to be the conduit; Alison's desultory attempt to acquire IT skills rapidly foundered, Charles took one look and turned away. The computer sits in the television room, thus converting this into the Allersmead twenty-first-century heartland. Ingrid checks the emails daily, and sends those drafted by Alison. No one is out of reach now; Allersmead tentacles embrace the globe. Furthermore, Ingrid has set up the Allersmead Cookery Courses website, which has brought in more custom than Alison can cope with. The waiting list is gratifyingly long, and those who at last rise to the top of it are all the more anxious to profit from this sought-after experience. Ingrid says that Alison should put the price up.

Back when the children were still there Alison somehow never envisaged a time when they would not be. Oh, she knew it would come — but she never considered the implications, tried out the idea of an emptied house, listened for silence. They went gradually, of course, so silence came gradually, and there were returns, and now there is Paul again so the silence is tempered. She has got used to it. You can get used to much — she has known that for a long while.

She is rather pleased at the way in which Allersmead has been reinvented, become useful in a different way — Ingrid's produce, the cookery classes. Once, it spawned children; now, it is differently creative. But it is still a shrine to the thing that matters — home-making. Alison regrets that her views on this were rather stonily received by the Mothercraft group; she would have liked to develop the theme by telling them — in the most abstract way, of course — how you can overcome those inevitable glitches in family life, by way of determination and common sense. But they were only interested in things like nappy rash and projectile vomiting. She will definitely pull the plug on Mothercraft, but plans a new course on confectionery, jam-making and preserves.

The house does indeed have empty rooms these days. The drawing room is seldom used; the television room is altogether more convenient. Ingrid has turned one of the attic rooms into a dedicated space for her sewing machine. Below, there are empty bedrooms, though Paul is where he ever was, and Charles long ago moved into Roger's old room. That four-poster matrimonial bed has come to seem something of a mockery. After Clare's arrival, Alison became rather resistant to sex; there had better not be any more children, on the whole.

And I always disliked the idea of the pill, so best to play safe. Charles often used to go off into the spare room, anyway, when he wanted to read and I wanted the light off, so it didn't make much difference.

They always startle me now when they come back — I've forgotten what they'll be like and there's this *adult*. Gina with a different man, and of course Charles had to have an argument with him but I suppose he doesn't much get the chance these days. One didn't like to ask what had happened with that David — Gina never did go in for confidences. Roger's wife is perfectly sweet, of course — I've tried her waffle recipe and she's going to email me more things she does. One gets absolutely used to that Chinese look, though it seemed odd at first, you didn't expect her to speak English like that, with a Canadian accent. Katie we haven't seen for ages, but she says maybe next year they'll get over. Clare seemed very kind of *foreign* last time she came, I almost thought she'd start talking French or something.

291

And of course Sandra is so elegant, but then she always was, even in school uniform — and the *presents* she brings, lovely food and silk scarves I can't wear, but Ingrid sometimes does.

Charles is difficult these days, but then he never was an easy man, you walked on eggshells half the time. It's a different kind of difficult now, not so much irritable and shutting himself off — he's more edgy, jumpy, he can't stand it when the dog barks and he seems so *elderly* sometimes. He's taken to stopping halfway up the stairs, sitting on the windowseat, and he's got this habit of putting his hand on his chest. There's nothing wrong, of course — Charles has always had excellent health — it's just some mood he's in. Plus, he's drinking again in his study, which he hasn't done for years.

Voices

Charles is writing. He doesn't feel too bad today — so thoughts come, words. He is having a mild attack of concurrence as his glance roams along the books on his shelves and falls upon names: Carlyle, Freud, Browne, Shelley, Stendhal, Malinowski ... all these disparate dead people who rub shoulders with one another and are present still because he notices them. Everything — everybody — carrying on concurrently. This notion has always interested him. Long ago he thought it might be the subject of his *magnum opus*, but he has never been able to get a sufficient grip on it, to garner enough material, so the *magnum opus* has never come about, in that or any other form.

He doubts that it ever will. In fact he knows it won't. But there is no reason not to get down a few thoughts, on one of the better days when these still occur.

Accordingly he writes.

"Thomas Carlyle died in (check date); (check sp. first name) Malinowksi died in (check date). These men lived far apart at different times, their intellectual concerns were in no way related, but their posthumous existence is concurrent — they are a part of the furnishings of my mind. Looking out of my window I can see a tree that I know to be an ilex (check botanical name), a tree of Mediterranean origin mentioned by Virgil (check reference), who also now joins this disembodied throng in a room in an English house in 2008. But the house is not of 2008 — its bricks and mortar, its stained glass, the marble floor of its hall, date from the 1890s, thus introducing a further element of displacement, of concurrence."

Charles stops writing, distracted; there is a more immediate concern.

Email — Gina to Roger

Coronary. Apparently he must have had a heart problem for some time, but never saw anyone about it. Well — sudden is the best way to go, I suppose. I went down this morning. Mum a bit off the rails, Ingrid and Paul coping. Funeral on Tuesday. Look, I know it's not easy for you to get away — we'll understand entirely.

Email — Sandra to Gina

Of course I'm coming.

Email — Clare to Gina

Performance that evening but a dep will go on — which is only for life or death circs but I've said this is, isn't it? xxx

Email — Katie to Gina

Arrive Heathrow Monday evening. With you Tuesday a.m. I think we should all do *individual* flowers. Can you get me white lilies? xxx

Email — Roger to Gina

Sorted. See you.

Email — Sandra to Gina

Thanks for offer but don't care for anemone idea. I'll organize in London and bring my own.

Email — Clare to Gina

White roses fine. Masses, please.

Email — Roger to Gina

Sorry don't know what ranunculus is but sounds good. Thanks.

Email — Corinna to Gina

Unfortunately Martin has a Senate meeting so impossible — sends apologies. I am cancelling seminars and a lecture and shall come. I'll be driving and need directions to crematorium please. Is it flowers or charity donations? If latter, which?

Email — Gina to Sandra, Katie, Roger, Clare

Right — here's the agenda.

Congregation/audience (??) takes up seats. Cellist friend of mine will provide music.

Paul reads Matthew Arnold's *Dover Beach*. (This is because he doesn't want to do what I shall have to do.)

Gina gives short address about Dad and his life (and no, I don't know what I'm going to say).

Cellist plays.

Sandra reads from Sir Thomas Browne's *Urne-Burial* (yes, I realize you haven't got a copy to hand — I'm emailing you the relevant text).

More cello.

Katie reads poem of her own choice (I know it's short notice but you're the only one of us who read Eng. Lit, at uni, so come on).

More cello.

Roger reads from Nabokov's *Speak, Memory* (this was on Dad's desk that day so he must have been reading/thinking about it. Don't panic, Rog — email text follows).

Possibly cello, or not. At some point there is pause while coffin disappears — don't know exactly when yet; there will be sheets giving order of proceedings for everyone on the day.

Clare reads from Tolstoy's *Childhood, Boyhood, Youth* — also in book-pile on Dad's desk (yes, yes — text follows. I hope you all realize I shall be typing texts till the small hours tonight).

Anyone objecting must kindly come up with alternative viable suggestions.

Paul says: She's insisting. Three-course sit-down lunch, the works, all stops out, the Limoges china — Christ, the Limoges china! What he would have wanted, she says. As if. Yes, yes — I know she said buffet would be fine, just some sandwiches, now she says she never did or if she did it was because she didn't know what she was saying. What? I know, I know, I've said all that. Gina, *you* talk to her.

Corinna thinks: It *would* have to be one of my Swinburne lecture days. Trust Charles. Oh, don't be so snide, the poor man didn't plan it. All the same, it is sort of typical. God, one's brother — *dead*. He's always been there. I mean, not that we were that close, but . . . Does one wear black? No, not nowadays. Flowers, not a wreath, that's naff. Peonies maybe — no, too pink. Chrysanths are boring. The French go for purple pansies. I s'pose all the children will come. I'd better go to the house after, Alison would never forgive otherwise. Will she stay in that vast house? What about Ingrid? That weird set-up. What *does* one wear? The dark green suit, maybe, with a pale shirt. Gladioli perhaps — except they're so stiff. I still can't quite believe it. Charles — just not there any more.

Gina says: It's all right, I've talked her out of it. I think. Fingers crossed. Compromise. It'll be sandwiches and other stuff and a dessert but not round the table.

Ambulant — people sit anywhere — kitchen, sitting room. That avoids any holding forth to everyone which otherwise . . . She's fairly hyper, isn't she? I know — and you're being great. Brownie points to last for years. Just keep it up a bit longer, OK? I'll be with you Monday evening. Oh, and ask Ingrid could she please make up a bed for me.

Email — Katie to Roger

Hope you got flight all right. I did — but a scamper. Whew! What a day. But it wasn't *too* bad, was it? I felt all weepy at the crematorium, and Mum was bright pink, like when she was about to erupt — remember? Oh, isn't it all a bit unreal — no Dad. Damn, I'm weepy again. And when I was looking at us all after it was over, standing around there, I thought — how has this happened, these *grown-ups*? Gina someone I hardly recognize, and Clare so thin and blonde and dancerish, and I don't think I've ever realized before that Sandra's beautiful. And you and Paul — men, huge great men. But this bunch of *adults* . . . Sort of all right, wasn't it, back at the house? You were brilliant with Corinna — goodness, she's *old*. I couldn't get over that either, grey hair and that hunched look. And she seemed defused somehow — I wasn't much scared of her. The cake moment was a bit dire — Mum suddenly producing it with a flourish, and the one candle. What *was* she thinking of? Always a cake, she said, for an occasion. For an awful moment I thought she was going to want us to sing. Remembering all those birthdays, dozens and dozens of them, and this wasn't. And Ingrid saying perhaps the last time everyone is here like this — she could always rather put her foot in it, Ingrid. Goodness, a married Gina, who'd have thought it. And oh Rog, I kept expecting Dad to walk in, wearing his Christmas face — that let's-just-get-through-this-somehow face. Damn — weepy again — I'm not used to it yet. Where is he? Where's he *gone*? But you're used to people dying; you're up against it all the time. I haven't met it much, and it's rather thrown me. Feel I must get over there more, see more of Mum. She was awfully wound-up, wasn't she? Fizzing. And then at other moments completely vague, out of it — like when Gina tried to talk to her about money, was everything OK, was there enough. Didn't want to know, changed the subject. Ingrid was pretty good, wasn't she, apart from the trademark heavy foot — she's obviously keeping things going while Mum's a bit astray. But them on their own together now . . . Sorry, I'm nattering on, just wanted to check in, now it's all over. Love to Susan.

Paul says: Yeah — she's a lot calmer, back to normal really. But listen — I got the job. Yeah — Wisley. The Royal Horticultural Society, no less. General duties in the gardens. What a turn-up for the books! They must be really pushed for labour. No — don't be daft, of course I sent them a proper CV, sober as you like. Live? Oh, I'll find somewhere to doss down, I always have, haven't I? So I'm off next week. Maybe this is the breakthrough. Paul Harper horticulturalist.

Email — Ingrid to Sandra, Katie, Roger, Clare

Paul has now gone to this new job which is good that he has it but at Allersmead we are sorry he is not here any more. Alison has started again the cookery classes. That is good too because the Bank is writing letters — not nice letters.

Email — Roger to Gina

Could you investigate Bank letters.

Email — Gina to Sandra, Katie, Roger, Clare

The long and short of it is that there's a severe cashflow problem. Dad's divvies have been going down and down, for complex reasons, mainly lack of management. Problem has clearly been there for some time, but ignored. Come to think of it — the house has been looking pretty shabby for ages, but one thought that was just their style. Repairs needed — but that's only the half of it. Income also needed. The cookery classes bring in peanuts. Ingrid proposes lodgers — indeed is quite gung-ho. Mum prepared to give it a try.

Email — Sandra to Gina, Katie, Roger, Clare

Lodgers potential rapists and murderers. Propose development of grounds — elegant newbuild at south end of garden, using prime architect.

Paul says: Look, I've had an idea. How about I set up a nursery garden business there — all that space, you could have glasshouses and growing tunnels — masses of room for planting out. Nursery is far superior to garden centre — you can do bare-rooted and the real connoisseurs are crying out for that. You'd specialize — just a few choice lines. Start-up capital? Oh well, you'd borrow, wouldn't you? Gina, you're so damn *practical*. Business experience? You'd learn on the hoof, wouldn't you?

Email — Katie to Gina, Sandra, Roger, Clare

I hate to suggest it, but Dad's books must be worth quite a lot.

Email — Clare to Gina, Sandra, Katie, Roger

The sitting room is big enough for a kids' dancing-class. You could come to an arrangement with a local teacher.

Email — Roger to Gina, Sandra, Katie, Clare

Lodger idea has legs, I feel, but caution needed (I take your point, Sandra). References essential. Students of some kind perhaps? Maybe talk to local language schools (are there any?), further education institutions, etc. Mum and Ingrid both used to the young — might even like having some around. Gina, please pass on to Paul (can't he get himself online?) and yes, agree thumbs down to nursery garden scheme, though well meant.

Email — Gina to Sandra, Katie, Roger, Clare

Progress. Ingrid in negotiations with local veterinary college, who are interested. Student hostel is oversubscribed — proposal is for three/four of overflow to come to Allersmead. B&B proposed, with option of supper also. Mum rather keen on supper. Health and safety inspection necessary — takes place next week.

Paul says: Have it your own way. Passing up a golden opportunity, that's how I see it — I could have made the family's fortune. Species roses and lilies, that was the idea. A stand at Chelsea — articles in the Sundays. Vet students will trash the place — just you see. A laptop for my birthday? Look, thanks awfully but no thanks — I hate the things. Can I have a weekend in Paris instead? Ah.

Email — Gina to Sandra, Katie, Roger, Clare

Shit. Allersmead has not passed health and safety inspection. In fact, has not just not passed but failed dismally on all fronts. Bathroom facilities are inadequate and require modernization, there is no fire escape from the attic floor, rewiring is necessary throughout, there are no fire extinguishers. And so on, and so on. For heaven's sake — we grew up there and lived to tell the tale. Vet college bursar is regretful but unless extensive improvements were carried out . . . So forget student lodgers, I'm afraid.

Email — Sandra to Gina, Katie, Roger, Clare

Commercial travellers probably less fussy, but more inclined to rape and murder. If newbuild is unacceptable, what about a self-contained flat on the attic floor? For rental purposes.

Email — Gina to Sandra, Katie, Roger, Clare

Mum would consider flat, but Ingrid points out that roof would have to be repaired before conversion. It's a bucket situation up there — I hadn't realized. Estimate for re-roofing — wait for it — £18K. And that's before conversion costs. But nice try, Sandra.

Email — Roger to Gina, Sandra, Katie, Clare

Roof situation does rather focus the mind. Not just income needed — capital also. Capital we don't have. Allersmead is an expensive pile — eats maintenance. Are the rest of you thinking what I'm beginning to think?

Paul says: *Sell* Allersmead? Mum'll never stand for that, will she? I'm not sure I would. *Sell Allersmead?*

Email — Sandra to Gina, Katie, Roger, Clare

It's obvious. You'd be talking a couple of million, I should think. Solve the problem just like that. Pity, but face the facts.

Email — Katie to Gina, Sandra, Roger, Clare

You *can't*. We can't. No, no. There must be some other way.

Email — Clare to Gina, Sandra, Katie, Roger

What! Allersmead? No Allersmead anymore? Oh, please not.

Gina drives in and parks by the front door. The gravel of the drive is a rare surviving substance now, peeking up here and there in between weeds and clumps of moss; tyres no longer scrunch. She remembers a delivery of gravel, aeons ago, and how they all waded about and helped to spread it. She notes that crack by the front door, and squints up at the roof, which does indeed signal distress — tiles slipped or missing all over the place.

Philip had offered to come too. No, she had said — thanks, but I'm probably best on my own for this.

She sees Allersmead with a curious marriage of detachment and intimacy. She sees this large house, conceived in another age, a time of vastly different social assumptions, when domestic service was a major industry, and an army of women existed for the maintenance of Allersmead-style households. The bell panel still survives in the kitchen: drawing room, morning room, bedroom I . . . she sees the house as an affirmation of the way things were back then, when a person was placed by the way they spoke or how they dressed, when most people took for granted such distinctions and when the polarization of wealth seemed part of the natural order of things. Allersmead speaks for affluence rather than wealth, perhaps. Gina thinks about this affluence: shades from Allersmead of another day float before her — ladies in capacious skirts and high-buttoned blouses, chaps in tweeds, children in pinnies, bowling hoops. A skivvy hauls scuttles of coal up the stairs — the old fireplaces are all still there, in the bedrooms. She sees the house as a consumer, over the century, gobbling up blacklead and polish and Brasso and Silvo (boosting the funds from which sprang Dad's divvies, now so sadly diminished); she sees it also as a producer, a restaurant that never closed, from which flowed forth an endless supply of breakfasts and lunches and dinners, a century-long aroma of toast and roast. The smells are perhaps the most assertive; she can pick up their own — Sunday lunch and coq au vin and Lancashire hot pot and macaroni cheese and apple crumble.

And the smells take her to a more intimate Allersmead, to the Allersmead-in-the-head, to a raft of private moments that come swimming up from the long darkness of the years, the strange assortment of glimpses that are known as memory. All of these are tacked to Allersmead; in all of them Allersmead is the backdrop — its rooms, its stairs, its furnishings, the deeply known places in its garden, the secrets of the cellar, where presumably the Daleks still roam.

I know what you mean, she tells Katie, and Clare, and Paul. I know exactly what you mean.

She is carrying a fistful of house agents' brochures: charming cottages with easily maintained gardens, compact town houses with quick access to shops, lofts with fibre-optic mood lighting and bespoke kitchens. She pauses on the top step, pushes open the front door.

"I heard the car," cries Alison. "I was just coming."

Email — Gina to Sandra, Katie, Roger, Clare

I've been. Floated it over tea in the kitchen — put out a feeler first, a little probe. Allersmead so big, and so costly to run. Lot to be said for small houses. Pretty cottages. Blank stare from Mum: "I don't follow, dear." Ingrid following very well on other side of the table; equally blank, but that's Ingrid. Eventually I had to come out with it — and flourished sheaf of pretty cottages etc. Mum then went from incredulity to outrage: "I can't believe what you seem to be suggesting . . . how can you even *think* of such a thing. *Sell* Allersmead! Live somewhere else!" Much airy dismissal of financial issue — "Money doesn't *matter*, it's your *home* that matters, and Allersmead has always been . . ." I know, I know, say I — and I do, I do, but . . . But, but. Unfortunately, money does matter. I try to explain this, I present some figures, and am evidently seen as on a par with slit-eyed mean-minded money-mad bank managers: "I had no idea you could be so hard-headed, Gina." Meanwhile, on the other side of the table, Ingrid is idly studying pretty cottage brochures — or maybe not so idly. So decided to leave it at that for the moment — changed subject, ate coffee and walnut cake, tried to restore personal image, received bag of veg from Ingrid and departed, having strategically forgotten to pickup cottage brochures.

Email — Ingrid to Gina

This week we shall look at places. Alison says this does not mean she has any intention, just there is no harm in looking. Some of the pictures she quite liked.

Email — Alison to Gina, Sandra, Katie, Roger, Clare

That one called a loft was hopeless. I mean, the kitchen worktop was made of *granite*. Granite is for mountains, isn't it? Not worktops. And every room lit up like a stage-set. Ingrid says we'd go mad. The house on the High Street was rather poky, kitchen no good for the cookery classes. Ingrid says probably anywhere we may have to think of a kitchen extension. Cottage in Hopton has a big one, though, and Ingrid likes the garden. It's got an Aga. Have always wondered about Agas. People seem to swear by them.

Email — Roger to Gina

If asking price for Hopton cottage sensible make an offer pronto.

Email — Ingrid to Gina, Sandra, Katie, Roger, Clare

It is good they accept. Alison says kitchen table here will just fit in and perhaps dresser also. Drawing-room curtains here are so old, it is not worth taking. I shall make new. Alison thinks pink floral nice perhaps. We shall need man with rotovator to clear ground for new asparagus bed. Alison says fruit cage if I want.

Email — Clare to Gina, Sandra, Roger, Katie

Listen, all of you — isn't this a weird situation? Here's your mum and mine fetching up together on their own. OK, I know this is what we never say, your mum and mine, what we never talk about. So I'm saying it, because maybe it's time. Your mum and mine. Apparently settling down together in a cottage with an Aga and a new asparagus bed. Minus our dad, and of course it was all his doing, and we don't discuss that either and never have. So here's my take on it, a few years late.

I'm rather glad to be here, so I can hardly hold it against him. Or my mum. I think yours had considerable cause for complaint. Actually, mine too, come to that. I think he shouldn't have, but if he hadn't I wouldn't exist and that's such a peculiar thought that I have to stop thinking. In the abstract, I think he shouldn't have — but look, goodness knows what things have been like for him — we've no idea, have we? I don't understand my mum. Why did *she*? And then why did she stay and how did she feel and I suppose I've got all sorts of Scandinavian relations but somehow I'm not very interested. We've never talked about it, she and I — never

ever. She knows I know — that we all know — and she's pulled down a shutter. And I don't mind — I prefer it that way. Does your mum know we know? If she does, my view is that she's not admitting it, least of all to herself.

There — that's my take. Clare bares her soul.

Paul says: Jesus! Bully for Clare — the whole can of worms, wide open. What do *I* think? I don't. I've always preferred not to. Otherwise I'd have chatted about it to the shrinks. Boy! — they'd have made a meal of it, wouldn't they? I don't think anything — just, aren't all families screwed up somewhere, when it comes down to it?

Email — Katie to Gina, Sandra, Roger, Clare

Oh, Clare — you should have said all that years ago. Well, *we* should. All of us — any of us. Actually, I think — poor them. All three of them. It can't have been much fun — knowing what they knew and not knowing if we did or not, or knowing and not wanting to. And Dad must have felt guilty — perhaps horribly guilty. And Mum — well, what Clare says, cause for complaint. And Ingrid — all *muddled*, perhaps. It's poor them, surely.

Email — Sandra to Gina, Katie, Roger, Clare

Well done, Clare! Sorry, Katie — no. No way did he feel guilty — he was out to lunch, all his life. In fact, they were all three of them out to lunch. That's my view.

Email — Roger to Gina, Sandra, Katie, Clare

Devil's advocate — there's a case to be made for Dad. Two women and six children — did he need that? OK — I hear ye, all of you. But give it a passing thought. And listen! I have news. Susan is pregnant. How's that? But this is not going to be an Allersmead-style launch — we plan two, conceivably three, and there will be no domestic assistance. Meanwhile, advise Gina arrange man with rotovator at once, contact fruit-cage suppliers, and get the max for Allersmead.

Email — Gina to Sandra, Katie, Roger, Clare

Paul proposes all families screwed up, more or less. Well, it's a thought. Spot on, Clare — thanks for lifting the veil, busting the taboo etc. We're an odd lot, aren't we? The elephant in the room, as we say these days, and all of us mute. Ho, hum, Sandra — I'm not so sure. Not so much out to lunch as in denial — my scenario. Same thing, possibly. And yes, Katie — yes I suppose to that too. Poor them. And the devil's advocate view has to be considered. How far can any of us say we knew Dad? I pass. OK, Rog — you've made a point — and that's terrific news! How open-minded can I get? Oh, plenty more — I'm trained that way. Suffice it that Clare has done us a service, I guess, and maybe we can close the file now. Or let it rest — it's always going to be there, I suppose. And right, Rog — rotovator and fruit cage will be sorted asap. And Allersmead too, alas.

Allersmead

A prestigious Edwardian family home, set in ¼ acre of garden with mature trees. Drive with turning circle and ample parking space. Marble-tiled entrance hall, imposing oak staircase to first floor.

Stunning drawing room with original fireplace. Panelled study with De Morgan tiles to fireplace. Further sitting room opening on to wide veranda overlooking the garden. Cloakroom. Large kitchen. Scullery and pantry.

Seven bedrooms and two bathrooms on the first floor. Five further rooms and toilet on attic floor. Extensive cellar.

A rare opportunity to acquire an impressive house of the pre-First World War period, with original stained glass and other period features, and grounds that could be delightfully landscaped, or considered for further development. Allersmead would also lend itself to institutional use, or conversion into flats. The property would benefit from extensive modernization, and is in need of some repairs, but offers a unique opportunity to the discerning buyer.

Price on application.

Also available in ISIS Large Print:

Our Precious Lulu

Anne Fine

Lulu's intolerable. From the outset she wormed her way into the affections of her stepmother and, with spite as her principal hobby, spent every childhood moment trying to undermine poor Geraldine, her dumpy and hardworking stepsister. Now she's an adult: sexy, long-legged — and ruthless. Jobs, lovers, fashionable clothes: Lulu picks any and all at whim and drops them with equal ease, all the while confident that Geraldine and her faithfully supportive husband, Robert, will bail her out of every passing problem. But not even watchful Robert has realised quite how much Geraldine's exemplary patience has rested on one simple but long-lasting assumption about her own family.

Could everything be about to change . . .?

ISBN 978-0-7531-8504-9 (hb)
ISBN 978-0-7531-8505-6 (pb)

The Family Man

Elinor Lipman

Henry Archer's ex-wife is unhinged. And impossibly demanding. And recently widowed. A hysterical phone call from her is the last thing his calm, well-ordered life needs. But there is one happy side-effect: the chance to get back in contact with his beloved step-child, her daughter, with whom he lost touch with when their wildly misbegotten marriage ended long ago.

Henry is a lawyer, an old-fashioned man, gay, successful, lonely. Thalia is now 29, a would-be actress, estranged from her crackpot mother and about to embark on a risky plan to further her career by posing as the girlfriend of a struggling actor down on his romantic luck. When Thalia and her complicated social life move into the basement of Henry's Manhattan home, she finds a champion in her long-lost father, and Henry finds that out of chaos comes life, and maybe even love.

ISBN 978-0-7531-8532-2 (hb)
ISBN 978-0-7531-8533-9 (pb)

The Truth About Melody Browne

Lisa Jewell

When she was nine years old, Melody Browne's house burned down. Not only did the fire destroy all her possessions, it took with it all her memories — Melody can remember nothing before her ninth birthday. Now in her early thirties, she hasn't seen her parents since she left home at 15. She's made a good life for herself and her teenage son and likes it that way.

Until one night whilst attending a hypnotist show, she faints — and when she comes round she starts to remember. Slowly she begins to piece together the real story of her childhood. Her journey takes her to the seaside town of Broadstairs, to oddly familiar houses in London backstreets and to strangers who love her like their own. But with every mystery she solves another one materialises, and Melody begins to wonder if she'll ever know the truth . . .

ISBN 978-0-7531-8416-5 (hb)
ISBN 978-0-7531-8417-2 (pb)

Consequences

Penelope Lively

Three generations of 20th-century women: a young woman, her daughter and her granddaughter, their contrasting lives and their achievement of love.

Lorna escapes her conventional Kensington family to marry artist Matt, but the Second World War puts an end to their immense happiness. Molly, their daughter, will have to wait longer to find love and Ruth, Lorna's granddaughter, even longer still: an enthralling examination of interweaving love and history.

ISBN 978-0-7531-7992-5 (hb)
ISBN 978-0-7531-7993-2 (pb)

Making It Up

Penelope Lively

In this fascinating piece of new fiction, Penelope Lively takes moments from her own life and asks "what if some outcomes had been otherwise?" What if her family's flight from Egypt in 1942 had taken a different route? What would her life have been like if she had become pregnant when she was eighteen? If she had married someone else? If she had become an archaeologist? If she had lived her life in America?

In this highly original piece of work, Penelope Lively examines alternative destinies, choices and roads not taken.

ISBN 978-0-7531-7495-1 (hb)
ISBN 978-0-7531-7496-8 (pb)

ISIS publish a wide range of books in large print, from fiction to biography. Any suggestions for books you would like to see in large print or audio are always welcome. Please send to the Editorial Department at:

ISIS Publishing Limited
7 Centremead
Osney Mead
Oxford OX2 0ES

A full list of titles is available free of charge from:

Ulverscroft Large Print Books Limited

(UK)
The Green
Bradgate Road, Anstey
Leicester LE7 7FU
Tel: (0116) 236 4325

(Australia)
P.O. Box 314
St Leonards
NSW 1590
Tel: (02) 9436 2622

(USA)
P.O. Box 1230
West Seneca
N.Y. 14224-1230
Tel: (716) 674 4270

(Canada)
P.O. Box 80038
Burlington
Ontario L7L 6B1
Tel: (905) 637 8734

(New Zealand)
P.O. Box 456
Feilding
Tel: (06) 323 6828

Details of **ISIS** complete and unabridged audio books are also available from these offices. Alternatively, contact your local library for details of their collection of **ISIS** large print and unabridged audio books.